Dermot Bolger

Emily's Shoes

VIKING

VIKING

Published by the Penguin Group
Penguin Books Ltd, 27 Wrights Lane, London W8 5TZ, England
Penguin Books USA Inc., 375 Hudson Street, New York, New York 10014, USA
Penguin Books Australia Ltd, Ringwood, Victoria, Australia
Penguin Books Canada Ltd, 10 Alcorn Avenue, Toronto, Ontario, Canada M4V 3B2
Penguin Books (NZ) Ltd, 182–190 Wairau Road, Auckland 10, New Zealand

Penguin Books Ltd, Registered Offices: Harmondsworth, Middlesex, England

First published 1992
1 3 5 7 9 10 8 6 4 2

Copyright © Dermot Bolger, 1992
The moral right of the author has been asserted

Set in 12/15 pt Monophoto Sabon
Printed in England by Clays Ltd, St Ives plc

A CIP catalogue record for this book is available from the British Library

ISBN 0-670-838179

To my friend and colleague
Philip Casey

PART ONE

The same dream has haunted me for years, the dream that I have killed someone. It had happened so far back in the past that I had almost forgotten it, or had willed myself to forget it. But now, on the eve of some great happiness, the sickening memory of it comes back. I am shocked, gripped with cold fear. The deed itself is obscure, who it was or how it occurred and even when I committed it. All I know is that the body had been severed into several parts and buried among the bric-à-brac of childhood deep in the earth beneath the long grasses of the gardens where I had grown up – in the same fashion as we had once buried cats as children.

It had occurred so long ago that I have been able to start my life again, to let the pain and terror of discovery gradually ease, to wake up at night no longer sweating as I imagined footsteps closing in beneath my window. But now I know that those gardens are due for redevelopment, that soon men with bulldozers and spades will move in like the older children who would dig up our cats in their plastic bags after a month to see what they looked like. How could I have been so stupid as to imagine that I could keep it safely hidden forever? I should have gone back and moved the body, I should have burnt it gradually or destroyed it, but I had been too afraid. I had just wanted to forget what had happened, had made myself believe that once I forgot it then it would in turn cease to exist. Or maybe I did move the body once, but had I left a part behind which I had not been able to find – the torso or the legs strapped together with old bandages?

Now I know that I have left it too late. I can do nothing but wait until the blade of the machine cuts the first plastic fertilizer sack in half, until the engines stop and the men form a half moon around the rim of the pit. My fingerprints will gleam on the plastic sack like a spider's web on a hedge after frost. My fingerprints are incubating like dormant germs beneath the earth, waiting to incriminate me.

I wake up suddenly in this apartment with an uneasiness which I cannot shake off. I lie in the dark trying to remember why I am still dreaming that same dream. And this is the most terrifying part – when I cannot remember if the dream is true or not. I am struggling between consciousness and sleep and my memory seems to be playing tricks. Is there something in the past which I am hiding from myself? I think back, trying to reassure myself, but a queasy sense of guilt persists, a garbled quiver of unease which remains perpetually waiting to catch me out when I wake for mornings afterwards.

The first memory: three faces, feminine, familiar, bending forward into my line of vision. The edges of their features are softened like in an old photograph, their smiles anxious. They must be sisters, leaning down towards me. My eyes close to several more years of darkness.

I am far older then, playing with clothes-pegs on the back garden path while she hangs washing on the line between the bushes. It is spring or early summer, sunlight making the concrete warm. The kitchen door is open, the heavy white enamel sink visible with the brass taps. I push the peg like a motor car towards the jungle of grass and think of school, an unknown word soon to be made flesh, a nun's wizened hand stretching out from a stack of black cloth.

The first dream dates from there: the dream of being left behind in the house when my mother goes to visit the grave of her elder sister, Betty. She has told me to be ready but as usual I have mislaid some item of my clothing. She calls up one last time as I search helplessly for it. I run down the stairs just as the front door closes, the lock so high up beside the pane of hammered glass that I can never reach it. I am alone now, the slightest of figures in the largest of hallways, and I know that when I turn around I shall see the woman's shadow begin to darken the stairs. I sink down to my knees as the eyes come around the bend of the landing. Slowly the whole of her whitened face and then her body is revealed, the features unfamiliar and yet instinctively known to me as one of the three sisters who leaned over my cot in my first memory. My dead aunt smiles as though bearing a secret, while she glides down the stairs towards me.

There is no terror like a child's terror, no greater inarticulation than to wake up unable to describe what you are frightened of. Because how can I tell my mother about the dream when I sense something in it that is shameful, some word like death which I cannot grasp but know should never be mentioned? On the nights I cry out and try to speak of it my tongue curls up, I stutter while my mother holds me, sitting on the bed in the light from the landing. Most nights I wake and just lie alone in the narrow boxroom where a square of light shines in through the ventilation hole above the door. I can never feel secure in bed with that cavity in the wall where, even with the door locked, her ghost could come swooping in from the landing. My eyelids are wet. I close them and begin to pray. I have faith at four and a half years of age.

It is one year later. We take the main street down through the old village. The new Corporation estates are unfinished, the children rough who play there. The road to the city plummets through woodland where boys cross a fallen trunk suspended above banks of nettles. A procession of young girls entrusted with prams watch them. We walk on by the dairy and soon the granite and black marble crosses begin to be glimpsed through the overgrown bushes by the stream. A long walk follows by the high cemetery wall until we reach the main entrance where a wooden sign announces the time at which the tall iron gates will be closed

A round tower points like a moon-bound rocket. Coffins perch in dry dock behind the rusty cell doors along the moat encircling it. We pass on through avenues of mud and plastic wreaths, the lemonade bottle of water weighing down my hands. Always we seem to get lost or perhaps that is just my anxiety about the clock on the gate lodge, as I trudge behind her, gazing at the cold stone carvings of Jesus and of Mary.

I never understand how she finds her sister's grave. It is unmarked by headstone or cheap wooden cross. I know this upsets my mother, that there is some quarrel over it which has left a distance between her sister Emily and herself.

'Pray for your Aunt Betty,' she says and I lower my head and always try to imagine Emily. Emily is an envelope from England arriving on my birthday, addressed to *Master Michael McMahon* with a postal order inside for ten shillings and the same one-line letter, *please send a photograph of himself, the Three Ms.* Emily is the reason we visit Woolworths, is why I sit with the present on my lap trying not to look startled by the flash of the bulb as my mother warns me to keep still through the curtain of the booth. Sometimes my mother takes down an old photograph of three girls at a wedding. *Young Emily*, she says and cannot hide her smile as I make her explain again that she is the bride in the middle and Emily the girl on her left holding the flowers.

When she has finished praying at the graveside my mother empties the putrid water and withered flowers from the plastic vase which once stood on our mantelpiece, wipes it carefully and fills it with fresh flowers. I pour the water in. I am cold, I want to urinate. The crosses circle me like an army of stone. I do not like this place where stooped yew trees block out the winter sun.

We walk back through the oldest part of the graveyard. Nothing grows here, not a wreath left or a blade of grass unburnt. The stones are tilted over, the lettering indistinguishable even if I could read. Is she annoyed with me? She turns and calls but no sound exists in my memory. Just a silence that strains at my mind. She waits for me and takes my hand. She smiles as we hurry on towards the gates which are about to close. On the walk home there may be ice-cream from the cottage of the old woman by the stream which we reach by climbing down steps of uncut stone. She shuffles out from her kitchen to the tiny parlour which is filled by the huge gleaming refrigerator. She lifts the heavy lid, raises the knife and cuts the block of ice-cream with silent concentration. She never smiles, holding the wafer aloft with her face as solemn as a priest with the sacrament.

It is two years later. The whispers of a dozen scattered

women lay claim to the murky church. I breathe in the stained light, the shuffling footsteps and the sharp tang of cleaning wax. An old woman mutters the Stations of the Cross as though they were a secret code known only between God and herself. We have stayed here in prayer for too long. My mother has sat back and taken my hand in hers. I feel her tremor entering my fingers.

'You're a good little boy, Michael. We'll just sit here quietly and make no fuss until the attack is gone.'

The old woman shuffles on towards the Crowning of Thorns. Jesus' bloodshot eyes stare at me over her bowed head as my mother conceals her pain.

Is Maggie six or seven in the first memory that I have of her? I cannot remember what sort of shoes she is wearing, but they make her taller, standing up bossily on the piles of concrete bricks in her father's back garden, her left foot on one tier, her right foot raised on to the next, the flash of white knee between her socks and pale skirt and her hands over her eyes counting to a hundred before calling out:

Here I come, ready or not.

Keep your place or you'll be caught.

And I with my penis still leaking away in my hand, the piss like the foam from a bubble bath running down the far side of the mountain of bricks. I shake it quickly, feeling the hot wetness staining my underpants as I button my fly and come out. She puts her head to one side.

'Were you doing a Number One or a Number Two job?' she demands to know.

Maggie with the tossed red hair and the chipped white front tooth, Maggie with the Leitrim mother who stored up jars of home-made jam and bought toilet rolls in bulk. I marvelled at the rows of cans and tins when Maggie opened the wooden press in her mother's kitchen. She selected two straws carefully for us to drink our milk through. A red one for me that was the colour of Jesus and a pale blue one for her own lips to suck through, as blue as the cloak of the Virgin Mary.

Maggie's mother nursed the mad in a rambling house with spiked gates and cattle railings on the edge of the countryside. Old women, Maggie said, who sat on commodes all day dressed up for their first communions with white purses in their hands as they told the nurses that the hospital was very nice but that they had to go home now because their mothers were expecting them in time for their tea. At night Maggie's mother had to pretend to chase Chinamen from under all their beds in the ward before they would get into them.

Maggie's father was a builder in England. He had been working at home with ten men on his books before the building game collapsed here. Maggie said her mother wanted to go with him as well but he claimed Maggie would grow up a heathen over there. Now only the dolmen of concrete blocks and stacks of rotting timber were left in the garden like a memorial to his dreams.

On Fridays when the postman came and Maggie's mother was still at work the bulky registered envelope would rest beside the clock on our mantelpiece. His handwriting was thick and large, the pen pressed down so hard it had almost torn through the paper. Even staring at the address frightened me as though if I were to so much as touch one finger against it that huge gruff man who never came home would materialize through the envelope. My mother hovered about in the kitchen, rinsing my clothes by hand, waiting for the hiss of the tap being turned in the kitchen next door before stepping through the back door with the envelope to reach across and rap on the window. She always looked relieved when she came back in and closed the door.

'The man has a fierce lot of news this week,' she would say, almost to herself, 'or else that's one thick wad of English banknotes.'

Maggie with the red hair and the lovely chipped tooth, with the father whitened by English cement dust, with the mother who shepherded the mad. Maggie who would boast about the money her family had in the bank, about the way she could make her mother move house away from us if I didn't do what she told me to. When her mother worked days Maggie lived after school in our kitchen. When her mother worked nights she slept through the afternoon while Maggie played quietly in our garden. And wherever Maggie was I would be with her, in the ruined hen-house with dried white shit still speckled on the felt or among the overgrown bushes behind the mountain of concrete bricks.

I cannot remember which one of us stole the birthday candles from her mother's store. The month of May seemed to last for eternity; the month of long fresh grass with the alder bushes between the two gardens in pale flowers, the month of makeshift grottoes concealed among those branches, the month of devotion to Mary, the Mother of God. Maggie confidentially whispering the details which she had overheard from her mother of the Virgin appearing to crowds near Annagary when her mother was a girl and tea was rationed. The sharp prickle of dried twigs cut into my knees as we both knelt before the jam-jar where the blue candles burnt. The plastic Virgin filled with Holy Water from Lourdes was propped up beside it, the halo of daisies and buttercups carefully threaded around her. Maggie composed in such deep prayer that it was hard to believe she would ever lure me to check if there was a loose thread on the back of her skirt before breaking wind in my face. Maggie with her eyes tightly closed, her hands joined and raised to cover her mouth in a perfect V ending under her nose. And me, a few inches behind her, feeling guilty for staring at the scratched freckled thighs that vanished up beneath her short dress.

'Maggie, there's a new game I want us to play. Let's pretend that one of us is sick and has to be undressed and examined by the other who is a doctor.'

Her eyes opened quickly and blinked. As she turned, the twigs beneath her knees moved, causing the Virgin to keel over. I lowered my eyes, I was blushing as I trembled. I lifted them again. She was so shocked that the blood seemed to have ebbed from her face.

'You dirty little boy,' she said, 'and us here praying to the Virgin Mary. The Holy Ghost is dwelling in my body and you want to touch it with your hands.'

'Maggie, no . . . I only meant it as a game. Listen, we can play some other one.'

'I'm going up to tell your mother and I hope she buys a bamboo stick from old Malone and beats you hard with it.'

'Maggie . . .'

'I want to cry I'm so offended.'

'Please don't tell on me, Maggie. I'll do anything that you want me to. I promise.'

11

She considered for a moment with her hands still joined in prayer.

'Well then, lie down there among the twigs and you keep your eyes shut. Just do it and stay quiet or I'll tell on you. You've fallen from a great height in an accident, you're unconscious now, you're my patient and I have to check if any of your bones are broken.'

I only opened my eyes once. The Blessed Virgin and I were both lying in the grass at the same angle. Maggie's smile was almost as secretive as hers. Her hand, like the coolest of dock leaves, fumbling in the heat of my unbuttoned short trousers. The feel of twigs snapping against my skin when she turned me over. My eyes closed again so that only the Virgin could see her exploring. The greeny sunlight of May through the overhung branches, the rustle of nesting birds in the bushes, the crack of distant sheets flapping on a line. When I opened my eyes again Maggie's eyes were still closed, her face serious, her breath coming short. Was it a tremor that I felt running through her? *Oh, Maggie, Maggie.*

The walled park with the pond and splashing birds was such a hazy memory that for years until I found the place again I was uncertain if I might have dreamt it. Only Maggie seemed to really understand my talk. I stuttered in class, words sticking like a communion wafer to the roof of my mouth. I was trapped by inarticulation, the butt of all jokes, sitting in a desk at the back by myself. I knew how worthless I was, standing alone in the concrete yard, grateful to be noticed by anyone. On Tuesdays and Thursdays when the teacher called me out I could sense their eyes watching as I buttoned my duffle coat.

Part One

That Tuesday it had been raining. I run from the classroom knowing that my mother has told me to meet her at the front door of the church. I step into the side porch, the entrance which I always use. The familiar smell of floor-wax and candles. The damp stain on my forehead as I splash the Holy Water on. Through the muffled glass panels in the doors I watch the old women shuffle on their stations. She is waiting around the corner of the building, though I do not realize it, clutching her handbag at the main entrance. I try to decipher the titles of the Catholic Truth Society pamphlets on the shining wooden rack: *Blessed Martin, The Story of Bernadette, How to Know if You Have a Vocation.* I shudder when my eyes see the snakes that twist about the feet of the plaster-cast saint. I look away, up at the infant Jesus shocking naked beneath the blue cloak which his mother has wrapped him in. I hear the clang of a coin falling into the metal box and wonder for whose intentions the candle is being lit and placed down in the wax-stained rack among the row of bobbing flames.

Meanwhile my mother has run back to the house in case I have gone there, catching her breath when she gets a stitch at the corner. She phones the hospital from a neighbour's house, apologizing that I will be late for my appointment. Sweets must be bought for the neighbour's children, the honour of a favour must always be repaid. She checks with my teacher, then wanders the streets nearly demented with fright before returning to the church where I am still patiently waiting. This time she passes the side porch and sees me there. I tell her that this is the door which we always use. How was I to know the front door was the wide door at the back of the church? Surely it should be called the back door? I can feel the hurt as she screams at me, while I stutter that the side door is nearer the front, the shame at failing to make myself understood.

It is my fault, I am too stupid to think, to work out which door is which. I am less than nothing, lagging behind her, still blubbering at the bus-stop. Another neighbour waits there with two children. My mother sits on the bus talking with her, insisting, despite her protests, on paying all the fares. Honour again is satisfied – despite being a widow she can hold her head high before the world, raising her son as well as any woman on the street, paying off the loan on her purchased house. She lets the neighbour's children trail the long bus ticket from the open window. I am squeezed into the seat beside them, my fists clenching under my coat with the dull ache of jealousy.

The hospital looms through a narrow archway where washing hangs from the windows of the buildings which we pass under. High up there are the sounds of children's voices, shouts and small faces peering from tall dirty windows. The lane-way smells of burning tar and echoes with the clamour of beaten metal. An old blacksmith still works at a forge, the white mane of a horse shimmering among the flames and the enveloping mesh of grey smoke.

She pulls me on by the hand, her face tight with worry. The waiting-room is dirty, filled with the squabbles of listless children. The speech therapist has a white coat and horn-rimmed glasses. He must have had a face if only I could remember. But all I can see are the model farmyard animals neatly placed behind their plastic fences on the table. He wants to see if I can shift them around from one field to the other, if I can put wooden shapes into holes and match up numbers and colours. I know that something is wrong. I wouldn't be here if I could only pronounce the words to tell them so. Other children with moronic faces stare blankly at the bricks in their hands, one boy placing everything that he is handed into his mouth. The therapist seems annoyed that I am finished so quickly. He instructs me to watch over the others. I feel a deep shame at having to be in that room, yet I know that if I didn't deserve to be here my mother wouldn't have brought me.

Back outside in the lane-way she tells me that she has not got the bus fare home. The sweets for the neighbour's children, all the fares that had to be paid on the way in. None of it would have happened except for my own stupidity. The doctors must be right to treat me like this, even though Maggie's mother had told her that I had a brain like a shiny penny. She quizzes me about everything that occurred in the room.

'They must know what they're doing,' she repeats to herself. 'Surely be to God they must know.'

For me the walk home will be a new adventure, for her it must be a Calvary. The warmth has gone from the day. Ahead of us is the long road out by the cemetery with the cars passing, the shame that a neighbour might see us from a bus as the evening chill presses against our cheekbones. But before that there is the walled park and the birds. Somewhere between the hospital and the cemetery road she brings me there, through a small entrance hidden at the end of a dirty street which seems about to topple down. There are broken benches to sit on, and a narrow concrete path circling the mucky expanse of water. This is all that is left of the canal which stretched down to the Broadstone, she tells me, this sealed basin where flocks of birds squabble as they flutter on the water. I stare at them through the wire mesh while she rests on the seat behind me.

What are her thoughts as she gazes at the back of my clipped hair? Regret now that she was too proud to borrow the few extra pennies from the receptionist in the hospital? A realization, after all the stress, of just how unwell she really was? A sudden longing that, if and when she was gone, I might remember the moment when a late shaft of sunlight lit up the grimy pavement and I turned, so excited by the water and the squawking birds that I forgot about how I had come to be there, and she smiled my joyous smile back at me, feeling faint as she opened her arms and heard the clatter of my feet on the cement racing blindly towards her?

That's the house that my father will buy. The same sentence which Maggie always said at the end of our walks, like a promise if she was in good form or a threat if she was annoyed. It never mattered which direction we started out in; through the old village or the woodlands where the dog barked in the haunted house, the lanes dissolving into countryside or the narrow road that led to her mother's asylum. Because always it was the old cul-de-sac off the main street where we would wind up, the houses there far bigger than ours, mature trees in the front gardens, the brass name-plate for the doctor with his surgery times. The Headmaster lived here, as did the chemist, along with men in suits with cars who drove home at five to six every evening.

The cul-de-sac curved like a river and narrowed at the

end. Only one house stood there obscured by trees, two pairs of chimneys on the roof, five tall windows at the front. An Alsatian stood up to bark at us, straining on a chain. To the left an old beech tree dwarfed the house, a tyre on a rope swinging from a branch beneath it. Even when there was no wind the tyre seemed to sway as though an unseen child had just abandoned it. We knew who lived there but we never saw her. *The Widow Lady* was how local people referred to her. The Widow Lady who had once owned all the farmland which our houses were built on.

How many decades had passed since the child whom the swing was built for had run down that path? How many years of nights had it hung outside the house like a bloated rubber noose? The Widow Lady had had only one child, Heather, a girl to ride horses against the best of the men in autumn at the local show. There was only one field left which the Widow Lady had never sold. Cows grazed there among the rows of new streets. The old milking parlour was caved in, fragments of rusted machinery glimpsed inside through the narrow slitted windows like in an old Norman keep. If you crossed the field by the huge antiquated bath which served as a drinking trough you would see the rock which Heather fell against from a piebald horse in 1941. Older people said that the ground beside it was always bloodstained. Although the grass grew high around the rock, nobody had ever seen the Widow Lady's cows lie down in that spot. If you passed by in the moonlight you would see them staring out at you, eyes perplexed as they waited to be butchered, their flanks turned against that sharp outcrop of rock.

17

'That's the house that my father will buy.' Maggie always clenched her hands against the gates of the Widow Lady's house and pressed her face so tight between the bars that they left two red marks when she took it away.

'My father says that it is beautiful inside. Everything there old and untouchable.'

Mrs Boran down the road had a television set and once we were allowed in to watch a film of *Great Expectations*. Maggie grasped my hand when we saw the old woman sitting stiffly in the chair, the wedding cake bedecked with clusters of thick cobwebs. We knew that it was the Widow Lady whom we were seeing, that it was her house in which they had shot the film.

Did she ever look out of the top window and see the two small figures at her gate? I never asked my mother if what Maggie said was true, I didn't want my fears confirmed.

'I know you'll be living in a much poorer house, Michael, but you can still come down and visit me every day. If you're good we can take turns pushing each other on the swing.'

I knew that on the day when her father piled their belongings up on a truck I would be losing her. I would just be the poor boy at the gate if I ever came to visit, the same Alsatian would snarl at me alone and have to be calmed by her. One night I dreamt that Maggie had moved and when I went to visit her the hall door of the Widow Lady's house was open. I passed through room after room with doors which creaked, old floorboards bearing only the imprint of rats' paws among the settled dust. There was one room in the house where I knew that she was playing on a wooden rocking-horse wearing only a light white nightgown. It became morning and all the light was turning into dust. Only in her room was the sunlight clear, igniting her red hair and the bright pictures on the walls. I was unable to turn back and so I went on, opening all the heavy oak doors along the infinite musty corridor, knowing that I had already passed by hers.

'That's the house that my father will buy. He's a builder. He has it all stitched up with the Widow Lady.'

Only once did we see a soul in that garden. It was an autumn evening, the dusk refusing to be postponed. From the curve of the road we saw that something was different, there was a wet hissing followed by a crackling sound. We saw the light cast by the flames before we saw the bonfire itself. It lit up the swing under the old tree, then cast the swaying tyre back into shadow again. We reached the gates. An old gardener stooped with a rake, piling the dry leaves on to the bonfire of old branches between two blackened stones.

'Hello,' Maggie shouted, 'I'm the little girl whose daddy is going to buy this house.'

She called out to him over and over as he stooped to gather the final loose leaves with his rake. I began to call out too for her sake, my voice almost as desperate as her own.

'Hello, Mister Gardener! Excuse me, Sir.'

Was the old man deaf or did the likes of us simply not exist in his world? Blow-ins staring at the gate, strangers, outsiders with their bright clothes and accents. He placed the rake in the old wheelbarrow and began to push it down the curved path. He had to pass within a few feet of us. Maggie waved and shouted, her face red, her eyes close to tears. His face never turned as he vanished past the swing up towards the dark bulk of the house. Maggie's hands gripped the bars of the gate so tight I thought that the steel must be cutting into her bones. I put my own hand up to cover hers.

'Hello, hello! Can you not see us standing here? I'm the little girl whose daddy is going to buy this house.'

The ventilation hole above Maggie's boxroom door has been wallpapered over but still I don't feel secure during the two weeks I sleep there. Maggie's mother cooks breakfast for us both, Maggie's bare feet touching my knees secretly under the table. I'm too scared to let myself be scared, I keep laughing at things even when they're not funny.

Maggie's mother has an ugly gleaming Hoover, the noise of which used to frighten me. I would stand with one foot on the step of her kitchen door and my hand over my face, peering at it through my fingers as though it were a dragon which would twist away from her and slither towards me. I am older now but in those two weeks suddenly feel small again and uncertain. I do not like her bringing the Hoover inside my house. On the last day of the fortnight she hoovers the two rooms downstairs that are carpeted. A fire is being lit in my mother's bedroom for her home-coming that evening. The grate has been unused for years.

'She always set a fire there,' Maggie's mother says, 'for the morning when your father was due back on shore.'

Evening comes with a neighbour's black car. My mother must lie in the bed, the neighbour tells us. She needs complete rest, she is still unable to turn her head. The bedroom empties of neighbours and I alone am left.

Part One

Cropped hair and scrubbed face, white shirt and red tie, short black trousers and V-neck jumper. The front door shuts downstairs. How good it feels to have her back with me again. I want to laugh with her and play tricks, to pretend that her absence was just a game. I think of how funny it would be if I remained in the room without her knowing that I am there. I drop to the floor, wanting her to catch me out, waiting to laugh with her about it. How long am I stretched on the cold lino with the pattern of coloured balls of wool, watching the roses twist and climb their way up the wallpaper? I hold my breath and try not to laugh as my pulse quickens with excitement.

'Is there anybody there?' my mother calls out suddenly. Her voice is different from what I expected; anxious, vulnerable, almost scared. It makes me too frightened to jump up now, too ashamed of having to face her. Her voice calls my name, with an edge of anger now but still uncertain and fearful.

'Are you there, Michael? Answer me, son. If you are then it's a cruel trick to be playing on me.'

How much I have longed in those past thirteen nights for her to come home, how many new ways I have thought up to please her. The tacky sugar bowl hidden downstairs which I had saved up to buy for her from the sweet money neighbours had given me, the cheap knick-knacks I had collected that were to be my tokens of love. I can still feel the coldness of the lino against my bare legs, the hot tears beneath the surface of my eyes, the horror of being trapped on her floor at eight years of age. How I long to run to the bed and throw my arms around her, yet if I move or make a sound she will know that I betrayed her trust.

21

'Would you make a joke of your mother's illness? Michael? Answer me. Is there anybody there?'

I can neither rise nor stay. I feel that I am made of glass and any single movement will shatter my life. Her troubled voice repeats my name, calling across the few feet of space that divide us, across a gulf of patterned lino.

Dogger, the Kisk bank, Fishguard, Fastnet, Faroe. Late at night I would wake to hear the radio through the bedroom floor, the reports from coastal stations of gale warnings or winds rising or falling. I knew that my mother would be at the small kitchen window washing up the few supper dishes, making the cramped kitchen spotless, scrubbing out the huge white enamel sink. Did she sometimes stop, cloth in hand, and raise her eyes to gaze out through the narrow glass towards the trees being tossed about in the wind? Beyond them, beyond the safety of lit streets where shoals of boys like me lay sleeping, beyond the darkness which lurked inside the green railings of my aunt's cemetery and even further out beyond the city of speckled light which began after that, the bay would be rough tonight. From the lonely Bailey light winking at Howth to the savage goats loose on Dalkey Island. And in between, the clank of Guinness boats tied up on one side of the quays, the passengers like beasts in the rain queuing in concrete sheds on the other. And out past them all, the fishermen beyond the Kisk bank soaked through their yellow oilskins as they dreamed of low-lit shuttered bars and after-hours pints in the harbours of Skerries or Rush.

Dogger, the Kisk bank, Fishguard, Fastnet, Faroe. Like the moment at a dance when your special song is played.

Part One

The broken boxed wireless was still mounted on the wall
above my mother's bed which he had promised to fix the
next time he came home. Why did I seem to know that
every night as a young bride she must have lain there gazing
up at that wireless, waiting for those names ... *winds
steady and falling* ... knowing that her husband, my father,
was listening somewhere out on those rough seas, a mug of
tea held tight so as not to spill it, a spent cigarette flung out
from the wheelhouse and carried off in a cartwheel of sparks
down into the dark waves.

He had stayed on in this country when almost all his
family left, yet he had stayed by having to leave his home
twice a month, trawling for cod and haddock off Iceland,
hauling in nets which felt slimy and cold as death, throwing
the slithering dogfish back in. A folded telegram to say that
I was born, a torn telegram back to her to express his joy. A
photograph of a tall Mayo man with a peaked fisherman's
cap, a souvenir of a stick of uneaten sticky rock with the
word *Reykjavik* curving down the side. These were the
remains of my father in a black wooden chest, which he
had once brought home for me to store my toys in, and
which now rested beyond my reach on top of the wardrobe.

Dogger, the Kisk bank, Fishguard, Fastnet, Faroe. I could
never ask my mother where the storm had struck. An engine
failure first, then a fire which, when they put it out, had
extinguished all the lights. Floundering in heavy seas as the
radio hissed out an SOS. They were all fishermen, they
knew what to expect. Never learn to swim, they say in the
West, it will only prolong the agony. Did they speak much
or did they talk at all? The radio operator's voice droning
away like an echo trapped in a glass. Men with wives, men

with young families. Maybe they tried to write them notes, to wrap them in oilskin somewhere deep in their clothes and hope they would be legible if their bodies were washed up. Or maybe they just screamed out their rage at each other, '*It was your fault! No, it was yours, you bastard, all yours . . .*'

Another boat came across them some hours after they had hit the rock. The yellow newspaper on top of the wardrobe said that the captain of it had missed them at first. They were past my father's ship when an old crewman started to shout and point back. They could see nothing but the old sailor swore at them until they turned the boat back. Some heard the cries first while others made out the hull. '*Like a black whale lying just above the waves*', the captain said in the newspaper cutting. The force of the waves kept the vessels apart, the white splash as occasionally a man fell off the hull or else tried to swim towards the lights of the boat. Three men were taken alive from the water, the rest had vanished when dawn began to grey the blue-green waves. Did my father cling on to the side of the ship until it pulled him under or die striking through the water towards the lights that bobbed in and out of sight? As a child I always wondered if he might have somehow been overlooked, a raised arm and a head sticking out of the water, waving but too exhausted to call as the ship finally sailed out of sight.

Somewhere beneath the waves there is a picture of me being held with a sour sunburnt face on the dunes above Dollymount Strand, a part of me which was already buried before I could pronounce the word death. I lay awake in bed and thought of my mother alone in the kitchen below, more tired-looking now since leaving the hospital. Yet she seems to have the smile of a young bride as the radio announces that winds are falling. The floor is scrubbed, the delft shining, the table, as always, set out for the morning as though for a home-coming.

The final day when the world was perfect. Maggie's mother in work nursing the mad and my own mother with her sleeves rolled up, wringing out sheets on an iron mangle.

'The corner of the street and no further,' she tells us. 'If I go to the front door I want to be able to see the pair of you.'

The sun is hot, the water from the flapping sheets evaporating within seconds of dripping on to the cement path. We stop at the corner and look back, then Maggie steps over the crack in the pavement on to the next street.

'I'm telling on you,' I say and she throws her head back.

'Cowardy custard. You'll have to catch me first.'

I chase her down towards the main road and then further and further on even though it is forbidden. Neither of us wants to be the one to turn back. For over an hour we walk until finally we are wandering through the main streets of the city. Nelson glowers from the crest of his pillar, oblivious to how little time he has left. A bus pulls away from outside Clery's, a last passenger leaping on to the crowded open platform at the back. Cinema queues form in the afternoon. There is the smell of grease from Italian chip shops, the clink of slot machines inside long dim arcades with glittering mirrors at the front. We ache to taste the ice-cream cones being sold by the old lady reading the magazine in the glass hatch outside the gaudy fun palace.

Alone together for the first time in town we feel suddenly grown up. Maggie takes my hand as though it were the natural way that we walked. A countryman drops an untipped cigarette and crosses the street ignoring the beeping traffic. I pick the warm butt up. Too scared to inhale it, I hold it between my fingers as we stroll until it scorches them. We get lost along the quays, begin to panic until we find a landmark which we know and then follow the twisting bus route home. We stop at the Addison Lodge opposite the Botanic Gardens and sit on the bench outside the door till we are ordered away by the publican.

Although we are already late we cannot resist a walk through the gardens. The Long Walk, the Mill Walk, the Herbaceous Walk, the Rose Garden. Maggie reads the names out for me. I can't be sure if she's making them up. The afternoon sun hangs as though suspended between the old trees in the arboretum. Gnarled and twisted trunks there seem to be in pain, an enormous tree constantly sheds its millions of speckled leaves with a slight whispering sound. We lie on the grass by the sluggish brown river and swap dreams with each other.

'When we grow up,' Maggie says, 'I want us to live on an island in a river together. No one bossing us or telling us what to do. Do you promise me, Michael, do you promise?'

Thinking about her words on the long walk home which can be put off no longer, walking up the steep Washerwoman's Hill with a clot of anxiety on my parched throat. What will my mother say about us being out so long, what will happen if she finds out how far we have strayed from home? She is folding the dried sheets at the kitchen table, a small brandy glass of lemonade on the white window-sill

26

behind her. I only ever tasted lemonade at birthdays or Christmas or when my Uncle Ned came over. Now the sunlight at the window flows through the liquid as though it were champagne. I can see the bubbles sparkle and burst in the glass. She turns to smile at me. I know that she is not cross. I am aching with thirst and hope.

'I've been saving some lemonade for you, Michael. I knew you'd be thirsty after playing all afternoon.'

I put the glass to my lips and raise it higher and higher. I can almost taste the bubbles, my longing is so much. I throw my head right back and yet still I ache for the taste of lemonade. My mother is smiling as she watches, waiting for me to get the joke. I struggle to drink from the glass again, almost biting into it with my teeth in bewilderment.

'Can you not see that it's a trick glass, Michael? Mrs Cotter bought it in Hector Grey's in town. She's been bringing it all around the street. Look at the layer of glass on top of the real glass. See how the lemonade is trapped. Isn't it very clever?'

She laughs and takes the glass from my hand. I feel betrayed suddenly and insecure. When I start to cry with thirst there is nothing my mother can do to make me stop. Even when she bangs on the wall and sends Maggie down to buy lemonade from the shop it doesn't taste the same as what I'm longing for. I drink the whole bottle down, never lifting it from my lips, still blubbering even as I feel it dribble down my chin. But my thirst is like a yearning that can never be filled, like an omen that nothing will ever be complete again.

It is my bedtime when the knock on the door comes. I listen to the voice of the only neighbour on the road who has a phone in her house. She and my mother talk in low voices at the door. I am half dressed for bed. I come to stand in the hallway, feeling the cold lino beneath my bare feet. The stars look huge in the square of sky above their heads. I know that something is wrong. The same thirst is still there, an unease which is gnawing within me. I am scared as my mother closes the door. She kneels down on the lino beside me.

'We must pray,' she said. 'Maggie's father needs all our prayers. The poor man has fallen from a scaffold in Birmingham. He's in a coma, son. That's like being neither alive nor dead. Now you be a good boy and go up to bed. I have to go inside to look after Maggie's mother. Pray for him tonight, Michael, he needs your prayers.'

I wake only once in the night. The feel of bedclothes being pulled back and Maggie's body, hot from crying, being placed against my own. I can sense her tears although I keep my eyes shut. The room darkens again as the door closes over. After a moment I hear her voice, pitiful and desperate for comfort, whispering my name. I don't know what to say or to do and so I pretend to be asleep, not sure if she believes that I am or not. She turns her back and lies a few inches from me, crying in silence. I feel a little stab of pleasure, knowing that she won't be able to move away into her big house now. Both of us stay awake for a long time, neither turning towards the other. When I wake again in the morning Maggie is gone.

'*An island in the river. No one bossing us or telling us what to do. Do you promise me, Michael, do you promise?*'

It is the feast of Corpus Christi and my mother and I are

searching in my bedroom for my Cub Scout cap. I have my pole with its Brian Boru flag, my neckscarf and blue jumper with the coloured badges, my thick corduroy shorts. As the tallest boy left in the Cub Scouts I will be leading them in the procession but I will be the only boy marching bareheaded, without his green and black cap.

'Where did you leave it?' she shouts at me again. 'The same every week, we have to look high and low for your uniform. People will think we cannot afford to buy one. Why must you always be losing everything?'

We are late for the church, I have to run up the side aisle to take my place. As the hymns end the priests begin to march with the host, the altar boys following, dispensing wisps of incense. Then it is the FCA followed by the Children of Mary in their pale blue cloaks. The rows of Boy Scouts rise in front of me and now it is my turn to leave the pew, marching in step at the head of the Cubs. Our feet strike the stone floor in perfect formation, I raise our banner high. But all I can feel is the bareness of my head and I know that all my mother can see is my freshly crew-cut hair. She kneels among the other mothers, her head down when I pass, ashamed. The badges on my jumper bear the name of ancient warriors from Na Fianna. I think of their valour and tests of courage and resolutions.

Next year I'll do everything right for you, Mother, I'll make you so proud to see me marching like a warrior at their head. Next year . . .

There would have to be a next year. The Cub Scout's uniform traded in for the Boy Scout's uniform, the small prefab classroom left for the big secondary school, the short trousers swapped for the feel of flannel against my legs.

And she would have to be there to watch over me, so I could see her pride at every step.

Next year I was a Fianna warrior emerging from the forests to be confronted by bewildering drips and hospital charts. I was a Fianna warrior stranded without a spear to fling at them.

Whenever somebody died on my road I always dreamt about them. I would see them appear about their everyday affairs, the men coming home from work to wheel their black bicycles down to the sheds, the women leaning across hedges to chat to one another.

'Don't you know?' I'd tell them. 'You're dead. I mean you're not supposed to be still here.'

They would smile at me and shrug their shoulders, then carry on with what they were doing while I stared after them. My mother was the woman who always organized the street collections for the funeral wreaths. *Deeply missed by her grieving neighbours* ... For weeks afterwards our kitchen table was where their dazed children were coaxed and bribed with chocolate fingers that the Johnston Mooney and O'Brien bakery man delivered in his van. A mashed banana browned on my plate, the taste of it sickening me as I stared at their chocolate treats. They never smiled as they ate them but they never left any behind for me.

Afterwards I would be told to play with them as they sat on the living-room floor surrounded by my few toys, their eyes always too large, about to brim over with tears. What age was my mother then, what age was any mother on that street? It is hard to imagine those women as either young or old, with their nondescript clothes, their nondescript styled hair. It is hard not to think of them as being twenty years older than they were; impossible to conceive of them as women, naked beneath sheets, making love on Sunday nights. It is hard to imagine their shoes.

In those years death seemed to visit our road at regular intervals like an insurance man. I lived surrounded by new widows and widowers, saw them after ten o'clock mass on Sunday mornings queuing at the bus-stop by the bank, beneath the sign for the local horse show which finished that year. They carried lemonade bottles of water in their hands, had flowers carefully taken from their back gardens and wrapped in last week's *Sunday Press*. Everybody talked to everybody on my street, but in that Sunday morning queue, which started up past the pub at the crest of the village, nobody ever seemed to speak. They boarded the green open-decked bus in silence when it came, never gazing from the windows as I stared after them, straining for a last glimpse of Maggie with the black mourning star sewn by my mother on to the sleeves of her overcoat.

Even now my greatest fear is the fear of worms. I have never been able to rationalize or control it. Slimy and red with blind open mouths, some nights they still wriggle about in my dreams. After Maggie's father had died there was a new recurring dream. I would dream that I woke cramped up in the bed, needing to stretch my feet down along the cool sheets. I'm afraid to do so without knowing why I'm scared. As my foot slips down it makes contact with the slithering mass of red bodies. But it's not just my foot but my whole body that is lying on them. Worms. Juicy red maggots. *Oh Jesus Christ*, I would pray, *please let me wake up. Oh Jesus, Mary and Joseph, my skin is crawling with them.* And yet always when I screamed awake and my mother came in I would just sob without being able to tell her why. Because if I said their very name I feared that I would make them real. *The worms are after me, Mammy! The worms! The red worms!*

It was a scuttery evening in autumn. The concrete in Maggie's backyard was glistening after squalls of rain. Maggie and I stood against the dripping wall, staring at the old tin dresser from the kitchen which her mother had thrown out, at the piles of lino, the sodden mass of old bedclothes from the attic which were being discarded for some reason. Light came through the narrow kitchen window where our mothers were conferring. So many words seemed to upset Maggie now that we had barely spoken all evening.

'There's something moving behind the dresser,' she said.

It was dark between the dresser and the abandoned mound of concrete blocks, impossible to see anything there. Both of us hunched down and glanced at each other. An old newspaper had blown in behind the dresser, it felt wet and crumpled like dissolving flesh as I pulled it out. Maggie screamed suddenly and we both jumped back. The kitchen door flew open. Maggie was sobbing. My whole flesh was quivering. I felt that I was about to be sick.

'What's wrong now?' Maggie's mother said, jaded looking and flustered.

Maggie pressed herself back harder against the wall of the house.

'Did Michael do something to you? I'll kill him if he did,' my mother said. She looked unnerved and harassed, glaring at me as she spoke. Maggie shook her head and started to sob again.

'When are we going away, Mammy? I want us to leave this place.'

But not even her words registered as I gazed, transfixed, at the dresser. I know now that it can't have been real, that it must have been a ball of wool or rags left out in the rain. Yet Maggie had screamed too, though I could never ask her if she had seen the same red ball of maggots who were eating one another as they twisted and scrunched up. Having dreamt about all the others, I had been waiting to dream of Maggie's father. When I dreamt about them once I was never again upset by their deaths. But now I was sure that the worms were Maggie's father come to haunt that backyard, that he would be waiting, twisting beneath those concrete blocks, another nightmare which, like all the others, I would never be able to speak of to my mother.

Canada. The land of open plains and of Eskimos, of singing Mounties on horseback and children skating on the frozen lakes. Maggie's aunt and uncle lived in Toronto. She showed it to me on the little map on the back of the folder for the airline tickets.

'I'm not going for weeks and weeks yet.'

Every day for weeks she said that. Her house had to be kept spotless now that potential buyers kept coming to look at it. I helped her to make up the beds while her mother was serving out her notice at work.

'I dare you to take off your skirt.'

'Well then, I dare you to take off your trousers.'

We tumbled together on the bedroom floor, the sheet stretched between the two beds to cover us.

'We're alone in a cave on an island in the river, Maggie. And there's ferns growing down over the mouth of it. See how the light is all greeny. I dare you to take off your socks.'

Both of us kneeling in our underwear. My hand grasping the iron rail beneath the bed. And now it was her turn to dare.

'I dare you to take off your underpants.'

I was trembling so much that I thought if I took my hand away from the rail I would tumble forward on the rug.

'I'll only do it if I can dare you to take off your knickers. If you get to see my willie then I want to see yours too. I've never seen a girl's willie before.'

Maggie shook her head. For a second I thought she was going to break into tears. She pulled the sheet down over our heads and covered herself with it.

'I want to get out of the cave, Michael. I don't like it in here.'

'Maggie, we're alone on the island together. Remember . . .'

'Michael don't you know that I've no . . .' She stopped. 'Michael, is that the sound of the gate opening? Let's get dressed. Maybe that's my mother coming home early.'

I'm not going for weeks and weeks yet. But the date and even the hour was marked out in biro on the missionary calendar in the kitchen. So how did I miss it? All that morning listening through the wall to the noise of the removals men, or standing around out on the street by myself, with Maggie forced to stay inside and help her mother pack. Three boys were kicking a football further up the road. I had no other friends on the street except Maggie, I had never needed any. Now I watched the ball smash against the gate as one boy scored a goal. They were playing Three-And-In, there was no room for a fourth player even if they bothered to speak to me.

'Oi, so your friend is leaving?' one of them called out. I ran up like a lap-dog, startled and grateful to be spoken to.

'We're going up the back field,' he said. 'Do you want to come along with us?'

'I've got to say goodbye to her. She'll be leaving at half-two.'

'Listen, she's only a bloody girl. Anyway, sure we'll all be back for that. I hear there might be sweets going.'

I tagged along, trying to seem like I was one of them. They waded through the nettles and the overgrown grass, trying to peer over hedges into neighbours' back gardens. Did I genuinely lose track of time? Did I just trust blindly that they would bring me back before she left? I laughed whenever they laughed, watching them clown and push at each other. The tallest turned suddenly and shoved me off the narrow path. I fell backwards into the nettles.

'So did you see her cunt, did you? Did you ever stick your finger up it, what?'

They leered at me as I lay there afraid to get up. What were they saying about Maggie? And what time was it? One of them kicked me as I tried to scramble up. I stumbled again, then got away from them and raced through the high grass. I ran down the hill wanting to scream *Maggie! Maggie!* The street was deserted. My mother was in the kitchen, I think that she had been crying.

'Where were you, Michael? The whole street was out to

wave them off. Maggie wouldn't get into the taxi, standing on the path waiting to say goodbye to you. She was crying in the back of the car all because of you when they finally set off.'

Two weeks later the new owner began to clear the concrete blocks away from Maggie's garden. I stood at the hedge and felt like shouting at him. *Leave those alone. They belong to Maggie's daddy who's dead and turned into worms that will get out and all come after me if you take them.* He turned and grinned at me.

'This old garden is a right wilderness, eh,' he said. 'How could that young girl have ever played in it?'

I saw that he was holding a blackened jam-jar with the stumps of birthday candles in it, all of them shades of blue for the month of Mary. He shook out the withered petals of daisies and buttercups.

'I'll have it cleared in a few weeks and then you can come in over the new wall and run around if you like,' he said. He flung the jam-jar into the pile of sawn-down alder bushes and the woodwormed timbers from the old hen-house. He unscrewed the lid from the container at his feet.

'Run up and ask your mother for a potato wrapped in tin foil and I'll bake it in the bonfire for you,' he said. 'Wait till you see the flames from this lot when we pour the paraffin over it.'

I was alone in that house and I wore nothing except her shoes. Infinite afternoons of childhood, my body pale as a

luminous Virgin's statue and the long unfolding factory railings through the lace curtains, sheer unyielding lines of spiked steel, broken only by the reflection of my flesh in the window pane.

I was alone in that house from nine when she left me till five-thirty in the afternoon, flanked by delivery trucks and English accents from the back gardens. That summer when I turned eleven among grey squibs of English streets named after car manufacturers. Vauxhall Terrace and Bedford Avenue, Irish assembly workers watching their children's accents and minds grow flat. Afternoons of yellow sunlight with the feel of patent leather against my bare soles. Hours to open slowly the drawer pinholed by long-poisoned woodworm, to feel my heart tense that the front door would open. Primary colours were what she loved best, the vibrant reds, the black, the sheer whites that were smooth and crisp as egg shells to touch. I hear the iron gates of the factories clanging shut outside. That noise of steel striking steel excites me still, a pale echo of that childish thrill, illicit and yet innocent, all prevailing, choking my senses without release, without the knowledge of how to come.

If I close my eyes I see it as a print, once black and white and now toned down to grey. A boy of eleven with slim ivory buttocks standing on a square of patterned carpet which was regularly turned around a rim of black painted floorboards to make the edges equally worn. And there among the heavy wooden furniture, like painted lips, a pair of startlingly red high heels are raising him inches above the ground. His eyes stare through the lace curtains, behind which time has ceased, while his hands are spread above the

37

finest down of pale hair out from which a slim bewildered
penis is pointing nowhere.

We played until after dusk and even then we carried on
until the ball was just a shape guessed at in the dark. The
fleeting swish of a body in flight and then the thud of a
football boot on leather as my instincts guide me to dive
towards one goalpost or the other. The ball collides with a
smart of pain on my stretching palms, or thumps the
makeshift woodwork or sends scatterings of twigs and small
leaves plummeting down from the plum trees behind the
goal. I search for it in the dark and thunder it back towards
my opponent's goalmouth, neither of us willing to be the
first to give up. My breathing is fast and heavy in my ears,
my blood pounding, my legs clad in bruises which will
deepen in colour when I sleep; my eyes cannot see but still
they stare blindly out guessing at where the ball will come
flying from next.

A back door opens in a frame of light and a voice calls
him in. *Tomorrow*, he says reluctantly, *we'll finish the game*
off tomorrow. Tomorrow is just a throw-away word, like
time, a certainty that will occur forever. There will always
be time for my new friend to drag a wet square of foam
from an old sofa through the goalmouth puddles and wring
it out on the touch-line, to fix the gap in the wire where the
ball might escape, to climb on to the roof of a neighbour's
garage at first light and retrieve the missing ball. There will
always be mornings when I will wake and hear his hammer-
ing as he rebuilds the cracked goalposts and know that as I
rush my breakfast he is laying down a line of whitewash
across the centre of his back garden, the makeshift flags are

being stuck in place, the cardboard numbers redrawn for the scoreboard in the corner, and I will always be able to sneak my way across what was Maggie's garden until eighteen months before, through the hole in the hedge and past the broken bricks and rubble in the narrow gap between the railings and the garage wall to climb out beside the corner flag.

The game would never end, that much was certain. Dusk or dawn or hailstones could only postpone the ball which would be chested perfectly down, the shot that would be low and hard to his left and like an arrow piercing the patched-up heart of his homemade net.

And although for a short while longer my mother might have to lie there recovering in the back bedroom, assured of where I was from my grunts and shouts as I played football, it was as certain as tomorrow morning that soon she would be up again – the smell of her baking in the kitchen, her voice calling me in across the hedge. The future was an infinity of summer mornings when she opened my bedroom door to call me, of winters of cold lino on my soles as I searched for shoes, of breakfasts in the small kitchen where gas jets played beneath the old kettle salvaged from a ship which had once sailed the Atlantic. What other way could it ever be, when the final shot had been saved and I climbed back across the hedges, than for me to stand, framed by the light from the kitchen window, and to gaze down at the streaks of mud on my legs and arms as though somehow they were tokens of my love that I was bearing home to her?

The feel of my father's brother's hand, his huge fist tightly encompassing my own. There was a question about where we were going that night in early June which I was afraid to ask him. I had lost my cap again. Rain on my hair, dribbling down on to my nose. Queues for the cinemas along O'Connell Street, more queues stretching down Aston Quay. The half-light of dusk making those familiar streets seem strange. Youths passing with shouts, girls calling jeeringly after them. He pushed me on as I turned to look back. A tramp deserted the Customs House steps, tattered pages of *The Herald* and *The Evening Mail* left in his wake like trampled grass where a wounded animal had lain. The dark shapes of gulls gliding above the stinking river, along which, from every side street and bridge, another cluster of men and girls marched with tied-up suitcases.

The quayside cobbles were slippery underfoot, the sheds lit by harsh light where we waited to board the boat. First Class, Steerage, then sheep and cattle. I could smell their fear, hearing their hooves slipping on the gangway, a last bellow echoing up from the metal belly of a ship. A countryman, waving a crumpled sheet of paper, tried to force his way past the boarding officials.

'I paid a man good money for this in the Liverpool Bar,' he shouted as they blocked his path. 'He said it would get me all the way across. I've work to go to in Liverpool. Glory be to God, you're not going to stop me getting to it now.'

The terror that I could slip on the gangplank, the lurch of the boat as it left the quay, and the smoky bar where, before the lights of Dublin faded, I had grown sick with lemonade. The clink of Guinness bottles and talk of the price of land. A man in the passageway played the spoons, a child was sick, not moving as she held on to a chair and watched the vomit dribble down her white dress. My Uncle Ned discussed me with the barman at length. Men turned on their stools to gaze as they would at a yearling in a fair. I stepped through the narrow door and went up on to the deck. Ireland was already lost behind me, the future was just a seamless horizon of dark water and air.

At the prow of the boat the salty tips of waves lashed over, the foam slithering down the deck towards my feet. Light came from high portholes, a lifeboat swayed with a rusty creak. I edged forward until I was gripping the railing with my fists, wind tearing at my hair, water splashing down my cheeks. I felt so cold there, and shaken and pure. No need for fears or thoughts about the months which had passed since Christmas, just me alone battling with the elements. If I slipped into the waves who would be left to notice that I was missing? Strangers with blackened potatoes I could barely eat during that succession of neighbours' beds. Then my father's sister, Aunt Maire, had taken me in. 'Just for the moment, anyway,' she had said on the first evening.

I kept remembering a television programme I had seen in Mrs Boran's house about a reformatory in the west of Ireland. The boys who were interviewed had small pinched faces and dead eyes. One boy had a scar across his shaved temple. He had run away once, he said. Miles of bog and walls of loose stones, climbing into a sty to see if he could steal some of the food that the pigs had been given. He described the lights of the cars on the bare mountainside, and how the guards had laughed, handing him back to the Brothers who had woken the other boys and crowded them down into the huge wash-house where he knelt, stripped naked, with his head down a toilet, and the way the other boys had been beaten too if they took their eyes away before the Brothers were finally finished with him. '*The Da was gone and the Ma just didn't want me,*' he had said.

A stout man with nicotine-stained fingers visited my school twice a week. The truant man, checking the attendance register, calling boys who had been mitching up. He had a leather strap inside his case, he had court warrants. Even the teacher seemed afraid of him. *The Ma is gone and people just don't want me.* After seeing that programme I would put my schoolbag up on the desk and try to hide my head behind it, waiting for him to call out my name, once even wetting myself when he stayed too long in the classroom.

My uncle's hands gripped me suddenly and pulled me back from the rail of the ship. His eyes in the light from the first-class cabins seemed genuinely afraid. I felt a little hot stab of power, imagining his terror at having to explain my absence to the two *émigré* families who were gathering to meet us.

'Are you cracked, boy, standing there waiting to be carried off by a wave? There's a man who wanted to meet you, a cook who sailed this very route with your father over twenty years ago.'

The important feeling of being ushered down below the deck, along passageways marked *Crew Only* and into the room where the sailors sat. The room swayed as the cook piled my plate up with chips, telling me that I was the spit of my Da, laughing with my uncle about stories from the past which I could not follow.

'Your mother was a lovely woman.' The cook leant over

the table. 'I was at your father's wedding. Now, did you know that?'

I couldn't eat anything after her name was mentioned. I didn't want to hear the cook talk anymore, I only wanted to be back out by myself on the deck. He gave me a bottle of lemonade as we left. In the dormitory men talked in low voices while others, trying to sleep, cursed them under their breath. I lay on the lower bunk, hearing my uncle shift above me, the soft tearing noise of a match being struck. I smelt the Sweet Afton placed between his lips. Although he had come to the house each Christmas and Easter I only remembered clearly one visit before those months. A wet Saint Stephen's Day with turkey sandwiches and rows of emptied stout bottles or 'dead men' as he called them. And Ned, slightly drunk, suddenly trying to play with me as he imagined a father might, chasing me into the front room and, when I stumbled, holding his foot on my stomach so that I was trapped on the floor. I never forget his laugh as he looked down at me and the way he seemed desperate that I should laugh as well. There had been no words between us, just his foot on my chest and his laughter until I started to cry and Aunt Maire came in to scold him out of the room.

My Aunt Maire with the neat bungalow which my mother would never visit. The unspoken tension between them each Saint Stephen's Day; both of them over-polite, anxious to get away from each other. My mother said that Maire had gone off to become a nun and not succeeded. When she had returned home my grandmother told her that it would have been better for her to come back into the house inside a coffin than to be disgracing the family. Years later she had married a schoolteacher in Dublin when her parents refused to allow the wedding in Mayo. It was my father, her youngest brother, who had given her away. Even when her husband died of a heart attack eight years later, cutting turf at the weekend in Wicklow, Maire's mother had attended the church but refused to set foot in her daughter's bungalow.

Despite her failure, the McMahon family had two cousins who were priests and an uncle a doctor in Mountrath. One Saint Stephen's night, when they had gone and my mother had allowed herself two Babycham, she told me about before they were married, the only time when my father had brought her to the family house. They had sat in the kitchen in Mayo while the kettle boiled, then my grandfather had made her laugh with jokes as he filled the china teapot. Aunt Maire came in as he was about to pour it and had flung the hot tea out into the sink.

"Since when in this house have we started using the good china for some poor farmer's daughter?'

I had thought of that story every evening during the four months that I lived with Aunt Maire. I would invent homework so that I could sit alone in her front parlour which was reserved for visitors. There was a smell of floor polish that always reminded me of death. Dust covered the wooden logs in the fire which she set every January to be lit on the following Christmas morning. Scurrying rickshaw men were frozen into raised plates of china above her heavy stained sideboard where a communion photograph of her only son in America was framed. I slept in his bed among his old copy books filled with cuttings about the exploits of English pilots in the last war. And when I woke I momentarily listened for my mother's knock on the bedroom door, before cursing myself for still remembering. In February, after Emily's letter came, Aunt Maire scrubbed my face and brought me to Woolworths. I had cried, surprising myself as I sat on the swivel chair, staring towards the eye of the camera.

'Dry your eyes quickly, Michael,' she coaxed through the curtain. 'Will you not try to look happy for your godmother?'

I had cried harder, staring pleadingly at the glass in front of the camera, thinking *she must send for me when she sees me like this*.

Now here I was on the boat. In the bunk across the narrow passageway two men discussed the devil appearing in a house a few streets away from my old home. I was frightened, I wanted them to stop. They droned on, smoking and passing a bottle back and forth while I lay listening to the throb of the engines as the ship lurched, until finally I slept.

It was just after dawn when I woke. The dormitory was silent now, trapped smoke near the ceiling caught in the slat of dusty light through a window. I was still clutching the empty lemonade bottle which the cook had given me. I followed the distant noise of voices out on to the deck. It was misty and freezing. The ship was docking at Birkenhead. An oldish man with a white beard stood on the quay. He frightened me even more than the figure behind him with the gun. Men pulled on the ropes which had been thrown from the lower decks. The gangplank came across. I was alone at the rails. The man with the white beard never looked up. He stared straight ahead as the first of the cattle crossed the plank. One was limping slightly as she stumbled on to the concrete. The man nodded once and the shot rang out. The frightened cattle parted around her as the blood discoloured the stone. Six times the man with the white beard nodded at limping beasts and six times the rifle was fired. No passengers came out from the dormitories or opened their cabin windows. The rest of the cattle had vanished, herded into the concrete sheds. The bearded man looked up as the ropes were being thrown back on to the lower deck. He smiled before he turned to walk in for his breakfast. From the heap of bloody carcasses a buckled leg twisted a few times and then stopped.

The ship sailed carefully on down the Mersey Channel. After a time warehouses and docks came into sight on the far shore. I found a piece of paper and carefully wrote my name and old address along with a short note: *Will whoever finds this please tell my Mammy I have been kidnapped.* I pushed it down into the lemonade bottle and let it dangle over the railing in my hand. A workman was watching me from the dock. I threw it out as far as I could but the wind carried it back to smash against the side of the ship. The man shouted something. I ran away into the dormitory where the men were rising, terrified that the man in the white beard would be waiting to nod towards me on the quay at Liverpool.

Before those weeks I had never taken the slow bus which strayed down through the estates, taking an eternity to twist its way beyond Phibsborough. Always with my mother I had taken the bus from the village which sped directly along the long road by the cemetery. Now, with a neighbour's hand on my shoulder as I stepped on to the back platform and the conductor rang the bell, I spent those December journeys staring in silence through the steamed-up windows, the streets beyond the glass distant and unreal, with my stomach sickening as we lurched towards the Broadstone.

There is a floodlit Virgin on a raised plinth high on the wall of the old train station, a harsh halo of electric light circling her head. I dread having to pass her, the guardian of a frontier between one world and the next. Beyond her lurk the smells from high blocks of flats and the uneven pavements where rough children run shouting through the dark. We cross a narrow road of poky shops where spinsters with cobweb hairnets gaze out over dusty trays of sweets. And then we reach the gates of the Victorian hospital, the original plans for which had been confused in London with those for an Indian barracks, the mistake only realized as the foreign turrets and domes were being erected under a rain-grey Irish sky. I do not want to look at them, I lower my eyes, almost halting on the gravel. I am the boy in the rain, too young to grasp the dread in people's faces, the way in which they hiss at me to hurry on.

Can I remember the feelings that I have about seeing my mother, or do I just recall being tired and wet and knowing I have to face the same long wait for that irregular bus back? No, despite everything, I can remember love as well, a love which I have made myself forget; the scrap of paper where I had written *I love you* over and over again and then filled it in with thousands of kisses, every inch crammed with tightly packed Xs until my hand ached.

I squeeze it into her hand in the hospital and she clasps

the paper, knowing that I don't want her to open it until everyone has gone.

'He's a brave little boy,' the neighbour tells her and I say nothing, just clasp her hand so tight that I know I must be hurting her. Nobody ever tells me what it is that is wrong. I listen to scratchy Christmas carols being played in the corridor, watch nurses stringing decorations above the line of beds. They have told me not to be frightened by the fact that she will be wearing a wig. Her head has been shaved for the operation. She jokes with the neighbour about the cost of it, saying that she will keep it afterwards in case she never has time to do her hair. The neighbour smiles and then looks away. Could she have known that she was so close to death? Was the last visit any worse for her or was each occasion the same muted torture?

'What a Christmas we'll have together this year, Michael,' she promises and then asks me whether I have been fixing up the front garden for her as I had promised. The last words I remember speaking to her are lies about how I have cleared the weeds from the flower-bed near the hedge and carefully cut back the grass which had grown long since the early autumn. I falter, desperate for her not to know that I am lying.

It is time to go. I don't remember her kiss or what final words she may have spoken. I have only a vague memory of being held very tight, the unexpected strength in her hands which I know now was terror. And of turning at the glass door to see her leaning forward in the final bed at the end of the ward, still frantically waving and smiling, trapped forever in my mind under those tightly wrapped blankets.

*

48

After the boat docks there is a day of trains and bewildering junctions, of black faces and endless redbrick cities. It is evening time and a band is playing *Long, long ago in the woods of Gortnamona* as the first couples dance in Saint Bridget's Irish Club in Birmingham. How long is it since I have eaten a full meal? An inventory of snacks in different houses. In the garden of one a young girl my own age shows me goldfish lying motionless as rocks near the bottom of a tiny pond. The backs of houses close in on all sides, their tiny gardens crammed with crazy-paved paths and plastic slides.

'What's your garden like?' she asks and I don't know whether to describe my mother's garden or Aunt Maire's to her. When I describe my mother's it is in a whisper so that my uncle cannot hear in case I am doing wrong.

The song ends to scattered applause amid the clink of cash registers. I keep my distance from the circle of strange faces that I have been told to call aunt and uncle. McMahons and McGills uncomfortable together. They listen closely as my uncle Ned speaks. What is he telling them about me? I feel as if I am being auctioned at the table as one of his sisters raises her head, her smile warning me to go off and pretend to play with my cousins. When I sneak back they are laughing.

'Mrs Paisley went to the dentist,' one uncle says. '"How is the mouth?" he asks her. "Oh, he's right as rain," she replies. "He's above beyond making a speech in Belfast."'

'Oh, a right Godshite,' another uncle agrees and lifts his half-empty glass. 'But he's going nowhere fast. Out throwing snowballs at Lemass and O'Neill. Them two men are the boys to sort him out.'

Emily looks as though she cannot possibly belong among them. The only single woman there, the lipstick making her teeth so white when she laughs. The band stops and the MC announces that the bingo will commence. The women begin to make room to spread out their cards among the queue of full rounds which are waiting to be downed on the table. It is safe to venture back towards my seat. I'm terrified that I will have to go home with one of the McMahons. I lean my head against Emily's crinkly plastic coat on the chair.

The sickening feeling of being woken in a public place. I blink in the harsh lights, the barmen shouting time, my stomach queasy from crisps and lemonade. The Irish national anthem is playing. I stand to attention like I have been taught in the Cub Scouts. I know that a decision has been made while I slept. The music stops and Uncle Ned touches my arm.

'I've trains to catch to get the morning boat, boy,' he says, 'but no doubt we'll be seeing you soon again.'

Emily catches my eye and smiles. I nod and then look down at her shoes. Outside on the street the cluster of relations begins to break up, the McMahons in one group, Emily's two brothers with their wives in another.

'When we all meet again let's hope it's a wedding and not a funeral,' one says as he winks at Emily and they all laugh.

I stand beside her, still gazing at her black shoes. Each uncle offers us a lift before starting their return journeys to different cities. My eyes hurt less in the night air as I let Emily take my hand. Both of us are nervous now that we're left alone, neither of us certain what to say next.

I close my eyes and my first memory comes back. Three

faces, feminine and familiar, leaning into my line of vision. Three sisters growing up on a Roscommon farm. I remember my mother telling me about the Sunday when the fishing hook got caught in their brother's eye and the three of them drove the loaded hay cart into town. The way the doctor's housekeeper refused to let them in and Emily, the youngest, had sat down on the hall carpet, not budging until she finally called the doctor out from his dinner. And how years earlier the three of them had stolen their mother's best pot to cook toffee in the fields and stayed out hiding till after dark, afraid to return home when the bottom of the pan got burnt. Three sisters in matching dresses on a Roscommon farm, old enough to turn the heads of local boys, sharing secrets as they peed among the bushes behind the cow byre. The dreams of the men whom they would marry, the quarrels about who would be the first godmother to whose child.

Three faces, feminine, familiar, bending forward over the cot where I lay. The edges of their features softened as in an old photograph, their smiles anxious. Could I really have remembered that, the eldest sister dead within a year of my being born? Three sisters delivered after their mother had carried seven brothers; the last, a seventh son of a seventh son, called in from the fields to cure mumps and ringworm. My christening was the last occasion when the three of them had gathered. A freezing February morning with frost underfoot as Emily carried me the quarter of a mile to the church in the christening shawl, which Betty had brought up from the farm. Emily protesting that Betty, as the eldest, should be the godmother. My mother still sore after giving birth three days before and my father, home on leave, walking beside Betty's new husband and hoping that the boy from the pub would arrive on time with the bottles clinking in the wooden box on his handlebars. The sailor who was my father's best friend asking Emily what she would sing afterwards.

'We've been best man and bridesmaid and now godfather and godmother,' he says. 'If this keeps up we'll become godhusband and godwife.'

Emily telling him to get away with himself as she tried not to look pleased, and afterwards saying that yes, she did sometimes come home from Birmingham, and no, she would not promise to be in Dublin when the ship got back from Portugal, but if she was then they would find out if he was as good a dancer as he claimed.

Emily later on that day, standing out in the freshly dug back garden and remembering the first train journey from Castlerea to Dublin and that house in Sydney Parade where the woman had wanted her to spend her evenings sitting upstairs in the boxroom. *'None of the girls in my employ ever went to dances. There's enough sewing to be done if time weighs so heavily on your hands.'* And the evening my mother had called with the soda bread for Emily and was told by the woman to go back down the street and through the lane to knock on the back door. The way Emily had phoned a taxi and sat in the hall on top of her case, not moving until the woman had paid her every penny due and then refused to leave by the back way, even when she threatened to call the police, until the woman was forced to open the front door for her. And how the taxi-driver had clapped when Emily walked to the bottom of the steps and had turned the meter off and made them laugh by impersonating the woman's voice all the way out to my mother's new home.

'How do you find England?' the sailor asks as he comes out from my christening party and offers her his last cigarette. She insists on him taking her packet, and he makes her write her address on the inside flap.

'I'll never smoke them now because the packet is too precious,' he says and Emily warns him never to say never. The future is unknown. Who could have known that when the three sisters next gathered in a church the eldest would be boxed in wood, that somewhere on the ocean floor a packet of Players No. 6 would be dissolving, wisps of flake drifting like plankton through shoals of flat-eyed fish?

Who could have known that a decade later only one of the three sisters would still be left, standing on a foreign street with the only child that any of them had borne? I open my eyes and Emily turns with a tentative smile.

'You looked so sad in that last photograph.'

I make no reply and she smiles again, as though embarrassed.

'Have you ever walked through a big city at night?'

I shake my head and we begin to walk. Windows filled with glamorous shop dummies with startled eyes. The strangeness of seeing men with turbans. The lights and warmth of an all-night coffee shop. The way her teeth shine when she lifts the coffee cup and laughs. The manner in which the man behind the counter winks. The light at the window beside our table flashes off and on. I take my cue from her, lift my fork when she lifts hers until she catches me and laughs again.

'Your mother was a terror for having everything right

and in its place,' she says. 'She was good at organizing things but sure I was always the scatterbrain. God knows I always meant to do things, but . . . funny the little things you fall out over. It hurt your mother, Michael, that Betty's grave never had a headstone, but she and I were no longer Betty's next of kin. I mean, the woman had a husband for two years before she died. The plot was in his name, we hadn't the right to erect anything. He left Ireland and married again soon after. I hadn't even got an address for him. She wanted me to be searching for him high and low across London, reminding him of his duties. If I had him in front of me God knows I'd have probably torn him to shreds, but sure I'd be no good at that Agatha Christie sort of thing.'

I try not to listen to what she is saying. I feel so grown up in this late-night coffee shop that the boy in the rain outside the hospital might have been somebody else. Emily sees how uncomfortable I am each time she tries to mention my mother's name. She talks instead of the clothes that she must buy me, of the way my hair will look if I grow it longer. She teases me that all the girls' heads will be turning within a week or two, seduced by my Irish charm. Two men have come in behind her. They lean on the counter and glance down, inspecting her neck. I outstare them with a cold unblinking look because I am a grown man of eleven years and she is my girl. One mutters something and they look away, grinning to each other, but I know and they know that I have defeated them.

Having never run away from home I could only imagine the suspense of sheltering beneath a dripping hedge, my small bundle for a pillow while I read my annual by the light of a street lamp high above the lane-way. And how my mother would be sorry now for the cross words which she had spoken as she fretted in the bright police station while detectives shone their torches down every back lane, always drawing in closer to where I lay. And although I was shivering and lonely I would be certain that soon they would find me huddled up there, that warm blankets would be placed over my shoulders, the night gliding past from the back of the squad car until their voices grew hushed as I ran, with all our quarrels resolved, into my mother's waiting arms.

One night, when I was nine, I threatened to go. My mother told me that I was welcome to, even found me a bag and said that she would help pack whatever possessions I wanted to bring. I can't remember what triviality I was sulking over, only the sudden terror when my threat was taken up. My anger had turned cold, I felt already homeless. I wanted to run to her and cry but I was determined that I was going to show her how I could manage on my own. I didn't pack any clothes, just my favourite toys, a tattered teddy bear I had not touched for years and the few torn annuals which I could still barely read. And all the time I kept waiting for her to change her mind. She couldn't just let me go, I thought, soon she must break down in tears. But she was calmly buttoning up my duffle coat. I went down the stairs to the hall door. I was old enough now to turn the knob by myself. The night seemed cold and vast as it waited to consume me beyond the corner of the street. I may have even walked as far as the gate. When I turned she was waiting, an amused smile on her lips. I dropped the bag and began to cry as she reached down for me to run into her arms.

'I'm sorry for all the things I said, Mammy. I'll never leave you. I'll never ever run away from home.'

'Come in, Michael, and we'll tuck you up in your own warm bed. You know that I'd have never let you go.'

It is a year since that night. I am sitting writing Christmas cards to both my new friends along the road. Soon I will go out and slip them in their letter-boxes. It is the Sunday before Christmas and I am wondering what presents I will receive, which day my mother will come home on, will she find the small present that I have hidden in the hot press for her.

I don't like being alone in the house. The key is left in the door for neighbours to come and go. A neighbour comes in and his voice sounds almost sharp.

'We have to go in to the hospital quickly now,' he says. 'Come on, get your coat.'

The smell of cigarettes in his car, the awful silence of the two women I am sitting between. I feel sick suddenly, I think of the Christmas cards left on the table, the bright colours of the reindeer and the sparkly snow. They are shoving me down the corridor. I have to trot and keep up with them, people staring after us, the noise of our boots on the stairs. My Uncle Ned is standing in the top corridor. His face is strangely hollowed. He shakes his head and as the women begin to cry their two husbands turn to comfort them. For a moment I am left alone, bewildered by all these adults suddenly grieving. I stare at my uncle but he can't look back at me. And when I cry I am crying because they are all frightening me. Where is my mother and why won't they let me see her? Nuns in white robes descend like seagulls over bread. There are nurses kneeling at her bedside. The rosary is being said. But who is this woman with the features of my mother, this woman in a strange robe with rosary beads twisted around her hands? When I pray I pray that my mother will come for me soon, that this confusion will all end. There is so little time between now and Christmas and we have so much to get done.

Back in the car each of the neighbouring women holds one of my hands.

'Come into my house now, Michael, and we'll give you a special treat.'

I wait until we have left the car before breaking free of them. They call after me. The key is still in the front door, I turn it and run down the hall. The kitchen is empty, the unfinished cards on the table. I am about to call her name when I stop. I walk up the stairs not knowing what I expect to see. The ghost from my first dream, the lady in white whose smile has haunted me? The bedroom doors are open, the sun dying in the boxroom. I sit on my own bed surrounded by my own things, that tattered teddy untouched since the night I had packed him to leave, the paintbox with the brushes, the toys and annuals. I hear footsteps in the hallway, anxious voices coaxing me down and I realize that home has run away from me.

For five minutes every morning that summer Emily's road was a black mass of men. A hooter sounded and then there was silence until the evening when they spilled out again. At night the lights of the factories shone, the hooter at three o'clock in the morning as lonesome as the distant sound of a train. Ever since it had woken me on the first night I would wake up moments before it sounded and listen for its muffled fog-horn moan. I relived the day's humiliations as I lay there. The torture of such simple things as queuing in a chip shop, trying to control my stutter as I asked over and over for a single of chips.

'What do you want, mate? A single chip is it, or a bag, or what?'

The shopkeeper looked at the queue behind me for support.

'A single,' I managed to stammer, 'just give me a single, or give me a one and one instead.'

I kept repeating the Dublin phrases in bewilderment until someone laughed and I ran from the shop.

Emily kept her copies of *She* and *Woman* in the wardrobe where she thought I couldn't find them, and once a week settled down on the sofa for a good read of the week old *Roscommon Champion* which she had to take two buses across Birmingham to purchase. Afterwards she would leave it out for me, saying that it would remind me of home. I struggled to read the notices of drink-driving cases, court cases over stolen turf and trespass of cattle, advertisements for fertilizers and new brands of sheep dip, meticulously kept parish notices, and tried to think of home. One evening she was convulsed with laughter when reading the court notices and kept refusing to say what the joke was. She cut out the article and tore it up before passing the paper over to me. Later when she was upstairs I tried to put the scraps in the bin together again. The only sentence I could make out was '*I was relieving myself in the corner of the field when the cow backed into me.*'

The column which Emily most lingered over was buried among the small ads and marked *Matrimonial*. She would read each entry carefully and then laugh with a shake of her head. I loved it when she laughed like that, loved the red sheen of her nails when she put her fingers over my face. Everything on the street outside was threateningly foreign. But I loved the snug feeling of being with her in the house. And even when she was gone I loved the scents and sense of presence which she left behind.

In the mornings I would hear her rise for work while I lay on. At lunch-time she hurried out from those black gates and across the road to be with me.

'If you were old enough,' she would always say, 'I could get you a job in the car plant for the summer.'

And then she would have to go at two o'clock, hurrying back before the noise of the hooter left me alone in that limbo. I would lean my head against the banisters and watch her go, smiling her anxious smile up at me. Those same eyes that all three sisters possessed. It was like my first dream now curiously reversed – with me at the top of the stairs gazing down at one of the sisters, who wasn't unable to leave the hall but unable to stay.

Did I haunt Emily's afternoons as she checked off the quality control sheets, recording the batch numbers, filling in the details of the safety tests? A woman at the stained counter beside the punch-clock, a woman in a white company coat ensnared by columns of figures to be ticked off, lifting her head over the hammerings and sparks from the assembly lines to gaze at the far wall in the direction of her home.

How could she have ever known? There were many afternoons that summer but when I look back they all seem to have merged into one. A boy that age is curious, an explorer in search of a world. Was I lonely? I never allowed myself to think of such words. I had a longing, a hunger which I could not trace the source of. And when I touched her shoes that yearning seemed to stop.

Always the first task was to remember the position of everything in her drawer. On the left were the soft piles of pastel-coloured panties with her tights beside them, and then the odds and ends of her life in the centre – the first ticket stub for the boat from Ireland, a broken necklace (the loose beads of which could be so easily disturbed) and an old menu from a company dinner-dance signed by everyone at the table – and next to that a torn envelope which I never opened. Beyond them to the right lay the cluttered assortment of sandals and high heels, of suede shoes and leather boots.

If they had been placed there in some order then it would have been easy just to lift a pair out and put them back when it was time for her to return. But unlike the neatly folded clothes in the other drawers, her shoes seemed to evade all attempts to organize them. Often she muttered to herself that she must clear out the drawer upstairs and then smile ruefully, saying that she had never been able to throw a pair of shoes away. But still I was too scared to take chances. I would kneel like an archaeologist in the rubble of a site and gently prise each shoe out, leaving in their place a thread of my hair to mark the spot where the heel had rested.

I put the shoes on the floor and closed my eyes. I was naked, I was Cinderella. Each slender shoe fitted my white feet. I stood tall in them, I tried to walk and found my body twisting into new shapes as I learnt how to balance. The crisp click of a heel on the stairs, each step amplified through the empty rooms. And the way I forgot everything except the feel of leather, the way it gripped my instep, supported me, made me strong and secure.

What did I wish for at that moment? Did I fantasize or was the moment in itself enough, the illicit thrill of standing behind the lace curtain terrified that she would return early, the new sensation of a penis throbbing with blood? Sometimes I imagined a country girl who might have fallen straight from the pages of the *Roscommon Champion* and sprained her leg. The bicycle wheel is still spinning among the nettles in the ditch beside the desolate bog. And there is nobody about as I come across her lying helplessly, half on and half off the road. She is frightened of my English accent. She tries to shy away as I kneel beside her in the grass but I catch a hold of her bare leg. She is at my mercy as I slowly prise her shoe off. Nothing else occurs between us but I can still almost feel her hot swollen shin, the smoothness of her ankle, her slight gasp of pain or release as the shoe is slipped off.

I open my eyes in Emily's sitting-room. Through the lace curtain I see the security man reading his newspaper in the hut at the factory gate. I panic suddenly, not certain of the time. Will I be able to get the shoes back in the right place in the drawer, will my face betray what I have been at? I am running in her high heels now, my buttocks jutting out as I clamber up the stairs. And life is a series of steps being climbed out of breath, a tingling which envelops all of my flesh, a line of red leather that cuts its way into my instep.

I remember little of the funeral beyond standing to attention and being told that I was a brave little boy, the grey stones in the mound of damp earth and the grave-diggers arguing with each other because they were not finished when we arrived. They had stopped and put a green awning over the grave, still annoyed with each other as they blessed themselves at the back of the crowd. A year before, John Kennedy had been shot and I remembered how touched my mother was then at the newspaper picture of the little boy who had saluted at his grave. I was wearing my Cub Scout uniform. I wanted to raise my fingers to my skull and stand stiffly to attention. I wanted her to be watching among the crowd, proud of me this time in my green and black cap.

I wanted to forget the previous evening when we had brought her from the undertakers to the church at six o'clock. A crowd of people waiting in the winter dark and at the back of them the two friends whose Christmas cards I had never posted. One waved and then stopped, uncertain if the gesture was correct. I read the inscriptions on the plastic wreaths which were piled in the alcove where the coffin rested, and watched the cards pile up on the varnished wood. A wreath had been sent from the Cubs and another from my class in school. I felt a thrill of importance that for once they must all be talking about me.

Afterwards, back in the house, the neighbours had passed around ham sandwiches and pressed red ten-shilling notes into my hand. And I had stood in the hall, still stupidly waiting for my mother to come home, even though I had seen her in the coffin and had been unable to kiss her unfamiliarly painted lips. In the kitchen behind me Aunt Maire kept washing and drying dishes, awkward at being there, needing to be doing something. My Uncle Ned kept repeating to people that he was only my father's brother, that all my mother's family were in England but he was expecting her younger sister to come back. He said it apologetically as though wanting to excuse his presence in the house. His face looked red, he kept wiping his palm over his forehead as though it were lined with sweat.

My home was a house filled with so many strangers that nobody heard the gypsy woman until she had knocked several times. She asked for my mother and broke down in tears when they told her that my mother was gone. She sat on the front step with a shawl pulled about her.

'I've lost the only friend I had,' she cried and when they tried to give her money she pushed it away, still sobbing as they persuaded her down the path. At the pram by the gate her young son stood, wearing my old clothing. He stared at me as he did every week before his mother pulled him away.

After the gypsy had gone people drifted back into the living-room. Aunt Maire was starting to scrub out the presses, standing on a chair, her eyes mesmerized by the cloth in her hand. I drifted into the empty front room where somebody had lit a fire which was now dying out. I was waiting for something to happen. Somehow I half-believed that the face caked with make-up was about to break into a smile, the eyes about to flicker open. When I closed my eyes I could see it so vividly that I convinced myself it was occurring. The lights would be dim on the side aisles, and the few old parishioners still left at their prayers glancing at each other as if to say that the knocking must be the heat in the pipes switching off. I pictured their shock when they heard the kiss of wood against wood as the lid slid back. Just like in the ghost stories they had told us when we camped out with the Cub Scouts, the mistake discovered at the last minute, the twist in the tale which always revealed a happy ending.

I opened my eyes. My mother has left the church by now, I told myself, the parishioners calmed and rejoicing after their initial fear. Her limbs would be stiff after all that stillness. I must be patient and let her walk home at her own pace. I tried to count the steps, imagining her in that habit passing the shops now, pausing at the corner, seeing all the lights on in the house like a ship in a port. How many steps was it from the corner to here, which house would she be passing next?

A figure came into view beneath the lamppost at the bend in the road. I gripped the window-sill with fright. Her height was right, the way the light shone on her hair. She was looking at the houses as though surprised to find herself lost. My mother was dead, they had all told me that she was. But it had been a mistake, a mix-up of bodies, or else she had heard me calling to her and was coming back. No, I told myself, it must be somebody else. But she was stopping at the gate. She opened it. I ran out into the hall, wanting to scream *'She's back, she's back!'*

The key turned in the front door and for a moment I was afraid to look up. Emily once said that when I did, the desperate hope she saw in my eyes filled her with terror. I never cried out, I just stared. Had the coffin changed her so much or was she somebody else? The features were so familiar, the same eyes and turn of the mouth. But they were like a jigsaw which had been patched-up wrong. The make-up and the hair, the red lipstick. We stared at each other, both shocked. Then she tried to smile.

'Do you know me, Michael? I'm your Aunt Emily, your mother's sister come from England.'

I looked at her face again. Behind the unfamiliar blackened eyelashes her eyes were identical, the same unmistakable blue.

'You're a brave little boy, that's what they all tell me.'

'I want my mother,'

'I know you do, Michael, and God, how I long for her too.'

I blinked. Cub Scouts didn't cry. We camped out in the woods and endured tests of strength like the old Fianna.

'I want to wear my Cub Scout uniform,' I said. 'And my cap. I'm the tallest boy with my cap.'

'Come on upstairs with me, Michael, and I'll help you put it on. And you can wear it tomorrow, if you like, when we ride together in the big car behind your mother. And there's nobody will make you take it off as long as I'm here.'

Aunt Maire stood at the kitchen door. She looked wrinkled, like an evil witch in a story. Emily nodded curtly at her and looked around with a smile of thanks at the neighbours. Emily put a hand on the banister and beckoned me to follow her. I walked behind her, my eyes downcast and never leaving the stairs. Her clothes were black, a sombre mourning coat, a short dark skirt and storm-cloud grey tights. But the only shoes which she could find in her haste, the ones that my eyes followed up each step, had the delicate stems of the slimmest high heels and were bright red as the most radiant lipstick.

That summer in Birmingham the pain of those long spring

months in Aunt Maire's house eased. The months of waking in the mornings afraid that I would be taken away, of waking at night to remember the red sheen of Emily's shoes on the stairs like an icon to cling on to. If I could only go and live with Emily I thought that I would feel secure. Now I was finally with her but I was still scared, unsure if my stay there was just a holiday or the start of a new life.

In the evenings I would have the potatoes peeled and boiling before she came in, the meat taken out of the fridge for her to fry, the can of beans or peas open on the kitchen table. Afterwards we walked in the public park or twice a week visited the cinema. On our way back she would always make her phone calls. The phone booth was on a corner with overhanging trees. I can smell them still, the way they were after rain. And the light inside the booth which shone on her hair as she cupped the receiver tight and spoke quietly into it. I tried to guess which relative it was that she was speaking to each time; was it one of her brother's wives or my father's married sisters? Was she pleading with them to let her keep me or beseeching them to take me off her hands? I leaned back against the rough bark of a tree trunk and tried to guess from the agitation of her hand with the cigarette.

There were words like Eleven Plus and O levels and A levels which frightened me with their strangeness. At the start of the summer she had sometimes mentioned them and laughed about her own schooling, asking did we still learn everything through Irish. 'We'll have to talk soon,' she would say and though several times in the park it seemed like she was about to discuss something important, each time the conversation had drifted away and she had laughed, as though at herself, and bought us both ice-creams as a treat instead.

The summer was half over and lately she seemed distracted. She would wash my hair in the sink, sit me down and blow-dry it into new styles as I tried not to stare at her breasts which pressed close to my face. I would feel the heat almost scorching my scalp and look up to find her staring vacantly at the drier in her hand. Once when I jerked my head away she smiled and stroked my damp hair.

'I'm sorry, Michael, I was just thinking that maybe you would enjoy a whole evening by yourself?'

I knew where she was going, knew by the length of time that she spent in her room, by the smells of lacquer and perfume which lingered there after she had gone, by the shoes heaped untidily on the floor after she had tried on pair after pair. I tried to guess what sort of man she was meeting by the pair which she had chosen. The slenderest and tallest heel, the most glistening black sheen. I wanted to imagine how she must feel walking through town in them.

I had many more evenings and pairs of shoes to imagine in the following weeks. I suspected that she had met him in work. I had her too well chaperoned everywhere else. Her nights became carefully spaced out as though she was playing us off one against the other. I thought of him now as my rival, a man with a beard perhaps and a Birmingham accent. I felt both jealousy and excitement when I thought of him touching her shoes under the table, and wondered if he knew about me, the other man in her life. Always before she went out Emily gave me a small present, chocolates or lemonade, with a guilty smile as she ruffled my hair. I could still feel her fingers there long after she had gone. I would put on her records and mime singing in front of the mirror, or roll socks into a ball and kick them against the wall during *Match of the Day*. I scored with my head and with scissors-kicks and when the crowd had stopped cheering I would lie sweating on the carpet and realize how hot the room had become. I would swing the door open and closed to create a draught and tell myself that I wasn't frightened on the nights when she told me not to wait up in case she was late. When I went out to stand at the open front door I pretended that I was just letting the cool night air in.

One night I dreamt that she brought her boyfriend home. He had a flowery purple shirt, an evil moustache and long hair. He called up the stairs and smiled when I came out on to the landing, luring me down.

'Hey, kid,' he said when I reached the bottom step. 'Come on in and take some drugs with us.'

The drugs were like cubes of sugar which he was trying to press into my mouth. I twisted my face sideways and fought to avoid his hands. He grabbed me in a headlock, pulling me into the living-room as he tried to force my mouth open. I knew that if I swallowed them I would be damned.

'You're going to be just like us, kid, you're going to be cool. What's wrong, eh? Come on, just try one.'

Emily was watching from the armchair. I beseeched her with my eyes but she shook her head as though to say *he will soon be your stepfather, we must obey him when he decides what is good for us*. But I knew he wanted to poison me so that he could have Emily all to himself. I would wake up with cigarette burns down my arms like the children in the newspaper story that my mother had cried over. I would be crazed with drugs and lying in a cardboard box beside endless lines of railway tracks and I would never find my way back. I screamed myself awake and found Emily sitting anxiously by my bed.

'What's wrong, Michael? Were you dreaming?'

The light told me that it was almost dawn. I knew by her clothes that she had only just come in.

'I'm frightened,' I said.

'Frightened of what?'

If I told her about the dream she might be angry and begin to feel trapped. Then she would send me away so that she could lead her own life.

'Just a silly dream,' I said, 'all about wars and tanks.'

'Would you sooner that I didn't go out?'

'No,' I lied. 'I like being alone.'

What else could I have said to her? But after that the house at night began to frighten me. Twice in the next week she remained out all night. I would wake at three in the morning and know that she wasn't back. I experienced the fear of being alone but also the thrill of feeling part of some illicit secret. I would snuggle down, feeling superior because I knew her secret and yet she had never guessed mine. The hooter would sound for the end of break for the night shift in the motor plant across from the terrace of houses. A solitary set of footsteps might pass, amplified by the still night.

The fear always started as a vague sensation in the back of my mind. I would try to keep it there , inventing objects to dwell on, multiplying shapes in my mind, while it prowled inexorably forward. I felt it gaining control the way a toothache takes over the brain. Was that a noise on the stairs, had a key been turned? My eyes stayed open, staring at the wall a few inches away. Behind me the white shirts in the open wardrobe were swaying souls. For now they hovered on the far side of the room but if I turned they would begin to float, white shapes sailing out from the darkness towards me. I knew that I was not alone in her house, that there was something, someone watching me as I lay with the blankets pulled over my head. I wanted to pray but the words brought back my mother's voice. I curled into a ball and tried to rock myself to sleep. Once I found a pencil between the mattress and the wall. I reached my hand further down to where there was a slight tear on the wallpaper. I pulled a small strip off. My writing was big and awkward in the darkness. *There is something in this house that I am frightened of. Pray for me if you find me dead. I am eleven years of age.* I hid it under the pillow wrapped in an old pair of my underpants. I wanted comfort, I wanted to be reassured and held. I longed for the strong feel of one of her shoes, to feel its patent smoothness under my palm, the cool unfeeling heel beneath my fingertips.

When sleep finally came I never woke again until the front door clicked shut after dawn. I would hear Emily pause to listen before she mounted the stairs, her shoes in her hand, carefully stepping over the one floorboard which creaked. Her bedroom door shut and I waited for it to open again after a few minutes, for the exaggerated noise of her deliberately going about her morning chores. She would tap on my door, a dressing-gown untied over her night-dress, and call me a sleepy-head as she asked what I wanted for breakfast.

She looked happy those days and yet under strain. She

didn't seem aware of the way in which she kept staring at herself in the mirror.

'How old do I look?' she asked unexpectedly one morning, the question itself making her suddenly seem old. Before that I had always thought of her as young because she was my mother's young sister, but now her words made me look at her coldly, as a woman, and I shrugged my shoulders nervously. I felt instinctively that the man she was dating was much younger. She smiled back, a little flustered as though she had spoken out loud by mistake.

'You've such lovely hair,' she said. 'I love combing your hair for you. You should go out more. What do you be doing sitting in here brooding all day?'

I tried to go out to reassure her, but I never went far. In the municipal park threesomes of grannies played crazy golf. I walked along by the muddy concrete pond staring so closely at the water that the girls there once suggested I throw myself in. In my pocket I still had Irish coins which shopkeepers stared at in disdain. Although Emily gave me English money it did not seem right to throw the old coins away. Anything I bought was in the supermarket where I didn't have to speak. In the small shops I lacked courage to ask for things. One morning I stood outside the newsagents in the local town centre, watching girls passing in bright clothes along the concrete shopping mall and van drivers unloading goods. Two youths leaned on the glass front of the newsagents.

'You missed it down at the club on Friday,' one said. 'A pound we all clubbed in together and bet Sharon she wouldn't do a strip. She had her blouse off and all and everyone gathered around the stage clapping in time when her brother walked in. She ran off the stage. Man, you should have seen the chick blush.'

I leaned against the glass pane as they moved off. I could see the girl in my mind, blonde hair and white skin, blushing as she undid the final button on her blouse, her bare legs stretching down to my aunt's black high heels. I knew that I was becoming erect. It was something which still frightened me, I had little experience and no knowledge of how to control it. I hunched down and sat on the path outside the shop. I felt that everybody on the busy shopping precinct was staring at me and whispering in their unlovely, incomprehensible English Midlands accents. A mother wheeling a shopping trolley passed like a tank, her well-built shoulders bare, children screaming and pulling at each other in her wake. Behind her an office girl came in a white blouse and miniskirt. I couldn't look up, I just followed the crisp clip of her polished shoes until they were lost among the grey worn feet of the shoppers.

Emily now stayed out on more nights than she was in. She had less time to cook our meals, was happy to let me eat crisp sandwiches for lunch. She spent hours in the bathroom and a whole evening once with her face caked in a mud pack. She had an anxious gaiety about her which was unsettling, a brittle happiness that she seemed terrified would be snatched away from her. For hours after she left the house I could smell the lacquer. Her hair, when I touched it once, had stiffened like a cloth left out on a line on a frosty night.

The 21st of August was Emily's birthday. It was a date which my mother had repeated to me every year. I searched the shops for something to give her. There were cheap statuettes inscribed *To the Best Mother in the World*. I held one in my hand for a moment to see if I would feel anything. *Mother*. It was a word I never used now, I felt only a sort of nervous embarrassment when anyone spoke of her. *Mother*. A woman in a church quietly offering up her pain. A woman, it might have been any woman, a woman whom I no longer knew. I didn't wish to think of her. It would open up a wound which I might not be able to heal. The little boy sitting beside her in the pew with cropped hair and short trousers? What had he got to do with me standing among the cards and gifts in a foreign newsagents? I was someone else now, somebody different, I had left that child behind.

I put the statuette down. On the next shelf there was a red ornamental candle in the shape of a shoe. My hand trembled as I picked it up. I knew it was the gift for Emily. It was her as I saw her, it was bright and sleek and glamorous. I put it under my coat. It was not that I wanted to steal it, just that I felt too ashamed to hand it to the bored girl at the cash desk, afraid that my secret would be exposed. I ran from the shopping centre convinced that I was being followed, my hand caressing the wax shoe underneath my jumper.

I opened her drawer again that afternoon and carefully took out the envelope which was next to her shoes. Her name was on it but it was addressed to the farm in Roscommon. It contained an old miraculous medal with a pale blue ribbon, a patterned handkerchief with the words *Dada's when he died* written in black ink across it, carbon copies of tax certificates which I could not comprehend, a picture of three sisters at a wedding in a country hotel and, held together with Sellotape, a tattered birth certificate. *Susan Emily McGill, born the 21st of August, 1927.* At the bottom of the envelope was a smaller envelope folded over. It had my mother's handwriting. I took out the small pile of passport photographs inside and watched myself grow younger, year in and year out, sitting in the booth in Woolworths. My hand was shaking with the shock of finding my past among the shoes in Emily's drawer. I felt sickened. There beside the impervious world of cold leather my face from the previous February had come back to haunt me with its tears and glazed look.

I had to buy two packets of birthday candles to get thirty-eight for the small cake. They lined the top of it like crosses at the Somme. I scrubbed the whole house as best I could. I had the potatoes peeled and boiling and stood at the window, watching for her to come home. She didn't know that I was aware of her birthday. She grilled the meat and opened a can of peas, preoccupied in herself, apparently slightly depressed. I felt the same giddy thrill as when I used to have a surprise hidden for my mother. The meal was over and she was about to watch *Crossroads* on the television when I lit all the candles and brought the cake in.

I waited until she had turned her head before I began to sing. Her eyes narrowed and I could see her count the candles as my voice dried out. Two characters in the *Crossroads* motel were having an argument. Emily raised her hand up to her face, then lunged out to knock over the cake. Tears began to smudge her make-up.

'Jesus Christ, how could you do this to me, you little bastard?' she sobbed.

I stood with the empty plate in my hand after she had

run from the room. A guest came down to check out of the motel and the two characters shut up but glared at each other over the bald patch on the guest's head. I heard Emily's bedroom door slam as I knelt down to scrape the icing off the wallpaper.

I left her present on the top of the television and went walking through the streets. Football leagues were being run on the common, a small knot of people gathered around each match. A man on a bicycle free-wheeled down to the main road with a pitchfork tied to his crossbar. I knew that he was Irish and from the way he winked at me he knew that I was too. He turned left into the traffic heading towards the allotments. I wanted to follow him but knew that I wouldn't know what to say. I stayed out until I thought that Emily would be gone, but when I returned she was sitting at the top of the stairs. I knew that she was late but had waited for me to come home. She beckoned for me to come up. I stood in front of her with my head bowed and she put a hand on my shoulders, drawing me down. I found myself blubbering against her shoulder while her fingers stroked my hair.

'I'm getting your dress wet, I'm sorry,' I said, 'I'm sorry.'

'No, Michael, it's me that's sorry. More than I can ever tell you. It's probably too late now, but if I ever had a son I hope he's just like you.'

'Will you send me away again? I've got nowhere else to go.'

She pulled my face up so that it was close to hers. She wiped my eyes with her palms though I felt that she was near tears.

'I don't know, Michael,' she said. 'It's what your mother

used to always hate about me. One minute I'd be up in arms and the next ... She was always trying to get me to decide things. It always meant so much to me to be your godmother, holding you in my arms when you were that small. I always said if anything happened ... I was always saying things.'

'Do you love this beardy fellow?'

I could feel Emily's breasts shaking as she suddenly laughed.

'What makes you think he has a beard?'

'I don't know. I just think that.'

She tilted my head so that I lay looking up at her. The laughter was gone. She looked near tears again.

'I used to think that when I'd grow up I would have no fears, Michael. God, I couldn't wait for it. Everything would be so clear cut. You lose all the old fears, Michael, but you trade them in for new ones. Do you know what my worst one is? I don't expect you to understand it, but do you know what it means to get old? I don't mean an old woman in a wheelchair in a nursing home, but just that little bit too old to do something you're longing for? To feel yourself every year getting left that bit more behind?'

'But you're not old,' I said, 'you're beautiful and glamorous. Any man would love you.'

She put her finger to my lips and tried to smile.

'And any woman would love you, Michael, the way you are. Sometimes I wish that you never had to grow up. I have to go out now, do you understand?'

'I wish you weren't my aunt and I was old enough to marry you.'

Part One

'It's my birthday, Michael, and so you have to promise me something. Will you swear never to tell anyone my age?'

I nodded and she looked anxiously at the slim watch on her wrist.

'I'll be over an hour late. He has a furious temper. Don't wait up for me, Michael. I love you, you know that?'

I remained sitting on the bend of the stair long after she had gone, my hand on the strip of carpet which still felt warm from her body. And I didn't stop crying for a long time.

That night was the most frightening I had ever known in her house. I can't explain my fear or even describe what I was scared of. But I felt a presence there stronger than ever before. There was a Western on the television in which they dug up an Indian's skull. I jumped up from the armchair, my eyes averted as I groped for the plug. Since my mother had died any image relating to death could convulse me with a sudden horror. The lines of a song from a war movie would not leave my brain: *The worms crawl in, the worms crawl out.* I plugged the television in again and changed channels, staying up until both channels went off the air. Their queen paraded on a horse during their national anthem and then the screen dissolved into a white dot. I withstood the high-pitched tone for as long as I could. In the silence that followed I stood at the front door. The high skylights of the factories across from me were lit up, I could hear the distant whine of a hoist.

I knew that I should go to bed but I couldn't bring myself to do so. She wouldn't be home till dawn, I had never been more alone. I was too afraid to switch on the light in her room. I knelt on the carpet in the half-light filtering in from

77

the landing and prised the drawer carefully open. I wasn't alone anymore and I wasn't afraid. I was Cinderella again. I tried on the suede boots, feeling so tall in them. I tried a pair of black high heels, walked towards the bed suspended on them three inches above the ground. My body tingled, I was absorbed, I felt delicate and firm as a new stem. I lay on her bed, naked except for her shoes. I pulled the soft coverlet over my body. One o'clock. Not a noise in the street, not a noise in the world. Before this I had just known that she was out with a man, now I imagined what they must be doing together as I lay there. Had she her shoes off I wondered, were her feet shockingly bare?

I felt uneasy for a moment, felt as though somehow my mother was watching me, reproachful and sad. I pulled the coverlet closer. It was as cosy as the womb in Emily's bed, I heard the same creaks and noises about the house but I didn't feel frightened of them anymore. I never meant to sleep with her drawer wide open and her shoes on my feet. But when I remember next she was coming into the room. She never even turned the light on as she pulled the dress over her head, kicked her shoes off and turned. We saw each other at the same time, both equally shocked and guilty. Her face was puffed from tears, she looked suddenly far older.

'You can stay,' she said, 'but don't try anything.'

The mistrust of her words startled me, turning me into a man. She climbed over me in her slip and settled down between the sheets. I lay on top of them wrapped in the coverlet. I know that she hadn't seen the drawer open, hadn't even looked at my feet.

'Oh, Jesus, Michael,' she sobbed suddenly. 'Oh, Jesus.'

I put my hand out to comfort her as she cried into the pillow.

'Go to sleep,' she said. 'Go to sleep.'

I remembered Maggie on the night that her father had died. I knew I should do something to help, but all I felt was terror at being discovered. I moved my legs gently, trying to prise the shoes off without a sound. I knew that Emily was awake, her eyes staring at the moonlit wall. *Don't try anything.* The words were still reverberating in my mind. The shoes made a muddled thud as they hit the carpet. I tensed but she never turned. I slept again and in my dreams I lay beside her, but this time both of us were between the sheets and while she murmured *No, don't try anything*, I put my hands up to touch her breasts. They felt like hard sculptured plastic, as smooth to the touch as patent shoe leather. She stirred when I touched them and whispered *Leave my shoes alone.* The sheets had fallen from us, her breasts were two starched, bright red caps.

I woke after I came over the coverlet. I felt the sperm sticky and hot on my thigh. I had never known the experience before. My body was saturated in drowsy pleasure but I was terrified. Had I hurt myself in some way, would my body ever be the same again? Would she know in the morning, would she send me back to Aunt Maire's bungalow? *Emily*, I wanted to say to her, *don't grow any older. Just wait till I grow up. You'll see how well I will look after you when I find a job and become a man. Nobody will ever hurt you again and you will never have to work. You'll rest yourself and be happy and be able to put your beautiful feet up. I promise you that I'll protect you and I'll build you a home.*

But I knew that not a word of it made any sense. I knew that she would never be able to make up her mind, that when school began again I would have to go away, that her letters would arrive, still addressed to Master Michael McMahon long after I had grown out of that name, with the same neat schoolgirlish handwriting and the same plea for a new photograph on my birthday. I was lost in her narrow bed. Her mouth was open, she looked vulnerable and old as she slept. I wanted to stroke her forehead and reassure her but I knew that I could not. I reached my hand down to the floor instead, and finding the shoe which she had worn, I pressed the polished leather against my cheek.

It is late afternoon. I raise my head from the sink in the bathroom. The small window is open, revealing the swaying tops of branches. As I dry my face I lean forward to glance at the makeshift goalposts beneath the plum trees, the pitch marked out with whitewash, the high wire netting surrounding it like a chicken run. I find myself staring at the glasshouses at the back of Aunt Maire's bungalow. I close my eyes and press the towel to my face. It has been six years since I set foot in my mother's house, how can I keep making this mistake?

Sometimes doing my homework I remember the chalk watches which I drew on the back of the wooden fireguard in my mother's bedroom. That week when she couldn't move and time stopped in a childish squiggle at half-three while I sat quietly on the lino with my stick of white chalk

guarding her bed. I glance up from my school books expect-
ing to see the wooden firescreen blocking the fireplace. I am
always stunned for a moment to discover where I am and
shocked that I could have forgotten. Six years and yet part
of my mind has never lost the sense of dislocation. I am
haunted by walls and old pictures that arrange themselves
around me when I am unaware. Occasionally I wake still
believing that I am there. If I stepped from my bedroom and
saw the plain white door of her room where I had been
delivered I would automatically walk towards it. I would
have turned the handle and stepped on to the lino before
realizing that it could not be real. And even there, when I
looked back, I would expect to see a ventilation hole above
a boxroom door filled with dusty sunlight like an empty eye
socket.

When I see myself in those years I see myself alone, a
succession of solitary images of different rooms and streets.
Even when I am among people they seem to be grey and
indistinct and it is just me who stands out, isolated within
their midst. The boy in the rain outside the hospital, the
naked boy in high heels in Emily's front room, the boy
alone on the rail of the boat after leaving her house at the
start of September, watching the lights of Ireland approach.
The same clothes that I had packed at the beginning of
summer, except that hidden among them now were the pair
of Emily's red shoes which I had stolen. Uncle Ned waiting
in the black and white of dusk at the quay to bring me back
to his sister's house. The noise of Aunt Maire fussing as she
made up the bed again in her son's old room and the way
that neither of them ever mentioned Emily's name to me.

When I had gone to England I had left behind that small wooden chest which held my father's last few things. Now I had my uncle take it down from the attic and leave it on my bed. All the way over on the boat I had used this one anxiety to cancel out all my other worries. Now when I was alone I dragged the chest across the floor and kept my back pressed against the door while I emptied out everything that was in it and hid Emily's shoes there instead. I dumped the old telegrams and press cuttings about the sinking that had been in the chest when I went for a walk that evening.

In the weeks that followed Aunt Maire only asked me once why I had got my uncle to take the chest down and I muttered something about keepsakes of my mother which Emily had given me. She never inquired again, but every night I was convinced that she must have heard the loud click of the padlock opening after I had lifted it out from under the bed.

Those years in Aunt Maire's house have fused into a single image in my mind. A nightscape in which the bedroom curtains are pulled back and, outlined through the small window panes, I can see the crooked branches of trees that yielded sour apples, the tops of neatly kept potato beds, and further back the roofs of glasshouses which stood on the scrap of land owned by the builder behind the back wall. Grey filtered light is coming through the lace curtains, the room is silvered and softened until it almost feels like home. And I am lying on the coverlet with my feet resting on the window-sill, encased in Emily's red shoes.

At twelve years of age and then thirteen and fourteen. Each year thinking that this is just a childish act for comfort which I will have grown out of by my next birthday. The image never changes, only the body grows longer, the shoes tighter. At fifteen and sixteen a cigarette burns in a saucer beside the bed, posters of pop stars start to litter the wall above my head. My aunt wheezes at night through the wall, the creak of springs as she rises to find her inhaler and the panic I feel when I cannot hear her return to bed afterwards.

Often when I heard her rise I would lie there, the end of the coverlet thrown over the shoes in case she came in, and wondered if I should go in to her. Only once did fear make me. I tapped on the door and found her sitting on the edge of the bed in an old night-dress. Without her teeth she looked like the ghost of herself. She was startled by my presence, embarrassed by the state which she was in.

'The asthma,' she rasped, 'sometimes I think I can't breathe anymore. Go back to bed now, boy, I'll be okay. You need your sleep for school in the morning.'

And every weekday morning I would pause outside her door with her tray in my hand, wondering if I would find her dead inside. Sometimes she might still be asleep and for a moment I would stand at the doorway, afraid to call her name, and when she stirred I would breathe again with relief and yet always feel ashamed at my sense of disappointment.

'What do you be doing by yourself up in that room all afternoon?' she would ask if I stayed in. 'Have you got no friends to go out with or visit?'

If she had not badgered me I might never have left my room in the evenings. But most nights I began to call at the house of a classmate called Liam who had a flock of younger brothers and sisters, a father who always laughed and told jokes in the corner of the room, a twin sister, Carmel, who perpetually fought with him, and a mother who made tea and toast at half-nine for everybody who was there. Other friends dropped in and out without a thought, yet no matter how much Liam's parents tried to make me welcome I still felt the same apprehension every time I approached their front door. I would rehearse excuses in my mind for calling, but often at the door I would turn away and begin to circle the block. In the end it would be only the thought of having to face Aunt Maire's worried comments if I arrived back too early that would force me to return to Liam's house.

When I found the courage to knock on the door one of the younger children would let me in without a word as though I were part of the family, and the others in the packed living-room squeezed up to make space for me on the sofa before the television. It is hard to describe the sense of happiness I felt at pretending to be part of a real family for those couple of hours. After a time Liam would nod to me and we'd wander out into the backyard. A pathway of loose pebbles led down to a corrugated iron shed filled with tools and scrap metal. A half-mended electric lamp high on the wall filled the yard with a faltering bluish light. His father would call out the kitchen door at us, pretending that he was about to come down as we puffed our way through illicit cigarettes, while Liam's younger brothers wandered casually out to wink and slag us that we were fooling nobody. Liam sat up on the work-bench and kicked out at them playfully until they left. I would close my eyes and inhale the smoke, taking in, along with the tobacco, the smell of stored paraffin and axle grease, feeling the flakes of rust peeling in my hand as I tapped at the bench with a monkey wrench which had been left out in the rain.

'There's a pervert in the neighbourhood,' Liam said one summer's night as we smoked. 'He fecks girls' underwear off the clothes-lines if you leave washing out. We're going to leave some of Carmel's out tomorrow night and watch for him if you want to stay over.'

That next night we zipped ourselves into sleeping-bags in his father's open-top trailer which was parked down beside the rubbish heap near the entrance to the back lane. Liam had stolen two King Edward cigars which cut against our throats and lasted for an eternity. The stars looked larger than usual. The night had turned cold. Lights were turned off along the terrace of houses. A young man came into the lane-way to piss while his girlfriend waited under the street-light at the entrance. We cupped the tips of the cigars, wondering would he bring her down into the shadows towards us. He called and she shook her head and walked on, the perfect click of her shoes loud in the night air. Whoever the underwear thief was, I didn't want him to turn up. I wanted to have to lie out there for summer night after summer night, no longer just an uninvited guest at the door but a watchman trusted to guard over the house.

'What was your mother like?' Liam asked from the sleeping-bag beside me after the young couple had vanished. I shrugged my shoulders, surprised at the question.

'Sure I don't even remember the woman.'

'But you must remember something.'

'No.'

'Do you miss her?'

'No.'

'Do you like talking about her?'

'No.'

We reverted back to silence. I tossed the butt of my cigar out among the old bricks and rubble. I loved to be allowed to sit among Liam's family and yet I thought of how uneasy I grew if I stayed too long, as though deep down I felt that they were involved in an elaborate charade, that their harmonious bickering was staged for my benefit, that when I left they all reverted back to the individual silent existences which Aunt Maire and I lived. I thought of how the youngest children would kiss their parents goodnight and retreat together into crowded bedrooms. I could scarcely imagine three brothers sharing a single room, breathing in the same air, listening to each other's stirrings in sleep. Liam's family fascinated me and yet I felt threatened. No matter how much they made me welcome, or how much I longed to be part of them, each evening I was relieved to escape back into the privacy of my own bedroom.

'No,' I said again, although Liam had not asked me another question. 'I don't miss anyone. I like living alone.'

'I thought you lived with your aunt?'

I said nothing and Liam thought for a few moments.

'The sick bastard isn't going to come tonight,' he said. 'Will we pack it in?'

I was relieved to walk back into Liam's kitchen and turn on all the lights, as if to warn anybody who might be lurking in the gardens. The door of Liam's bedroom was open. I could see his two young brothers curled into the shape of each other in the top bunk of the bed.

'You can kip down there on the floor in your sleeping-bag if you want,' he offered and I shook my head and said that I would head back to my aunt's bungalow instead. I paused under the street-light at the lane-way leading down to Liam's garden.

'*The sick bastard.*' Liam would be getting into bed now, listening to the breathing of his brothers as he tried not to wake them. I thought of the wooden chest hidden beneath my bed. I felt cold and sick and worthless.

I was sixteen when I purchased my first pair of women's shoes. It was a sale of work for old folks in the local church hall, the hot crush of bodies packed against the long wooden trestle-tables which were piled with useless second-hand goods. And there among the knick-knacks and comics and torn paperbacks lay a single pair of white high heels. The woman behind the counter was selling raffle tickets, calling over my head to the crowd of elderly women who were joking among each other behind me. I hadn't the courage to pick the shoes up, I just stood with my hand on them until she finally realized I wanted to buy something.

'Them?' she asked incredulously.

'They're a present for someone.'

'But will they fit her?'

'Just tell me how much, please?'

I tried to keep my hand from shaking. When she turned back with my change I had already slipped through the crowd, the shoes under my coat as I walked, imagining that every person there was watching me, that every laugh I overheard was at my expense. I sweated as I ran home through the afternoon heat, unwilling to unbutton my coat. Aunt Maire looked up from the kitchen.

'Is everything okay?' she said, as I panted, still holding my coat closed in the hallway.

'Homework,' I said. 'I've forgotten to do my bloody Spanish homework.'

It was the first time I had ever cursed to her. I ran down the hallway to my room and, dragging open the wooden chest, crammed the shoes in on top of Emily's. At the sale of work they had seemed elegant, but now I saw how battered and ugly they were. The heel was low and stout. They must have been worn by a woman in her fifties with plump feet. I tried to stop my body from trembling as I heard my aunt follow me along the hallway. I hardly had the chest back under the bed and hadn't been able to lock it before she came into the bedroom.

'I feel a bad attack coming on, Michael. Will you run down to see if you can find a chemist open for me?'

She remained leaning against the doorway of my room after I had walked reluctantly past her. The chemist in the village was open. I was served at once and cycled back fast. I opened the front door and startled my aunt who came out of my bedroom. She seemed out of breath and perturbed.

'I was just resting on the bed,' she said. 'I was remembering the way the room was when Patrick was a lad. The way we both stood at this window watching the flames from the North Strange bombings. That's why they built Cabra so fast. It was the Germans made them build Cabra. You're a good lad, Michael.'

She took the paper bag from me and, walking slowly down the hall, closed the door of her own room. I felt too flushed and guilty to examine the chest. My tea was on the kitchen table. My aunt didn't leave her room all evening. It was late at night when I finally got down on my knees beside the bed. I couldn't be certain if my aunt had opened the chest but it seemed to be facing the wrong way round. I felt sick with worry that I might be found out.

I did not have to be here. I could be out with Liam and my other school friends. They would be in town now queuing outside the Apartment Club. I should be with them if I could just bring myself to leave that room, I should be eyeing up the lines of girls standing in the bubbles of spinning light, growing outwards and away from that wooden chest. But I was frightened and it was so easy to open the chest and imagine their dancing feet without the dangers of failure and ridicule.

And yet if my aunt knew of the shoes then how could I face her tomorrow and all the other mornings to come? Already there were so few words between us; her daily question about how I had got on in school, my nightly remark about the dinner being nice. I knew that she would never mention the shoes but still she would know. I would see them thrown back at me in her troubled expression. The new shoes were ugly but at least they fitted, unlike Emily's which now hurt and left red scars on my skin. I tried them on and lay there, not wanting to think about tomorrow. When would I give this stupid game up? Would I still be doing the same when I was eighteen? No, I told myself, it was just a phase, a habit left over from childhood which I would soon outgrow. It would fade away like those old scraps of prayers which still clung on in my skull.

From above the mantelpiece a cross-eyed Jesus with a bleeding heart watched over me. I thought of my aunt's religion, the musty prayer-books and Nine Fridays, a litany

of saints for all occasions like a cabinet full of pills. I
didn't just hate it anymore, it made my physically ill. The
bodies crammed together at mass, babies crying, the
stifling boredom of people waiting to leave at communion.
Yet there was a void within me that I didn't know how to
fill. The words my mother had taught me. *If I should die
before I wake* ... How safe I once felt closing my eyes
afterwards ... *I beg the Lord my soul to take.* I had nothing to replace that feeling with. If there was a god then I
had no words of my own to say to it. I just had these
shoes to banish that phantom pain. I felt alone and cold
and without feelings, lying in the moonlight in that pair of
white shoes.

The bed creaked in the next room and I suddenly knew
that my aunt was about to come in. I threw both pairs of
shoes on to the floor and tossed the coverlet over them. I
was half sitting-up when she came in. I was trembling, I
knew that I had been caught out. I expected her to be
transformed, enraged and shrieking. Instead she staggered
at the doorway, unable to breathe.

'I'm dying,' she gasped, her voice barely audible, 'dying.
Oh, Good Jesus, dying.'

She walked over the coverlet and staggered when her
bare foot landed on one of the shoes. But she didn't seem to
notice anything in her terror. She was holding her inhaler
but had been unable to get the refill in. I took it from her
and filled it, then held it to her mouth. The sound she made
when she inhaled didn't seem human. She frightened me as
she lay against my shoulder. For the first time in years I
found myself praying to her God, not that he might save
her but that she wouldn't look down and see the outline of

the shoes under the coverlet. My aunt looked up. Her hand gripped my shoulder with sudden sharp claw-like strength.

'Michael, you're all that I have to look after. It's everything I live for, just to cook and wash for you.'

In the years that I had lived off her I had never kissed her once. I had barely even looked at her. She was just the woman who had poured the tea from the china teapot down the sink on my mother all those years ago. I realized how much I had withheld affection from her. I had been punishing her for something which happened before I was born.

'I'm sorry,' I said.

She looked so old with her teeth out and her hair dishevelled. How little she ever spent on herself. She had never touched the money from the sale of my mother's house which was in the bank, waiting for me when I was twenty-one. She seemed startled by my words.

'Your poor mother and I, we never got on.'

'I know,' I said.

'In the country it's different from here. There's different ways. It was never easy for me, I was never respected. There you always had to look down on someone else to be respected.'

She closed her eyes again. In the four years since my summer with her, Emily hadn't written once beyond the standard one-line card and postal order on every birthday. She had married without inviting any of her family and then almost as quickly had separated. And yet I still thought of Emily as my real aunt and this old woman as someone to be endured for as brief a time as possible. I leaned down to kiss her forehead and hated myself for the sense of nausea I felt. She looked up in surprise and I held the inhaler to her mouth and pressed it in.

'You have your mother's eyes,' she said. 'I think that I'm dying. Will you run next door and get Mrs Kelly to phone an ambulance?'

It was Mrs Kelly who travelled with her in the ambulance. I walked around the streets that night with the white shoes under my coat until I found a skip to dump them in. I was finished with all that, I promised myself. I was going to start behaving like an adult. I waited up for one of the Kellys to come in with word for me. Mrs Kelly came home in a taxi. My aunt hadn't died but she was going to be kept in, possibly for weeks. That morning before going to school I went out again to dump Emily's red shoes in the skip but I couldn't part with them. I put them back in the chest under the bed and locked it. On my way to school I found a drain and watched the key sink down through the black layers of muck.

Now in school I suddenly became somebody, I was the Boy with the Empty House. Every Saturday of those first weeks when Aunt Maire was in hospital Liam and I would spend the afternoon moving everything breakable down into her bedroom, turning all the cabinets and presses towards the wall and rigging up lights and extra speakers on to a friend's record player.

Most of the people who arrived weren't known to me, but I was still grateful to them, welcoming anybody who followed us back from the pub, laughing with strangers on the front lawn as I searched for the key and nervously watched for neighbours to appear. Although in the daytime

I had begun to creep up and down the street, at night when I was drunk I didn't care about any of them. They were dull and ordinary with their humdrum lives, but I was different from them. I was above all that, with no ties, no commitment and no family.

I had never even kept a photograph of my mother, had avoided all memories. I had honed her down until she was just a faint unease, never to be mentioned. I grew up but she did not. Standing in Aunt Maire's kitchen, watching bottles being opened and someone being sick in the sink, there was a satisfaction in imagining her disapproval, her fossilized 1960s outrage. She was my prisoner, locked in time while I drifted towards each new experience. Yet it was she who set the boundaries, not of my behaviour but of how I perceived it. When the last stranger had gone and I had put a blanket over the curtains to block out the light and felt the residue of alcohol coursing in a hot flush through me, it was through her eyes that I weighed my actions. Without her memory there would have been nothing to put against the guilty satisfaction of wrong-doing; I couldn't have drifted towards sleep and woken on those Sunday afternoons knowing that I would have earned my place in her eyes among the truly damned.

And yet most of the time at those parties I was still alone, still an outsider walking around ignored by my guests, aware that most of them didn't even know that I was their host. One night somebody set the chimney alight. Someone else tried to put it out by climbing up on to the roof from the shed with a whiskey bottle full of water which he poured down it. People gathered in the back garden shouting at him to jump. He moved along the roofs and, as Mrs Kelly opened her bedroom window, he jumped from directly above her head and landed tumbling over on her lawn. Everybody else drifted back in, leaving me to stare, open-mouthed, back at her.

She never told my aunt, nor did anyone else on the street. But they all discussed me and I loved that. Because I was no longer just the orphan, I had become the wild boy in number forty-one. Sometimes friends called in at two or three in the morning, people crashing out in my aunt's bed. But more often nobody called. I would stay in all evening, pacing up and down the hall, waiting for the doorbell to ring. And at half-twelve I would have the screwdriver out and be frantically trying to prise open the padlock on that wooden chest.

My aunt came home after a month and smelt the sheets on her bed.

'Somebody has been sleeping in here,' she said, deeply offended. Even more offended, I denied it. She said nothing more, just washed all her bedclothes and hung them on the line and got down on her knees to wash and rewash her bedroom, though the doctors had told her to rest. I ate my dinner in silence.

'Are you not going up to that friend of yours?' she asked when I stood up to go to my room afterwards.

'No,' I said, surly, 'I've too much study to do.'

Liam and my two other best friends had joined the FCA. Now they talked only about guns and the way it felt to parade up and down the square in McKee Barracks. Sometimes in class Liam would mention where they had been out the night before and then, seeing my face, ask if nobody had remembered to invite me along. They urged me to join the FCA but I felt that in the masculine world of rifles and farts and blue jokes I would surely be caught out, my secret unmasked, that I could never pass myself off as one of them.

Two nights before my aunt came home they had been sitting in my living-room, talking for hours without bringing me into the conversation. I went out into the hall and listened to hear if they might mention me. They continued talking about the parts of guns. I couldn't compete with their strength and so I tried weakness. I let myself fall with a loud thud. The talk continued for a few moments as I lay there and then ceased. They ran out and knelt down beside me in the hall.

'Are you all right, Michael?' Liam sounded genuinely concerned.

'I think I must have fainted,' I murmured. 'I'll be all right now.'

They helped me into an armchair and asked if there was anything they could do. I could see them glance at each other over my head. I said that I would be okay there, I would just take it easy. After inquiring again if there was anything they could do, they all left together. I crept down the hallway to listen to what they would say about me. I heard Liam lighting a cigarette at the gate.

'That sergeant is a right bollox all the same,' he said.

'Yeah,' one of the others replied, 'but sure it's great crack. See you there tomorrow night. Good luck.'

I remained with my back against the hall door long after their voices had drifted out of hearing. Then I got a hammer and broke open the padlock on the chest.

I had never asked myself how old Aunt Maire was. She had

been old before she was middle-aged and never seemed to age any more. She still rose for mass at half-seven every morning, when her asthma let her, no matter how cold the weather. She still knelt with a scrubbing-brush in the kitchen within hours of being released from hospital.

Her past was as closed as the confessional. Apart from what my mother had told me, I had only a single glimpse of her childhood from a story which she told me one Christmas. A night of flames filling the McMahon farmyard, the English accents of soldiers jeering from the lorry as the roof of the house caved in, and the bad teeth of the grinning sergeant who held the can of paraffin with drops splattering over his boots. I could see her there as she spoke, aged nine, cradling the infant who was my father in her arms while she stood perfectly still in case she dropped the revolver wrapped in the freezing oilskin cloth beneath her night-dress.

For the next year she was in and out of hospital, her releases as unexpected as her attacks. I studied alone for my Leaving Certificate in a submerged world. For days on end I wouldn't open the curtains in the bungalow, dishes piled up as I worked my way through all her sets of old china, the pieces of fried meat drying-up in the oven each evening as I queued for chips in the chip shop beside the pub at the end of the street.

I lived in her best room, eating my meals there, leaving the dishes on the carpet as I lay on the sofa to watch television. My old clothes piled up around the sofa, teacups with fluffy mould starting to grow in them, school books covered with blocked-out doodles of high heel shoes. I felt becalmed there, often too apathetic to go to my room at night. I would wake up on the sofa to face the white unblinking dot on the television screen. My stomach felt sick from the food I ate, my mouth was sticky with nausea. I would go to the front window and watch for the postman. I have no clear idea what I expected him to bring; news from the real world, some magical letter that would transform my life. It may just have been a carry-over from my first year there when I had waited for a summons from Emily. Most mornings he passed without turning in, but on the mornings when he creaked the gate open I would duck down under the window, then slouch my way out to the hall and curse as I picked up the gas or the ESB bill or the circular about subscriptions to the foreign missions magazine. If anybody called to the door during the day I hid, trying to catch a glimpse of them from the window when they left, and then, if I knew them, having to bang foolishly on the glass.

I always planned to have the bungalow spotless for when Aunt Maire came out, but I lacked the will-power to start cleaning until the last moment. Sometimes she would arrive home a day early and I would come back from school to find her sitting among the chaos with all the windows open.

Just before my eighteenth birthday my Uncle Ned called. My hair was long, unwashed for weeks. I looked pale. Dishes were strewn in the kitchen behind me. He shifted uncomfortably.

'I promised your mother I would look after you,' he said.

'Leave my mother out of this.'

'Your aunt. The doctors think she shouldn't come back here. It's too much for her with her breathing. It's care she needs, attention. They've given us the name of a nursing home.'

We looked at each other. I knew the accusation in his eyes. Was it the asthma or me that was driving her out of her home? After he left that evening was the first time in over a year that I visited Liam's house. I hesitated for a long time before knocking. Liam opened the door himself, grinned and then looked closely at me.

'Jesus, Mick, have you got bad news or what?'

Instead of bringing me into the living-room he cleared his young brothers out from their bedroom. He vanished for a moment and I sat on the edge of the bunk-bed, resting my head against the rail. I wanted to cry, I wanted to lie down and never move from that spot. I hadn't been fully aware of the grief inside me until he had spoken. I had always told myself that I didn't even care for my aunt, had never allowed us to get close, had just expected her to be there forever.

Liam came back and said that his father wanted to know if I would like a drink. I shook my head.

'Is anyone dead?' he asked and I shook my head again.

'Is it a woman then?' he said after a moment.

I needed to invent a story.

'A married one,' I said. 'I've been having an affair with her. She's pregnant now, she's carrying my child and her husband thinks that it will be his baby.'

I looked up to see if he believed me. I think he did. I wanted to believe it myself.

'We always felt you had a secret somewhere,' he said.

'Don't tell your parents.'

'No, I won't.'

'What can I do? I'm just a schoolboy. She says it's too dangerous for us to meet again.'

'Do you love her?'

'Yes.'

'And does she love you?'

'It's killing her too.'

'You won't do anything stupid, will you?'

'No, I'll be okay now. I can cope with it.'

'You were always a dark horse, eh.'

I nodded and got up from the bed. I felt better. Liam swore that he would tell nobody and I thanked him. He went into his parents for a moment and left me staring through the open door of his sisters' bedroom. He came out again and I could sense him gazing after me as I walked towards the dark corner. I could hear his sister Carmel come out to accuse him of something. Now I knew who I was. I was a dark horse. I had just invented myself.

I walked the half mile to the house where I had been born. Six years had passed since I last stood outside it. The front lawn which I had never finished cutting was gone. A car was parking on the concrete inside the new gates. The door was still the same. The brass numbers which Maggie's father had put up years before, the same pattern on the pane of hammered glass. In my first dream I had stood on the other side of it, gazing up the stairs, waiting for the figure to appear. The road was empty. I stood at the gate and defied that ghost to appear. I wasn't scared of her any longer, this time I would not scream when she came fully into view. My hand gripped the gates as I stared at the door. I cursed her and God and everyone. But only the silent street mocked me. I was alone.

I took out Carmel's shoes, which I had stolen. I put them on and tried to walk. The streets were deserted. On the main road I walked on in the glare of the headlights from the cars, staggering as though drunk. I don't know what I wanted. For someone to stop, someone to recognize what I felt, someone to explain it all back to me.

PART TWO

This wasn't supposed to be the way it ended: with me leaning my head against the damp wall to catch the sound of mourners cluttering up that small kitchen where Nick sat on days when it was too cold to haunt the front step. For four years I had lived with his radio coming up into my flat from there, the sound of him coughing sometimes in winter, the strains of grand opera from his tape recorder at unlikely hours. Now the muffled voices were bizarre. I closed my eyes and I could see every feature of the room, the heavy wooden sideboard like Aunt Maire's with its sheet of glass on top, the clutter of old Reader's Digests, Irish Independents *and opera scores under the stool that he would always pull out for me to sit on, the fireplace which he had built himself from Wicklow granite scavenged during the war, grey photographs dulled by half a century of smoke beside colourful new snapshots of grandchildren with English and American accents. They were his own family inside in that kitchen now, his daughters home from London and Boston and those grandchildren, and yet somehow their presence felt like a violation, their hands lifting up and replacing objects which he had cherished and that now, without him, seemed battered and worthless.*

'How old are you?' he would ask. 'Twenty-three? Sure I was married at your age. Cycling in from Bray every morning to Francis Street. Some days I think I could cycle it still. Last year the daughter takes me up to this specialist in London. Students watching from a balcony as he has me up

*on the table. This test and that test, bleeps and dials flicker-
ing. Eventually he tells me I can get up. "Mr O'Shea," he
says, "You're eighty-seven years of age and do you know
all that's wrong with you?" Well, I lit a cigarette and I
looked at him. "SFA," I said. "Sweet Fuck All. Sure I could
have told you that two hours ago."'*

*SFA. That isn't how you spell loneliness. I was only the
passing tenant. It was I who was supposed to leave Nick,
not Nick who was meant to leave me like this. Often I
thought that it was only Nick who still kept me in Breffni
Street with its tumbledown back lane where flowers nestled
in the crevices in the brick wall of the abandoned flour
mills. My bedsit looked over those empty silos aimed
towards the clouds. It was long past time for me to move
on from that flat at the top of the stairs where the ceiling
wept in winter and the outline of the attic beams seeped
through in damp stains like an X-ray of bones. The other
flats in the house had all changed hands, the landlord was a
figure like death who silently crept in and out at unexpected
hours seeking money. There were no ties to keep me there
except for Nick. Because I knew that at no matter what
time I slipped out with my bags he would still appear like a
ghost on his doorstep with a story of how he also had left a
house just like that on a similar night some forty or fifty
years before, and all the events that had befallen him
afterwards.*

*And how could I finally say goodbye and leave him on
his own? Because even though neighbours called and family
friends arrived in cars, my door was the door that was next
to his. And in the years which he had knocked on it for me
he had never used my name once.*

'Is he there?' he would say and whoever answered from another flat always knew who he meant.

'Old Nick is at the door,' they would come upstairs to tell me. Old Nick. Often he could have given the devil a bad name with his talk. One hour, two hours, it was all the same with him. Yet he wasn't ashamed to say that he was lonely, that was what made him special. There was no bullshit there. It is hours before nightfall, talk to me. The kitchen is smoky and full of ghosts, talk to me. The winter is here and I hate days alone that feel like Plymouth on a wet Sunday, talk to me.

And how could I leave a man behind who was as honest as that, who divided out his time between the old tapes and radio in his kitchen and the front step, a man who you knew was lingering in winter beside the old paraffin heater in his hallway with ears on the alert for any knock next door?

Inside his kitchen a mourner laughed and others joined in. There was a rattle of cups, the conversation paused and then moved on. I lifted my forehead from the wall. Nick was supposed to miss me when I left, not leave me stranded, suddenly aware of how he must have felt on those nights when Joe lived in the flat downstairs. Nick and I, both in our rooms, listening to the noise of poker hands being dealt across Joe's table. And on those nights when Joe gave me a knock and I ventured down I could always imagine Nick standing in the way that I was standing now, with his forehead close to the damp plasterwork as he listened to the laughter and clink of glasses coming through the wall. And I knew that he would be smiling at the jokes which he could barely hear and the volley of curses as people were forced *to stoke the pot, that he was taking pleasure from our pleasure and that our voices were making him feel less alone.*

Sitting among those card-players it was his isolation that I felt more than their company. Because I too had stood behind so many doors, listening to life happening elsewhere. Across from Nick the white dot on his ancient television would remind him that it was late and that darkness beckoned in the big bedroom up the staircase which was thronged with absences. Somebody would raise the pot and coins and notes would be slammed down as people suspected a bluff and Nick would turn for bed with a sigh. Often, just as he hung his cap over the brass bedpost, he would hear voices filling up the street as Joe's card school broke up. And standing in the hallway watching the gamblers file out, I would imagine Nick half undressed underneath that high damp ceiling, cursing himself bitterly for giving up when he might have appeared from nowhere at his door.

Sleep was a tunnel of dead voices to be passed through, the morning a monotony which might or might not be broken by a letter. When Joe went in I would open the front door and wait, knowing that Nick would be dressing again, wondering would anyone be left and could he still lean for one final time that night against his door, light up a last cigarette and, gazing skyward, talk about how clear the stars were one night when he had walked the high mountain road from Anamore to Laragh during the war. And when he did come down to the door, even though he had told me it before, I would listen to him describe the drone of a German fighter-plane that had strayed across the blue sky, the engines crippled and almost out of petrol, and how the pilot must have known that he would die, peering down at those Wicklow forests and crags obscured by the darkness. And how the crash on the far hillside had looked no more than if someone at the top of the lane was putting a match to a pipe and how loud the water in the stream had seemed in the silence afterwards.

I lifted my head from the plaster as the kitchen on the far side of the wall went silent.

'A fierce man to talk,' I heard a mourner say and the voices rose again as if in a wave of agreement. I smiled, remembering myself trapped there in the moonlight before him, already regretting having waited, as I tried to judge the moment to interrupt. But even as I cursed him silently I would feel like a subject paying homage, bending my head slowly to listen to a king among his words.

It is a spring Saturday after the clock has gone back and the light is a willowy sheet of darkening air. I am twenty-two years of age. Cars speed through the Phoenix Park towards Parkgate Street. Sunlight sifts through trees bearing the mellow scent of evening. A young man sits on the park bench set back from the road, his girlfriend sitting facing him on his knees with her bare feet resting on the grass behind them through the bars of the bench. Her white skirt is spread out to cover them. Two bicycles rest entangled against a tree trunk. A deer strays out from the trees for a moment and surveys them before scampering silently back. The girl throws her long hair back and laughs before kissing the young man again. It's impossible to tell if they are rocking innocently or secretly having intercourse.

Will the phone box be broken, I wonder, or will there be a queue outside it? The air is polished and clear after the gloom of Inchicore library where I have been working, the evening so alive with possibility. I pass through the park gates on to the start of the North Circular Road, the sweet-shops on the corner crammed with children. I pass the hotel and reach the phone booth. I put in the money, lift the receiver and press button A when her voice answers. The coins jangle down into the metal box as I say her name after a pause.

I know that if she agrees to go out then we will end up in bed. Her breasts are perfectly pointed, she always smiles to herself during sex and only ever comes once. I don't think of her as my girlfriend, she is the girl that I have phoned a dozen times over the previous six months. I can't explain her, there is something in her personality which is unnerving. I don't know if it was drugs or nerves but there is something in her past that has never been explained. And yet it is this quality which attracts me to her. If she is strange, then I feel that I can be myself, getting her to keep her shoes on in bed, putting my hands down to touch them as she kneels before me on the sheet.

I walk down past the ugly church to my bedsit in Breffni Street, passing through back lanes of tumbled walls and crooked angles. Nick from next door, who spends his life hovering on the front step, is talking to someone on the street. I nod and dodge him, getting the door open quickly before the stranger moves off. I listen to the other tenants moving about in the rooms below as I dress. The house is let by a young man who bought it in an executor's sale. He only half cleared the house out before dividing it up into five flats. We keep turning up items from the lives of the old couple who had died in it. Once Joe in the flat downstairs came across an envelope under the old newspapers lining the chest of drawers in his room. When he opened it he discovered a man's death certificate for 1962. Months later when I pulled up the lino in my room one night I found a Post Office receipt for a lodgement of money in the same year, obviously the insurance that was paid out to his widow.

Joe and I are all that are left of the first tenants in the house. The other flats have changed hands often in the last eighteen months. The night we moved in, Joe had a party and we explored the whole house together, joking as we took down the old religious pictures that hung in our rooms and stored them in the shed. Now a bright square of wallpaper with a dustmark still watches over me when I sleep. On the landing upstairs a little table is laid out as a sort of altar. There are bottles of musty water with hand-written labels for Lourdes and Knock, old rosary beads and two bog oak crosses, a tattered prayer book and a small silver container in which some sort of liquid has congealed. The white cloth on the table is covered with the dust of a decade. We laughed about it then but the table looks so bizarre that nobody has ever had the courage to shift it.

I finish dressing and walk into town. I meet the girl outside Clery's. She comes forward, smiling, in faded dungarees with a black leather purse tied around her neck. I glance down towards her shoes. My conversation is always cautious and neutral, trying to avoid anything that could be taken for commitment. Permanency is a word which terrifies me. I am a man without ties after four years of living alone.

I want more from her than just a one-night stand and yet I can't give anything of myself. I tense up if she seems to want to get too close. In the mornings we are always awkward. I find a taxi for her as soon as she wakes. I watch it move off and always think I won't see her again. Yet two weeks later I'll be queuing outside that same phone box.

The traditional musicians warm up in the room above the pub. I bring back two pints of Colt 45 from the hatch, a new strong lager which is bound to get us drunk. As at the start of every evening, she tells me that she cannot stay the night. The atmosphere is tense between us as I work towards the moment when I ask her to change her mind. The musicians start, a hundred people crammed around us in a windowless fire-trap. I urge her to drink up, refilling pint after pint.

'Will you stay the night?'

'If you really want me to,' she replies in her Drogheda accent.

The street outside is lurching, crowds appearing from everywhere. I am euphoric. As I take her hand she turns towards me and vomits. She looks more surprised than I am. I tell her that it's my fault, that I should never have made her take so much drink. She brushes past empty crates into a narrow back lane. I hear her being sick again. I follow her in. She is almost in tears.

'You had better go home,' I say. 'I'll get you a taxi.'

'I'm sorry,' she keeps saying. 'I know that you're disappointed. It was all the drink with the tablets I'm on.'

She puts her arms around me and I pull her close, ignoring the vomit that is now staining my jacket and jeans. We rub noses, unwilling to kiss with the smell, and I work my hands down into the back of her dungarees, feeling the cool white globes of her arse and the wetness further down between them. Somehow she has worked my penis out of my jeans. Her hand is kneading it as I catch her calf and pull it up until I'm holding her shoe in my hand. We are caught in the headlight of a taxi turning the corner. People whistle and shout as we fix our clothes. Her shoe has come off and I'm still holding it. The taxi-driver has dropped his fare and is about to pull off again. I hail him and get her into the back seat, pressing the money for the fare into her hands. She is still looking back at me standing with her shoe under my coat as the car speeds around the corner.

A tall girl is coming down the far side of the street. She is wearing a dark blue cloak and stylish black shoes. I know her face but my mind refuses to make the connection. I cannot bear to go home alone to that bedsit. I begin to follow the girl from a distance. The way she walks is beautiful. Her name hangs over me like a drop of water in a Chinese torture. I know it but it just will not come. She begins to run and I'm frightened that she has seen me. I should turn back but I start to run through the crowds as well. If I can just get another glimpse of her face her name will come back. We turn into Abbey Street and she puts her hand out for the bus which is moving off towards her. The driver stops in the middle of the road and I see the sign for Clonsilla.

I stop running. People are staring at me. I get my breath back and walk home. When I get there I put the shoe on the mantelpiece. Below me I hear the northern accents of the card-players in Joe's flat. I know that I would be welcome but I lack the courage to go down without being asked. I lie awake on the bed for hours just trying to place the girl's face.

*

111

On the first day that the house was set out in bedsits we all decided that Nick was a nuisance. Nobody was sure if he was a spy for the landlord, marking our comings and goings. We were the third house in Breffni Street to be turned into flats and windows had began to sprout *Will Resist Flats* notices as people in the local shops eyed us with suspicion. And yet Nick, the oldest resident on the street, seemed genuinely friendly, even pleased that there were young people in the house. During the first week every new tenant had been cornered in turn for an hour on the front step. Some people began to concoct elaborate strategies to avoid him. By crouching down and opening the letter-box with a knife you could peer out and see if his door was closed by the reflection in the window of the house across the street. In the mornings the girl in the bottom flat used to check the letter-box and then, mounting her bicycle in the hall, would have someone open the door for her and cycle straight out on to the path. She would be several yards down the road before Nick could get his door open to shout a greeting after her.

One evening I arrived home from work at the same time as Joe and the black African, who had the top flat upstairs, were coming in. Nick was waiting in his doorway. The three of us hurried our step, each trying not to be the last down the path. The African and I made it first and slammed the door in Joe's face. We lay on the hall floor with our feet against the door, preventing Joe, who had turned his key, from pushing the door open. We heard Nick speak to him briefly and then go in. Joe thumped on the letter-box and cursed us in his Tyrone accent when he got inside.

'That's not funny. The old man isn't a fool, you know.

He could see exactly what you were doing. Now if you want to talk to him or tell him to fuck off that's your own business, but if you're going to insult him then leave me out of it.'

His words sobered me up. I felt guilty all evening. Next morning I was working late in the library. It was one of those wet, sullen April days that disguise themselves as December. I knocked on Nick's door and asked him if he needed anything in the shops. If he knew why I was there he said nothing but just grinned at me.

'Where are you going?'

'Wherever you want.'

'The butchers. Tell them old Nick sent you, that I want a piece of steak that I won't bang my head off the wall trying to eat. And would you mind getting me some carrots and parsnips mixed in the shop by the Post Office?'

When I came back he said he had the kettle boiled. I refused his offer of tea. I had done enough to ease my conscience. I went back inside and watched him through the letter-box, surveying the empty street like it was his kingdom, standing there as though waiting for somebody. After a time a car pulled up and, suddenly serious looking, Nick closed his front door behind him and got into the back seat without speaking.

It was several nights later that I opened the front door to get some air before going to sleep. Nick was in his garden, watching the same car drive off. I was about to slip back inside when he turned.

'A sad night,' he said quietly. 'We've had a bereavement here in the house. The Missus, she's after passing on.'

I had always presumed him to be a widower. I was

shocked, not knowing what to say, so I said all the usual trite things, and asked was there anything that I could do.

'I had her home with me this Christmas,' he said. 'The nurses in the hospital said that I wouldn't be able to manage, but of course I did. Sure this was her home, the woman was my wife, she couldn't have spent Christmas anywhere else. There wasn't much she could do for herself, just sit at the table with a bib around her, but I mashed up her food and fed it to her. We had turkey and ham and sprouts, all the things that we always have. Only this time, you know, it was the best Christmas that we ever spent.'

He looked down and smiled at the memory but I could see his hand tremble on the gate. I knocked on the door of the other flats and told them. I just figured I had to do something.

Joe and I stood at the back of the crowd during the funeral. Nick's two daughters were home from London and America. At the family plot one of them pointed down as the grave-diggers scraped against wood.

'Look, Daddy, there's Uncle Larry's coffin.'

'Ah, never mind that old bollox now.'

Nick put his hand out to touch his wife's coffin with such dignity in his grief that he seemed to dwarf all of us present.

Clonsilla. I knew nothing about the place. It was a new suburb still in the process of forming. Unfinished houses, unfinished roads. But unlike where I grew up there was no old centre, no village street for the estates to swamp. They were estates where you might never know your neighbour. An eerie stillness filled the afternoon before a shoal of cars nosed in at six-fifteen. Those evenings when I had nowhere better to walk I took to walking there. If my excuse was that I was hoping to spot the girl again then it was just a vague hope, enough to give a sense of purpose to my journey but not enough for me to feel disappointed when I finally caught a bus back to my bedsit.

One of the estates had a granite boulder at the entrance with the name carved into it. Cherry blossoms had been planted on the path leading up to the houses and were now at the height of their brief bloom. The gutters were filled with tiny pale petals and each time the wind blew more drifted down. The surface of the narrow main road had been broken by the trucks and earth-movers which used it. It was a mile from the bus-stop where I got off. I liked to pause there and have a cigar, leaning against the boulder before heading back. I liked the anonymity of that corner with its new lives and new starts, rooms where nobody had ever lived before.

On the Wednesday night when the girl came down past the cherry blossoms it was the walk which I recognized first, then those same black shoes. Yes, I knew her face but still I couldn't place it. I felt embarrassed to be caught there, waiting for her to pass me. She reached the corner and looked over. I knew that she was trying to place me too. Then she crossed the road towards me. A name came to me but I rejected it. She stopped with one foot on the road and one on the pavement. She tilted her head sideways to look at me.

'Mick?'

'Maggie?'

'I can hardly believe it.'

We both started to grin and then were suddenly awkward.

I didn't know what to feel. Over fifteen years had passed since I had seen her last. Yet her face was the same and possibly so was mine. But I could barely remember the child that I had been then. A vague sense of guilt came back.

'I'm sorry I missed your leaving.'

Maggie had to think back before laughing.

'I forgave you for that after a decade or so.'

There was still something little-girlish about her. So much was flooding back to me. The memories felt good. How long was it since anything felt that good?

'It's funny,' Maggie said, 'I always thought you'd grow up taller than that.'

I smiled self-consciously. As a child she had always tried to tower it over me, but now she actually did by a good two inches.

'What are you doing out here?' she said.

My smile vanished. I couldn't tell her. I just shrugged my shoulders.

'Are you home on holidays or have you come back?'

'My mother came home last year when she retired from her job. Coming home has been all she ever talked of. It's for my sake, she says, but I don't think she really settled in Canada. We live in the third house back there in the estate. Do you want to come in? I'm sure she'd be delighted to see you.'

'No.'

I felt a tremor of panic at being confronted by my past. Maggie looked disappointed.

'How does she find it?' I asked.

'A bit strange. I think she thought the country was going to stay in a sort of time warp until she came back, that the girls at the airport would all be sporting beehives. She keeps getting angry a lot of the time about things I can't understand, things on the news and in the papers, things that wouldn't have bothered her in Canada. She had friends and a life over there. I don't think she will ever fit back here either.'

'And what about you?'

Maggie shrugged her shoulders.

'One place is as good as another, I suppose. I don't know though, I spent most of my life getting slagged for being Irish in Canada. It's hard getting slagged for being Canadian here.'

We both dried up. Despite her Canadian accent her voice was the same, I thought. The cigar had gone out. I flicked the dead ash off and flung the butt away. I didn't know what to do with my hands.

'I was sorry to hear about your mother, Mick.'

'My mother?'

'We heard in Canada. One of the neighbours wrote.'

'That was years ago. I can hardly even remember the woman now.'

'You must do. I remember her well. I'm sure it was hard for you. Who reared you?'

'I reared myself.'

I didn't mean my voice to be as sharp. Maggie flinched slightly. She waited a moment, then said goodbye and began to move away. She crossed the road and took the temporary gravel path. A truck passed, blowing her red hair back in its slipstream. She was almost out of sight when I ran after her.

'Maggie?'

She stopped and turned, a little defensively.

'Would you like to go out some night?'

'I don't mind,' she said.

117

We fixed a time and place. I wanted to reach forward and kiss her lightly. I knew that she expected me to, but I was suddenly shy. I took her hand instead and shook it, feeling incredibly silly. It was obvious that we were both going to town but I turned and walked the other way, out towards the countryside, waiting until a bus had passed before walking back to the stop.

The librarian was cursing the students who were in studying for their exams. A new pair of ladies' shoes had been left behind by a borrower and stored in a plastic bag under the counter beside the reserved books. None of the other assistants had seen them being taken as they shunted between the old wooden catalogue drawers and the desk. I spent the rest of the day shelving the adult non-fiction in the corner beside the tramp who walked from library to library and sat in the warmest corner of each, deliberately reading books upside down while old ladies complained of the smell.

I remained in the staff-room until the girls were gone, then walked out, feeling self-conscious with my jacket bundled up under my arm. I knew that this was ridiculous. I could lose my job, I could be so publicly shamed. But I kept walking, feeling the pulse of my bloodstream quicken. I locked the door of my bedsit and put a chair against it. I checked the curtains twice even though they were tightly pulled. The borrower's shoes were cream with a fussy silver bow. They pinched my feet as I lay face up on the bed.

I listened to the tea-time noises, Joe coming in and putting his motorbike helmet in the hall, reggae from the African's stereo, opera blasting from Nick's tape recorder through the wall. In two and a half hours I was supposed to have my first date with Maggie. What was I doing here locked away, closing my eyes, trying to keep time suspended? I was scared. This wasn't like going out with any other girl. I was going to have to explain myself, to try to contrive a life.

No matter how friendly Joe or anyone else was in the house I always felt that I was merely tolerated. I felt comfortable only with myself. How could I even try to share my life with anyone? I opened my eyes and closed them again. A red-haired girl standing up on the piles of concrete bricks in her father's back garden, her left foot on one tier, her right foot raised on to the next, the flash of white knee between her socks and pale skirt. I opened my eyes again but the ceiling was blurred. The tears tasted salty in my mouth. I felt as if I'd just woken to find that I'd been drifting for years inside an iceberg of loneliness.

That night after our first date, lying on the sofa in Maggie's mother's house. The eager way that she had kissed me in the cinema and now was letting my hand wander beneath her skirt. The pale stockings which emphasized the whiteness of her legs, a shoe still on her left foot and the right one shaken off on to the carpet. When I tried to slide my fingers into her panties she had laughed and lifted my hand away, whispering that I had to slow down, I was going too fast, and I was surprised to find that I wasn't disappointed. We lay together, trying not to move because of the way the leather squeaked, and told each other about our lives.

Maggie was working as a nurse's aid in a private nursing home. It was always presumed that she would become a nurse but she had never finished her training in Canada. This was her fifth job since coming to Ireland. Even that

119

first night she spoke about getting herself a flat, a small room somewhere away from her mother.

'She's too protective of me,' Maggie said. 'Watching everything I do. I'm twenty-three, I keep telling her, I can look after myself.'

She had once lived alone by herself somewhere in Canada. The details were sketchy. I knew that there were things I should not ask.

'I always remember you as being so dependable,' she said. 'You were always there. Are you still the same?'

'I'm just myself,' I said. 'Not up to very much.'

'It's nice to see you again. I always thought we would meet somewhere. I was on the pill in Canada, I want to go on it again. I haven't had any reason to until now. Can you wait till then?'

Maggie's sense of humour could be shocking. The more public the place was, the more passionate her kiss became. On the evening when she finally persuaded me home to meet her mother again, Maggie had worked my penis out when her mother had left the room to get an old photograph album. She had it sucked half erect before walking to the far side of the room as her mother's steps came back down the stairs, leaving me to try and stuff it into my trousers. I looked at old black and white photographs of the pair of us in my mother's garden, sitting tightly up against the edge of the table, unable to lose the erection as Maggie smiled innocently across at me.

In the library everybody said that I was a changed person.

'Someone once told me you were only twenty-three but I

never believed them,' a new girl confided in me. 'Now I do. Have you done something to yourself? Your whole face looks different.'

Maggie loved old Nick but she never liked Breffni Street. On the first evening that she called over he had cut the best rose in his front garden and given it to her. The three of us stood talking in the late sunshine and I felt proud of her.

'I'm working nights for the next week,' she said when we went inside. 'I'm starting tomorrow but I told my mother it was tonight.'

The girl in the front flat was watching a quiz show on television. I could hear the bursts of applause as I entered Maggie's body for the first time. It was messy, we were both too tense. When it was over she began to cry softly. I stroked her hair. I remembered the only other night when we had lain together, the night her father had died. Just as then, I didn't know what to do.

'Are you sorry we did it?' I whispered. 'We don't have to again, you know. Not until you're ready. I don't mind.'

'No, it's not that, it's . . .' She wiped her eyes and tried to smile. 'It doesn't matter. I'm sorry, Mick, for going to pieces on you.'

A little later there was a knock. It was the African wondering if I wanted to go for a drink. I had pulled my jeans on before opening the door. Maggie smiled at him from under the covers. He ducked back out on to the landing but she called him in and said hello.

'The pair of you go on,' Maggie said, 'I'm tired. I'll stay here. I'll see you later.'

The pub on the corner hadn't changed since the days when I used to pass it on the bus with my mother. The instructions beside the telephone detailed the charges in old money and gave the dialling code for Skerries. It was filled with old countrymen. Joe sat in the corner next to one with ripped trousers and the saddest face imaginable, who nursed a Paddy whiskey and responded to greetings by almost imperceptibly lifting his eyes. At closing time the three of us strolled back up Breffni Street. Nick's door was open and the light on in his hall. When we opened the gate he emerged with Maggie behind him. She had dressed hastily and had a blanket wrapped around her shoulders.

'You'll be all right now, Miss,' Nick said. 'Thank you for the chat. It was a pleasure.'

Maggie stepped over the fence as he closed his door. She looked embarrassed as we stood around her.

'I got frightened,' she said. 'I was scared to be in the house alone. I swear the place is haunted. That damp stain above the bed looks like the devil's head. And even though I locked the bedroom door twice each time it swung open by itself.'

I expected the lads to laugh but they seemed to respect the genuine fear in Maggie's eyes. I put my arms around her as we went in. My bedsit looked the same as when I had left it except that the door was open. The two girls who had flats in the house were out. The four of us sat in the African's bedsit drinking coffee with brandy in it and then decided to search the parts we could of the house. We went through each of our three flats carefully, joking about the state they were in. Yellowed faces stared out from the newspapers under the carpets, a 1912 farthing rolled out from under Joe's wardrobe.

I dreaded them reaching my room. I wasn't frightened of

ghosts, I was frightened that they would find that same locked wooden chest under my bed with Emily's shoes still inside it. There were old shutters on the window, covered with so many coats of white paint that it seemed impossible to shift them. Joe found a crowbar which bit softly into the wood. With a creak they finally opened, spilling dust out over us. There were carcasses of long dead insects, an old comb with broken teeth, a horoscope out of a women's magazine and a tattered envelope which none of us wished to open.

'There's money in that,' Joe said. 'Every old biddy in the country has money stashed somewhere for masses for her soul. We might as well have it ourselves as the bastard who bought the house.'

I looked at Maggie. She had retreated back to the bed. I knew that she wanted me to tell them not to open it. Joe handed it to the African.

'You open it. At least it won't be your god we'll be offending.'

'Shag off, man, I was taught by the Christian Brothers in Kenya. You must be joking if you think I'm touching it. You do it.'

Joe tried to hand it to me but I wouldn't take it. He put it on the bed beside Maggie. Downstairs we heard a girl come in with her boyfriend, their laughter shrill in the silence.

'Give it to old Nick,' Maggie said. 'He'll know what to do with it.'

'We'll show it to him in the morning.'

'No,' Maggie replied. 'Get him now. I'm not sleeping here with that in the room.'

Nick came up the stairs slowly, gazing around him. Even

though it was us who lived there and he was our guest, his presence made us feel that we were the intruders. He turned the envelope over in his hands for a moment before opening it. He drew out what looked like an old bandage decked with various religious medals. As he unfurled it, it was hard to prevent objects from falling on to the floor. Scapulars, a broken cross from a set of beads, a twist of greaseproof paper with a baby's tooth inside it and various tattered memorial cards. I remembered Emily's drawer and wondered would those photographs of myself still exist, secreted away in some corner after her death? The thought made me uncomfortable. Near the end the bandage grew bloodstained, clotted heavy blood which stained the wad of old pound notes that Nick drew forth from the centre of it. I looked at Joe. He had been right that there would be money in it. There was a piece of folded paper with it which Nick flattened out and read. He held it close to his face under the light-bulb and seemed to go over the words several times. We waited.

'I suppose none of yous pray?'

We shook our heads.

'Give me that stuff off the floor, will you?'

He collected the objects which had fallen and replaced them inside the bandage. All of us knew that we shouldn't ask him what was written on the paper. He said goodnight to us and retreated down the stairs. Joe managed to get the shutters to fit back into place. None of us said much. After the two boys had gone back to their own flats Maggie stood at the window.

'Turn the light off,' she said.

I did and joined her, standing with the curtain pulled

back. The light was on in Nick's back kitchen. It lit him up as he dug a hole in the flower-bed. Although he was old he used a shovel expertly. When he got two feet down we saw him place something in the hole and then fill it back in. He knocked the loose clay from the shovel and put it back in the shed. I saw him stand for a moment gazing over the tumbledown wall into the garden below me which was covered in weeds. Then he went in and the kitchen light was switched off.

It was half-three in the morning when Maggie woke me. Her face was tense and scared, yet there was nothing hysterical about her.

'I didn't dream it, Michael,' she said. 'I saw what I saw. I woke and there was a woman sitting at the end of the bed. No, not sitting, more like hovering an inch or two above the blankets. I couldn't see her face but I knew that she had been watching me sleep. And then she was just gone.'

'You were dreaming.'

'No. I don't like this house. Put on the light, Michael, I'm going to sit up until daylight. Have you a radio?'

'You'll wake the whole house up.'

'I want to hear living voices. I want to hear music.'

I plugged in the electric kettle. The room felt cold.

'Maybe you did see something,' I said. 'I don't know.'

I made tea for us both and found some biscuits. We sat up on the bed in our underwear.

'Remember the cave with green ferns growing over the opening?' I said.

'No.'

'It was between the two beds in your mother's room, and I almost got to see you naked.'

125

'I remember the island in the river,' she said. 'The day my father died. When we grew up we said that we'd live there, just us alone with no one bossing us. Our own island in the river.'

I sipped the hot tea and put my arm around her. She was shivering slightly. She drew the blankets up over us.

'You're different,' she said. 'In some ways deep down it's like you've never changed, never grown up and yet somehow you're different. And so am I.'

This was the moment to tell her everything, about Emily's drawer, about how my life had tilted off. But even though I wanted to I knew that I couldn't, not so soon at least. I had money gaining interest in the bank which I had never touched; all the money from the sale of my mother's house, and money from the sale of Aunt Maire's bungalow which her son had insisted on me having a share in. I could buy Maggie that island in the river. Not just a run-down flat but somewhere where we might live in comfort together. Yet when she talked about leaving home again I said nothing about us sharing somewhere. She leaned her head on my shoulder.

'Next time we make love it'll be better,' she said. 'When I find a flat of my own.'

'Next time there'll just be the two of us in the room.'

We both laughed and then glanced uncomfortably at the image of ourselves in the wardrobe mirror through the old brass bedstand at our feet.

Over the next fortnight Maggie found her flat and lost her job again. Losing the job happened first, at the end of that week of nights. She had told me that her mother never liked her working in nursing homes. When they had first come home she had tried to enrol Maggie for secretarial and bookkeeping courses.

'She said that seeing those wards and locked doors would upset me.'

The words had been puzzling. But now Maggie's mother seemed to be right. Whenever I met Maggie after she had finished work she was upset from all the hours in the day-room minding the old women who sat staring out from armchairs seeing nothing through the window. Old women waiting for dinner, waiting for visitors, waiting for death; the grandeur of the reception rooms downstairs giving way to the threadbare carpets in the wards beyond the old staircase.

On the third night of that week an old woman had died on a commode while Maggie was watching her. The woman had been obsessed with constipation and had badgered different visitors to sneak her in powerful laxatives. She overdosed on them and, when her heart failed, had put her hands out for Maggie to catch her, gasping very faintly as she keeled over.

Maggie never told me exactly what happened afterwards but at the end of the week she was asked to leave. The following Friday she called down to tell me that she had a new job in another nursing home, this time on the north of the city, and had paid a deposit on a flat in Fairview. Her bedsit was as small as mine except that the furniture was different. Everything from the original owners had been long since sold off and the cheapest of plywood furniture installed in the rooms. The house was a hundred and fifty years old and looked it. Her flat was on the first landing.

I helped her move in, waiting for her when she arrived with her bags in a taxi. I was relieved that her mother wasn't in the car. There wasn't much to carry up the stairs. I had bought a bottle of wine which we opened when we had finished unpacking.

'Thirty-eight flats I looked at before this,' she said. 'Our own island in the river, Michael, even though the deposit has me flat broke and the soles of these shoes are worn away.'

She kicked her black shoes off on to the floor. I bent down and picked one up. It felt warm inside and slightly moist. I had read somewhere that when the foot sweats it releases secretions like those from the sexual organs. Her scent excited me. She watched me curiously as I ran my fingers over the shoe.

'What is it with you, Michael?' she asked. 'Is there something you're holding back?'

In all my life I had never told anyone about my obsession. It had been as impossible to mention as the feelings after the death of my mother. And it had always come between me and everyone, trapping me into a loneliness which I longed to break from. But how could I explain something to her which still made no sense to myself? Maggie was watching, her face serious. I knew that if I didn't speak now I never would.

'Your shoes,' I said.

'What about them? Are they dirty? I'm sorry.'

'No. I love them.'

She laughed, a little nervously, and took the shoe back from my hand.

'No, I really mean I love you, Maggie, but I love you

through them. That's how I see you. Like . . . I don't know, like maybe you can be snatched away from me again but your shoes can't. Listen, I can't really explain what I mean, but have you ever been engulfed by something? Some days when life feels good I suddenly get this stricken feeling. I don't know, I want to cry or something. It's like as if the very sense of happiness makes me aware of the pain I'll feel when I lose it. And the closer I get to anyone the more I think that I'll be left with nothing when they're gone. And that's why I love the feel of shoes. Because they can't change and it's like I can cheat time in them. Christ, Maggie, you don't know how pathetic I feel talking about it, how frightened I am of losing you.'

Maggie sat stiffly on the narrow bed.

'That's silly,' she said. 'I'm sorry but I can't make sense of it.'

'I'm not asking you to.'

'Do you want to wear my shoes?'

'No, not when you're here. I'd feel so stupid, self-conscious.'

'Then do you want me to leave the room?'

'Maggie, please.'

'Well, what else am I supposed to say? That this is great? Let's open a shoe shop together in our little island in the river? Jesus, I've enough troubles of my own.'

Her eyes were troubled. She looked scared and yet seemed about to break into nervous laughter.

'Maggie, to hell with your shoes, it's you that I want. I've been lonely all my life. I'm so happy you're home that I don't know how to say it. But leave them on in bed tonight. For me, Maggie. Just for a while when we're making love.'

If I had known more about her past I might never have spoken. Since meeting her, I'd felt that I was gradually curing myself. So why did I have to drag her into my old world?

She nodded cautiously after a moment. We undressed with the light out. When she knelt on the bed in the darkness I could see out through the lace curtain on the small window beside the bed; the few lights of the extensions built out into the back gardens, a square of wallpaper in one, dishes in a sink and a loaf of bread in another. All those distant, isolated lives. Below Maggie's raised buttocks I could see the scuffed soles of her shoes. They faced towards me, nakedly exposed. The miles that she had walked in them since coming home, from temporary job to temporary job. The steps which she had climbed hoping to find this small room that she could call her own. The times when they had been resoled, made to last beyond their lifetime so that she could save enough for a deposit on her dreams. They seemed to offer me her life story, saying this is who I really am, neither ashamed nor proud. I felt such tenderness as I entered her flesh, felt that we would never be more naked to each other than with her shoes between us, that we could never surrender such perfect trust. Maggie trembled slightly, I knew that she felt awkward and unsure. A girl came to the sink at the window of one of the flats below and began to slice the bread with a black-handled knife that was too short for the job. She looked out into the darkness, seeing nothing. After I had come I lay curled against Maggie's back. I reached my hand out for hers, drifting towards sleep.

'I love you,' I said and placed my lips softly between her

shoulder-blades. It was only the second time that I had ever said those words to her, but it was an almost careless remark, the right words for the right occasion. I nestled against her, waiting for her to repeat them back. She was silent, her shoulders slightly tense.

'It's too soon,' she whispered, 'I can't just say things like that.'

I had no right to feel hurt but I did. She could sense it and grew annoyed.

'When I say those words, I'll mean them,' she said, 'not like you.'

'I do mean it,' I said, angry now. 'How the hell can you say I don't?'

'You love me because you want to, because it suits us now with the way we are. It's too easy just to say them. Love is a big word so let's not cheapen it.'

I lay awake for hours, insulted and self-righteous.

I don't know why I hated the shopping expeditions so much that followed along the seafront stores at Clontarf. I would become restless and resentful almost before we were inside the shop door. An electric kettle, cups, plates, two large French posters to cover the damp stains on the wall. These essentials I didn't mind but anything else made me uneasy. Plants for the only shelf in the room, cushions for the single battered armchair. I liked them when we got back to the flat, it was just the acquiring of them which I found so hard. It felt too settled, too much like the actions of a newly married couple. Each shopping trip with Maggie was threatening. I wanted us just to exist together, floating in a single moment of time.

'Which saucepan do you like?' she would say. 'Come on, Michael, just pick a saucepan. Why the hell are you so frightened of a few pots and pans?'

I would sulk, refusing to be of assistance to her while she grew progressively more cross. Standing in the shop I felt trapped on an invisible ledge. Outside on the street I would be happy again, suggesting ways to celebrate our new acquisitions. And back in the flat I would take pride in them, helping her to hang the curtains or putting up the new posters with Blu-Tack.

She always referred to the flat as ours and yet she insisted on paying the rent alone. She wouldn't put her name alone on the door but as she was afraid to add mine in case her mother called, the metal slot beside the bell remained blank. She had never suggested that I give up my own flat and I knew that she would never move into Breffni Street. She told me that I was free to come and go whenever I liked, that both the flats were too small for us always to be in together in either of them. I wasn't sure if Maggie wanted to have time by herself or if she sensed my unease and was afraid to lose me if I felt ensnared. I was so used to being alone that at times I found her company hard, especially the fact that she always talked so much. But now I was able to enjoy a double life. I spent most nights in Breffni Street, dodging Nick on the doorstep and sometimes having a drink with Joe or the African if they invited me. And when I got lonely I always knew that Maggie would be there, like the princess in the tower ready to let down her hair.

Sometimes I felt guilty, when I woke up by myself at night and thought of her having left the comfort of her mother's house so that we could be together. Yet I always remembered the first night in her flat when she refused to return my whisper of love. I told myself that she had made her own choice. I hadn't asked her to leave her mother for that tiny flat and she would probably have done so if we hadn't met. But I loved to wake up some nights when I was working on a late shift the next day and listen to the wind twisting among the old girders in the mill behind Breffni Street. I would suddenly decide at two in the morning to walk across to Drumcondra and down Richmond Road, knowing the welcome that I would receive when I reached her flat.

When I got there I would open the front door and walk quietly up to the first landing. Parcels of moonlight filled the hallway, framed by the ornate fanlight over the door. I turned the key in the lock but her door was always chained. Maggie's voice would be fearful, dredged up from sleep.

'Maggie, it's me. Let me in.'

Her delight was unquestioning. We laughed like schoolchildren, squeezing up in her single bed. She would try to quieten me, saying that I would wake the old woman downstairs, and I would jangle the bedsprings louder to flaunt my presence. Then at half-six in the morning she would quickly dress for work, skipping her breakfast while I lay on, and run out the door, knowing that she was going to be late. At half-eight I would stir, hearing footsteps from upstairs hurry down the stairs. When I woke again around eleven I was always aware of how small and bare Maggie's room was, how the bright posters and cushions could not disguise its stark utility. The rigged electricity meter which she had fought with the landlord to get fixed, the two rings of the little cooker with the grill underneath. Often the taps omitted a shrill hiss for hours on end. The flat was cold, any sunlight blocked out by the ugly extension next door. And I would grow melancholic as I dressed, aware that this island in the river which we shared was really a fragile ark that I could not allow just to drift. I would have to help to steer its course but didn't know which way to steer for.

An omen occurred in early August. I still can't explain the noise I heard to myself. I had brought Maggie to a party that a friend of the African's was having in a house on the Swords Road. Everybody there seemed to have huge slabs of hash and nobody had thought of buying cigarette skins. I knew a few people from seeing them call on the African in Breffni Street but there was nobody whom Maggie knew. Yet she seemed happy and relaxed to be there, sharing a few dances with me and then after a time just contentedly reading a magazine in the corner.

On the way home as the trucks heading for the north sped past us, she took my hand and motioned me to sit on the bench outside Whitehall Garda station. I knew that she was trying to tell me something but couldn't find the courage. That is it, I thought, she's pregnant. I felt the night close in around me. Maggie squeezed my hand.

'Michael, something happened in Canada. Something happened to me I can't explain. I've been wanting to tell you. I had a breakdown.'

I wanted to get up and put my arms around her and shout with joy. My relief was so great I hardly took in what she said.

'I don't mind. You're here now and you're fine. That's all that counts.'

And when I thought about it on the walk home I really

didn't mind. It seemed to make us equal in my mind, both with secrets which we would help the other to overcome.

I'm not sure at what time that night the noise woke me. I lay, looking up at the ceiling, trying to place it. It was like the drone, not of one but of a whole squadron of planes circling low over the city. There had to be a simple explanation for it, yet I felt suddenly scared. My movements in the bed woke Maggie.

'What is it?' she said.

'I don't know. I'm trying to make out that noise.'

She listened, my anxiety making her nervous.

'Well, it's like a plane, is it?'

'It's more than one. It's like dozens of them circling overhead. What are they doing there?'

I looked out of the window; all the flats were in darkness, the narrow strip of sky between the buildings empty and cloudless. I was filled with an irrational terror.

'What time is it?' I asked.

'Oh shit,' she said. 'The clock has stopped. We were too drunk to remember to wind it.'

All the pirate stations were off the air except for one that was playing pieces of classical music with no commentary between them. There should have been DJs with bad American accents presenting half-hour specials on blind musicians who had learnt to sing the blues in jail. I scoured the wavebands and then left the radio hissing away to itself.

'What's wrong with you?' Maggie kept saying. 'It's just the noise of a few engines.'

I couldn't explain my unease. I didn't honestly imagine that the country was being invaded. But the sound was so unnerving that I felt vulnerable, waking up beside a girl whom I suddenly felt I had to protect from so much and yet not even sure if there was anything menacing us. I wanted to walk out on to the road by Fairview park where people would be moving about and cars passing, to stare at the sky and reassure myself that there was nothing to fear. But I was afraid to take the chain off the door. Maggie put her hand on my shoulder.

'Hold me tight, Mick, I'm scared. Of you, of the way you're trembling. Please, Mick.'

Next morning when I went out to buy a newspaper there was no mention of anything unusual occurring in the night. I asked the shopkeeper but he just shrugged his shoulders. I never met anybody who had heard that same drone.

Maggie lost her job in the new nursing home. For three weeks she nursed an old woman privately in her house, then she found herself idle. Kebabs had become the new craze in Dublin. A late night take-away had opened across from Fairview Park and most nights when I stayed with her we found ourselves walking down for one. We sat on a bench and tried not to get the sauces on our clothes.

I didn't want to accept that Maggie's personality was changing but I could see it in the way that other people were looking at her. She was restless, perpetually needing to talk. I would sit on the bench and listen to every piece of trivia from her day being repeated and enlarged upon. Her words were giddy and bright like a child's overwound toy spinning out of control. She was more affectionate than I had ever known her to be. Her face radiated such happiness when I entered her flat that it frightened me. Yet also there was a hint of darkness. Canada was mentioned more and more like a jigsaw that I had to make sense of. Although I understood that she had had a nervous breakdown, there was something else, something that I could only guess at.

'Remember the first time we made. love,' she said one night as we sat on our bench, 'the way that I went to pieces on you? You handled that so well, you weren't put out by it at all.'

I remembered her eager sensuality on our first afternoon in the cinema, the way she had barely waited for the lights to go down before sliding her hands under my clothes, the time that she had stunned me when her mother was upstairs. I knew there had been a moment that first night in Breffni Street when she had become suddenly distant and upset but so much else had happened the same night that I hadn't thought much about it. Now it seemed the tears were all she remembered.

We walked home and went to bed. Just as we were drifting to sleep Maggie's tongue crept into my mouth for a final lingering kiss. Inside my dreams I felt her wet aftertaste draining from my tongue like a warm tide going out. And when I woke I was terrified for a moment that she had been taken away from me. I pressed myself against her with such intensity that she woke. I don't know how long it lasted but for a few seconds it seemed she no longer knew who I was.

'Maggie?' I whispered, suddenly scared, 'Maggie?'

What dream world had she been locked inside that made her look at me with such terror? She raised her hands as though the space above her was filled with arms which were trying to hold her down. I put my hands out to reassure her and when they touched hers she almost screamed.

'Maggie,' I whispered again, 'it's me, Maggie.'

Her eyes focused on me in the half-light.

'Dreaming,' she said, 'I was dreaming. Did I wake you?'

I put my arms around her to hold her close. She nibbled at my neck. Her skin was glistening slightly with sweat and my penis had grown hard. When I went to enter her it felt like the life had suddenly left her body. She didn't resist but seemed to withdraw inside herself. I stopped.

'Maggie.'

'Go on, do it if you wish.'

'Maggie, I want to give you pleasure.'

'Do it, if you're doing it. Please, Michael, just get it over with.'

I withdrew and leaned my head back to stare at the cracked ceiling. After a time she took my hand.

'I didn't feel very much the first few times with you,' she whispered. 'I was holding back, I was scared . . . not of you, but of memories. I was cold down there but now you've made me feel warm. But you've made other things come back too, things that I want to forget about. It's good with you, Mick, good like the way it used to be. Only every time that I open myself to you the memories come rushing back and they hurt. God, how they hurt me.'

'What happened to you, Maggie? I want to know.'

She was silent for so long that I thought she wasn't going to answer.

'I can't remember all the details. It was that winter in Halifax, Nova Scotia. Packed snow for months on end so that the streets were impassable after five in the evening. I was leaving Toronto, I promised myself, leaving my mother, I was going to start my own life. I found a room not much bigger than this, an attic bedroom of a wooden boarding-house. It's a cold city, Halifax, it's hard to make friends there. I spent the evenings walking alone through the old docks. At least I was away from my mother, away from having to train to be a nurse, I was starting a new life. These were the things I kept telling myself to keep going.

'You had to work hard even to find a drink in that city. There was a big old hotel there, the Lord Nelson. Full of little old ladies trying to feel British, wearing funny hats from the 1940s as they held tea-parties to celebrate Queen Victoria's birthday. It had a mezzanine where you could look down on the foyer. I used to sit there with a little bottle of brandy that I'd smuggled in and drink capfuls of it when I thought nobody was watching. I always expected somebody to throw me out but nobody ever did.

'One Sunday afternoon I found this bar down near the docks with the windows blacked out and a sign advertising topless dancers. I went in and sat at a table by myself surrounded by all these men looking terribly embarrassed. The girls were bored looking, far older than me. I could do that better than any of them, I thought. I sat there for hours sipping the one brandy. The bartender was sorry that he'd served me. He never came near me again, even to get the money. I didn't know if I was there looking for a job or a man or even just so as not to be alone for a few hours. I always wondered did they follow me home from that place?'

'Maggie, what happened to you? I want to help. Tell me.'

Somebody came in the hall door downstairs. We could hear them stagger slightly as they groped for the light-switch. The bulb on the landing came on, filling the outline of her door with light. Two pairs of footsteps clambered up past the room. One stopped and we gripped each other's hands, suddenly vulnerable.

'I'll catch you up,' a voice muttered and we heard the sound of urine splashing into the toilet in the cubicle outside Maggie's door. He climbed up after his friend without flushing the chain. We both felt violated after he had gone. It was hard to coax Maggie to say anything else.

'I remember trying to find my way back to my room in the snow afterwards. One or two o'clock in the morning. Every street looking the same. White roofs, little daggers of ice hanging from the window-sills. And the way my body hurt even though the doctor said there was no evidence of anything. And Mammy scolding the nurses in the hospital when she came for me. And then flying back to Toronto, having to get an injection in the toilet of the plane and the passengers looking away when I kept on singing.'

'What happened to you, Maggie? Let me help you, just tell me.'

She turned her back on me again, her voice growing distant.

'Why did they keep telling me that it was nothing?'

It was two weeks afterwards that I met her in town on a Friday evening. She was wearing the same dark blue cloak as on our first date. She began waving when I had barely come into sight at the end of the street. She ran forward through the crowd calling my name. She had started a new job in a different nursing home that week. I sensed immediately that something had gone wrong but she wasn't going to tell me about it. We ate in a small Italian restaurant with plastic red and white tablecloths.

Maggie wanted to hold my hand throughout the meal. She talked incessantly but she appeared so happy that I was content to sit there and try not to show my irritation. She brought my hand up to rub it against her cheek.

'I've bought new shoes,' she said so loudly that I squeezed her hand to hush her. 'Shoes to wear for you in bed tonight. You'll love seeing me in these.'

The two young men at the next table paused at their meal. I saw one grin to the other before they began eating again.

'They're like that woman's shoes over there,' Maggie pointed. 'Only mine are far sexier.'

The two men put their forks down and started to laugh as I waved at the waitress for the bill. In the safe darkness of the cinema Maggie curled up against me, giggling as she kept taking the shoes out of the bag and trying to press them into my hands. The row behind us were starting to mutter and twice people tapped me on the shoulder. Over the previous months I'd felt that I was gradually curing myself of the grip which shoes had held on me. I was finally growing up and away from them, or at least most days I convinced myself that I no longer had a desire for them. I stopped waking at night and imagining that I could reach my hand out to touch cold shoe leather. Now it was Maggie's flesh which I touched, hot as a furnace beside me in her narrow bed. One evening I had even walked up along the canal past the cider drinkers at dusk, carrying that old wooden chest like a child's coffin under my arm. I hadn't opened it for six months. I climbed on to a wooden lock gate and held the box out, wanting to throw it down among the debris trapped in the water below. I couldn't do it.

141

Somewhere in England Emily had a set of photographs of me which stopped at sixteen and back here in Ireland I was still keeping her shoes. But they were no longer sexual items, I told myself, they were one of the few mementoes of the past which I possessed. Everything else had been thrown out from that box on the night I returned from England as a child.

So now in the cinema I was mortified by her behaviour. I wanted to leave. Maggie put her foot up on the seat in front of us and tried to put a new shoe on. I gripped her foot and pulled it down, knowing that I was being rougher than I had to be. After that she went silent and watched the girl on the screen who, unable to decide between her husband and her old lover, ended up alone in a cheap foreign hotel room.

On the way home from the cinema Maggie spoke only once.

'That film was like me,' she said. I didn't ask her to explain, I was tired. I didn't want any further complications. The evening had been a nightmare. I just wanted to go to bed with her and to wake up tomorrow, hoping that she would have calmed down again. In the flat I got into bed before her.

'This is the way the dancers stripped in that bar in Halifax,' she said as she began to remove her clothes. Once I would have enjoyed it but now I only wanted to get the light out and not have to deal with her. There would be time to make up any quarrels tomorrow.

Before Maggie I had been trapped, ashamed of my desires. The girls that I had sought out were ones with whom I didn't have to feel small. They were lightweight, unimportant.

I watched Maggie undressing with a sudden stab of

treachery in my heart, wondering how much longer I could take her swaying moods, her constant chatter. There were new girls who had started in work, smarter and prettier. I now felt confident about asking them out.

Maggie approached the bed naked and put her hand down to pull back the sheet. When I spoke it was just a way of getting at her, it was more my irritation spilling over than any real desire.

'What about the shoes? Where are these famous shoes I've heard so much about?'

She looked down with the assurance and gaiety leaving her face.

'They're in the cinema,' she said quietly. 'I spent every penny that I had on them for you and now I've left them under the seat.'

I was more relieved than upset. But still I was tired and frustrated and it was a chance to show my annoyance with her. I turned over, slamming my fist into the pillow. I waited for a few moments, then turned back to forgive her. She was sobbing on her knees beside the bed.

'Come on, Maggie, get into bed.'

'You think I'm stupid, don't you, and worthless?'

'Come on, Maggie, get in. We'll go back for the blasted shoes in the morning.'

'You don't love me without them.'

'Listen, will you just get in.'

I didn't mean to shout but my voice was so loud it startled both of us. Even before her tears my nerves were frayed. She put out the light and climbed meekly in beside me. I could feel her wet face against my bare shoulder. I knew that I had been mean and was ashamed of my anger.

'I don't mind about the shoes, Maggie. Is there anything else wrong? You've lost your job, haven't you? Is that why you're crying?'

'I've let you down again like I'm always doing. I'm sorry, Mick, sorry.'

I pressed her close against me and she lay still. It was after midnight and people were starting to come into the house, muffled voices along the stairs, the clink of six-packs. The curtains were not drawn fully and a single beam of weak light divided the dark floor in two. I couldn't get her to stop crying, even though I said every word of comfort that came into my head.

'Maggie, is it your job or is it us or this flat that's getting you down? You can tell me, Maggie, I want to help you.'

She twisted herself out of my arms and turned around so that I couldn't see her face as she lay staring at the wall. I stroked her hair and kissed the back of her neck. Somebody paused on the landing outside our door. I couldn't be sure if they could hear her sobbing. I pressed Maggie's shoulder to warn her in case they knocked but she kept on crying.

'I want the radio on,' she said, 'I want music.'

She rose up and put some pirate station on too loudly. I argued with her that she would wake the entire house and she switched it off, then when I had turned over she put her cheek to the transistor on her pillow and began to blare it again. I let her carry on until the people upstairs banged down.

'Maggie, for the love of God, you've got to stop this,' I said and she sobbed about it being her home and not mine, that I only used it whenever I wished to. She flicked the waveband so that it was left on between stations. The hiss of static filled the room.

Listening to it, I realized how tortuous the last six weeks had been. Maggie seemed to have freed me from the past but in return all I had done was bring back the past to haunt her. Tomorrow we were going to have to talk rationally. I would help her if I could, but I was going to have to make a break.

After a long time the convulsions ceased and she lay so quietly that I thought she was asleep. Then she spoke in a voice that was completely different from her own, older and more cold.

'You were a good man, Michael, I'm glad that I met you again. A good man, do you know that?'

I thought that she was going to turn and crush her body up against mine, but she lay on her back a few inches apart from me. In the half-light I could sense that her eyes were open and she was still crying, but it was different from before, as though everything inside her were slowly dissolving. I called her name once or twice and got no reply.

After a time I must have blacked out into sleep and it was her soft moaning which woke me. As I leaned over her I don't believe that she knew who I was. It felt as if all the terror that was trapped inside her imagination was escaping. I put my arms around her body, trying to protect her, but I knew it was useless. Inside my embrace her mind was disintegrating.

I am not sure what occurred next. My body was so drowsy that I could not prevent myself from falling back asleep. So I do not know if I was dreaming it or whether I did wake again to find her leaning over me, whispering words which I couldn't comprehend. I only know that for Maggie her bedsit was no longer an island in the river. It was indeed an ark, but an ark which had broken loose from the moorings of reality, an ark bound for hell. And the features of the devil frantically tugging at the smashed helm which she was staring at were my own.

That night seemed to last forever. I was calling her name but I couldn't even hear my own voice now. Then there was the final blackout into a sleep without dreams and the pain of waking to remember everything early the next morning. The house was quiet. Maggie was dressed in her brightest summer colours. There was an uncanny gaiety about her which was frightening to witness, like a child let loose in an adult's body. I didn't know what to do with her so I walked out and found a taxi. All the way over to Clonsilla I kept trying to maintain a conversation and yet not speak about anything which had happened. I got the driver to stop on the corner of her mother's estate.

'Is this where we are?' Maggie said. 'I think I might call in and say hello to my mother.'

'You do that, Maggie. It might be wise.'

I watched her walk past the boulder towards the house.

'Canadian on holiday, is she?' the driver asked. 'Are we waiting here or what?' I should have gone with her, I should have explained everything to her mother. But I was a coward, I was that little boy again. And I knew that her mother would know as soon as she saw Maggie's eyes. I knew now why I felt so uneasy in that woman's presence, knew that she had been waiting for this to happen again.

'No. Drive on,' I replied.

Part Two

'Where to?'
'I don't know.'

I had paid off the taxi from Clonsilla at the canal and walked home. Nick was in his front garden. He looked more agitated than I had ever seen him, profoundly annoyed with himself.

'I've locked myself out,' he said. 'Can you believe it? Half a century living here and I've never done that.'

I let him in through the house and we went out to the back garden. The wall between the two gardens was half tumbled down. There were pieces of old piping stretched across it that the roses had twisted themselves around. I climbed over them easily and, getting my hand through Nick's small kitchen window, managed to prise open the handle of the big window. I walked through the hallway and opened his front door. It felt funny to be standing at his hall door waiting for him to come out of mine.

He asked me to stay with him for a few moments and we sat down on the hard chairs in his hall. I felt shattered and sick, and was cursing inside that I had seen him, but I realized that it was not loneliness which was making him want to keep me there. Mislaying his key had upset him. And now the agitation he felt frightened him because of his heart.

'The only weak thing I have in my body,' he said. 'The doctors told the Missus thirty years ago that I could drop dead at any minute. A scaffold collapsed when I was on a building site in Limerick. I was hanging there three storeys up for five minutes until they rescued me. It left the heart dodgy ever since. The doctors said I was to rest up fully for six months. How in the name of the lepping Jesus do you

147

rest up fully when you have two young daughters to be fed? I'll take my chances with the work, I told them, because the rest will surely polish me off.'

He stopped and looked at me.

'What have you been at, boy? You look washed out.'

'A rough night with someone whose daddy wasn't as lucky on the building sites as you.'

'How's that?'

I wanted to tell Nick what had happened, but I wasn't even sure of all the details myself. I kept persuading myself that Maggie would be all right, that it had just been a bad night and her mother would be able to cope with her at home. Nick lit a cigarette and got up.

'I'll be grand,' he said, and showed me out to the door. I climbed over the fence and put my key in the lock. Nick saluted.

'Thanks for baby-sitting me.'

On the morning after my first date with Maggie I had come downstairs in Breffni Street to find a card addressed to me in the hall. Even before I picked it up and read my name I knew that it was from her. I remembered the way she had lifted my hand away the previous night on her mother's sofa, the nervous way she had retreated back into herself.

'*The big girl in me wants to run to you,*' the card read, '*but the little girl inside can only take tiny steps.*'

The thoughts I had harboured about leaving her were gone. Perhaps in the future I would, but how could I leave her like this now when someone actually needed me? I had been afraid to phone her mother. I felt guilty as if it had all been my fault, the result of the pressure which I had put

Maggie under. I could still see the anxiety on Maggie's face when she told me that she had forgotten the shoes in the cinema, the way that I had turned over, selfishly dismissing her.

How much would she have told her mother about me? It was always the same, my own fear of discovery overriding every other concern. The next evening I had gone back to the cinema and collected the shoes which she had never worn. They were still in the green cardboard box, wrapped in the crisp tissue paper. I returned to her flat like an intruder. The cups we hadn't washed before going to bed, the radio lying on the floor, her clothes from a previous evening scattered on the chair. It was just like the way I had treated my mother's illness, I should have known all along where it was leading but had made myself ignore the signs. And in the same way as years before I had convinced myself that my mother would return, there on Maggie's single bed I pretended to myself that Maggie and I would soon lie together again beneath those soft French posters which she had chosen.

I undressed and I put on her new shoes. The strength I had felt to resist them was gone. I lay there on the unmade bed with my eyes closed. How long since I had felt a tight strap across my instep? Maggie, who when she undressed seemed almost overweight, Maggie with the most perfect breasts I had ever seen, Maggie whose absence formed a dull ache in the room. The rent was due that evening. I left money in the rent book on the counter beside the door. I took the shoes home with me. It didn't seem right to leave them there.

It had taken me two days to find the courage to visit the

149

estate in Clonsilla and even then I was unable to bring myself to call on Maggie's mother. I cannot recall any incident in my childhood when she was unkind, yet in all the memories which my mind selected she was someone to be wary of, the woman scolding Maggie and me from the bedroom window for making too much noise if she was sleeping after her night shift, the woman whose Hoover frightened me with its strange sucking noise, her harassed glare as though I had touched her daughter on the night when Maggie cried out after we thought we had seen a ball of worms behind the old press. I blocked any moments of kindness from my head. She brought back too many memories which I had made myself forget. She was the only person left who remembered me as that naïve boy in his Cub uniform. In her presence I always felt reduced back to him.

I had waited at the end of the estate until I saw Maggie's mother leave her house, then I knocked at the next-door neighbour's and said that I was a friend looking for Maggie. That was how I found out which hospital Maggie was in and how she had run down the street in her night-dress when the ambulance came.

In the shop in Santry I had paused at the cheap bouquets of flowers, fingered the cuddly toys, tried to find something which would explain how I felt both to her and to myself. I had put the flowers back and pointed to the giant cuddly crocodile over the assistant's head. She had pulled it down and tried to find a sack big enough to wrap it in.

In the end I had taken it the way it was and stood at the bus-stop, trying to ignore the schoolgirls sniggering behind me. The crocodile was four foot tall. Motorists beeped their horns as they passed. I felt as foolish as if it were an inflatable doll.

The hospital was low and flat, out in the fields towards Swords, a cluster of buildings spread out with large plate glass windows glinting through cherry trees. The driveway was long and curved. Patients with tuberculosis had been brought here after the change of government in the late 1940s, blinking in the strong light like prisoners in the newsreels released from Europe's camps, still carrying with them the smell of dank wards where they had been marked down for death. Now the trees were mature, a gardener with a mower scattering wisps of grass.

I did not know which ward she was in or if she wanted to see me, or even where to ask or what to say if someone questioned me. There was a bench with peeling green paint beside an old copper beech. I propped up the crocodile for company and sat there. Five minutes passed and then the door of one of the wards flew open. She stood on the steps looking out at the crocodile and me and then, as if in slow motion, began to run.

The big girl in me wants to run to you, but the little girl inside can only take tiny steps.

It was bizarre to watch her, like viewing an old film of a Chinese girl whose feet had been taped and her bones broken until she could only totter. And then I realized how stiff from illness and drugs Maggie's limbs were and that she was racing, in the tiny steps which were all her body would allow, towards my arms.

Maggie's gratitude when I came to visit her every day was frightening. The drugs had puffed her face up. I would be waiting on the bench by the copper tree at six o'clock after work. I never spoke to another person there. It was ingrained in my mind that I was guilty of something. Whenever anyone passed in a uniform I kept expecting him to order me to leave.

And every evening when she came out she said that the prospect of my visit was what had helped her through the day. We took the same route between the two lines of trees, Maggie leaning on me like an accident victim learning how to use her legs again.

'Remember how upset you got the night when I wouldn't say that I loved you?' she said one day. 'Well, I can say it now with all my heart because you're still here even when I'm like this. At night when I get lonely I take the crocodile into the bed for a cuddle. The other girls in the ward get so jealous of me that sometimes I have to pass him around.'

The words which I had wanted so cheaply back then were being given with such weight when I least wanted them. Now they would cost too much to return. All I wanted was for Maggie to get well, for a day to come when she could walk without leaning on my shoulder, when I didn't have to be strong for her.

'I was thinking today that when I get out of here I'd like to marry you,' she added. 'Or else one of the doctors here. I can't decide between you. He's got such lovely brown hands. We could have a house with a few kids on some estate out near my mother. If I just get through this I know I'll be strong enough to bear them for you.'

It was close to her mother's nightly visit. I said nothing as I led Maggie back. She asked me to go with her into the ward. I wasn't sure if I was allowed but was too frightened

152

of upsetting her not to follow. Some women lay on their beds staring ahead of them, some chatted together in a haze of cigarette smoke. One woman in her thirties was making herself up. Her clothes were glamorous. She applied her make-up with quiet precision. Another woman sat with her face to the wall. She looked as if she had been sitting like that silently crying since early morning. Yet there was nothing in any of their faces to mark them out as unstable. They seemed no different from the women I passed in the supermarket or the street.

It was in the ward that Maggie told me how she thought she was pregnant. Things had slipped away from her in the weeks before her breakdown and she wasn't sure if she had remembered to continue taking the pill.

I managed to control myself until I had left the hospital grounds. The bus-stop was deserted. Nobody heard the scream as I pressed my forehead against it. I had two brandies in Swords before getting a bus back to town. I despised myself for caving in but I got off at Griffith Avenue. The church there was a hated place and I a bloodied soldier with a white flag. I stood in front of their crucified god, despising myself for trying to bargain with him. Just let her period come, I prayed, and there was nothing which I would not do. All the things that I might have prayed for, and yet the only thing which had driven me back to that altar was to beg God that another life might not begin.

In work people were noticing the difference in me, the way that I snapped at children in the junior library. One morning the cleaner asked me if I had forgotten how to smile. And even when Maggie remembered that her period had come the night after she went into hospital my mood didn't ease. I was no longer just myself. Now I was the man she leaned on for strength, the man whose duty it was to be waiting at six o'clock on the bench, the man whom she often dismissed after a few moments by saying that she was tired. And even when I had gone to her flat after the first weekend to discover that her mother had removed everything and left a note for the landlord, I was the man who had torn up the note, the man who still forged her signature every Friday when I left the rent, the man who had never been able to bring himself to wash the two cups left on the draining-board.

Three weeks after I began to visit her she said that the doctor wished to see me. She went into his office first and I sat in the corridor, watching her fingertips which were distorted through the hammered glass panels as they tapped against the door. When she had gone I went in. The doctor was an Asian in his thirties, my rival for Maggie's affections. I wondered if he knew it.

'What do you think is wrong with your girlfriend?' he asked.

'I don't honestly know. I just want her to get better.'

'You do know this is not the first time she has had a breakdown?'

'Yes, it happened once before in Canada.'

'Three times. The first when she was seventeen. Each time it occurs after she has tried to leave home. I have to warn you that there is a pattern to these cases, a pattern of ever decreasing circles.'

'I'm just trying to help her get over this one.'

The doctor leaned back. There was a file in front of him with her name on it. From somewhere in the building I could hear the faint noise of a man sobbing. It sounded more harrowing than if he had been screaming in the corridor outside.

'You have to think of your own position,' the doctor said. 'Not just of Maggie. I am not saying that you cannot have a future together but you must be aware of the risk . . . in fact, of the certainty.'

'I just want to help her now. I want to do what's right.'

'You may not be helping her by coming here every day. She feels that you are putting her under pressure to get better at your pace and not her own.'

'But, I never . . .'

'Every day you ask her how she is feeling and every day she feels that she has to have progressed that little further for your sake. I know you have tried to help, Mr McMahon, but Maggie feels it is now time that she stopped leaning on you.'

I realized that it wasn't the doctor who had wanted to see me, but Maggie who had asked him to be her messenger. I had been keeping my voice low, thinking that she was waiting in the corridor. Now I knew that she was gone and the doctor was politely waiting for me to leave.

'What should I do?'

'Wait for Maggie to contact you if and when she is ready.'

It was far later than I had ever remained at the hospital before. As I reached the bus-stop Maggie's mother was about to cross the road. I hoped she might pretend that she hadn't seen me but instead she approached. I waited for her to strike me or at least scream abuse. Instead she put her hand out to shake mine.

'Thank you for all you've done for Maggie,' she said. 'You've grown up into a good man, Michael.'

It was the same phrase Maggie had used on the night of her breakdown, in the same voice and the same tone. I watched Maggie's mother walk through the hospital gates as she had been doing all her life. The young trainee nurse from Leitrim; the wife nursing the senile in Dublin when her husband took his dreams abroad; the Irish widow coping with the gleaming equipment and new textbooks in the Toronto hospital; the mother, finding it humbling to be wearing her ordinary clothes as she walked along the waxed corridors, searching for the ward with her only daughter.

I no longer felt like a criminal. I felt nothing. For those three weeks I had ceased to be myself, I had lived only to be there to help Maggie. I hadn't let myself think of the future.

That night after the doctor dismissed me, I sat up like a scarecrow in the window of her bare flat. The body which I had held was now smothered inside a blue hospital gown. All that remained were her shoes which cut into my flesh. They were all that ever remained of anyone I loved. Finally I fell asleep, sitting upright in the single hard chair. I dreamt that Maggie's bedsit was a cabin on my father's sunken ship. Fish without eyes swam through the murky green water. And when Maggie came towards me her skin had been shredded by a surgeon's scalpel. Although my body was still sitting there I felt that I had left it and was floating overhead, looking down at my own limbs swaying in the plankton-infested light. When we tried to kiss, our teeth scraped against each other and broke apart, sinking slowly down into the muck on the floor. Maggie moved past, leaving my body swaying there, only now it was swaying on an old car tyre on the branch of a tree. She vanished through the darkness of the ship. I was floating after her, trying to follow, but it was no longer my father's ship, it was the Widow Lady's house and I knew that while Maggie was there I would never find her. I was the poor boy left at the gate while she was playing in her white night-dress on the back of a rocking-horse with her red hair glinting like seaweed in the splinters of light squeezing between the shutters.

And so I waited for word from Maggie, trying to fit back into my old life but discovering that I hadn't really had one. Joe left the house and a new couple moved into his flat downstairs. At night when they weren't making love loudly they were quarrelling. From early morning they played Country and Western albums. I promised myself that the first morning they played Kenny Rogers before eight-thirty I would leave. The atmosphere of loss which used to linger in the house was gone, as though the ghost of the old couple hadn't been able to withstand all the changes in their world. The house was rarely silent. Only the altar at the foot of the landing remained, another year's crop of flies' corpses crumpled up in the water-font.

But Nick was always there and these days it was often I who sought him out. Most evenings after work I called to see if he needed anything in the supermarket. I would jig up and down on his doorway, presenting myself at his service. Often that was the only time in the day I would laugh. He would order yellow pack white bread and tea, full milk – real milk, as he called it – carrots and parsnips mixed, which he ate with almost every meal, and, at the weekends, a Madeira cake in case visitors called in. The clocks went back and Nick stood in the early dusk, cursing the policeman who owned the four houses in flats at the top of the street.

'Mean as the back of his balls that only ever knew shit. It does my heart good some nights to see the young ones doing a runner on him.'

One evening as I talked to Nick a neighbour who was even older than him came up the street. I knew the house where he lived, overgrown and ramshackled at the start of the main road. A Morris Minor which hadn't been moved for thirty years was growing back into the wild foliage in the front garden. A broken brass plate for the *Crinoma String Band* was attached to the railing. He looked like he hadn't changed his shirt since President Kennedy's visit. Nick leaned out over the gate to stare at him.

'Do you know what, Johnny Flynn?' he greeted him. 'You're fucked.'

The old man had trouble breathing. He looked at Nick, then took a seizure of both laughing and coughing.

'I am that, Nick,' he said. 'I'm rightly fucked.'

Four nights later I saw the squad car parked outside the old man's house and the guard emerging through the broken-down door to beckon to the driver of the ambulance which was turning the corner.

I had given Nick a spare key to my flat, and he was delighted whenever I locked myself out. He had already had a key to the front door for over thirty years, which the landlord never knew about. He would coax me down to his kitchen and produce some old book or newspaper, anything that would keep the conversation going. What he most dreaded was the onset of winter. When the snow came early in November I walked the hushed streets searching for paraffin for the antiquated heater which kept his hall warm. He would stalk about the house with his hat on to keep the heat in and grin when I returned, having thought up some other chapter from his past to tell me about. If loneliness had him caught by the balls then he fought every inch to shake its grip off, never giving in to easy despair.

Nothing was too far-fetched for him to try to get company. Sometimes late in the evening, when I wanted to be alone, I would know by the knock that he was standing outside. One night he had a hotel guide from 1910. 'Here, you're a librarian. Have a gander at this: *"Taps and water closets available in each room."*' I accepted the gift before finally closing the door in both guilt and relief, imagining his return to the infinite torture of his kitchen in the hours before it was time to sleep.

Or else he might try and coax me in for a drink, even though he was a teetotaller himself. He would go through the old presses and uncork bottles of wine which had been used by some priest a quarter century before to celebrate mass in Latin in the house. Dead insects floated in sediment in the glass which I would edge away from me as I sat back in that smoky kitchen to listen to him speak. Was there any village in Ireland which he hadn't worked in, any road he had not driven down in wartime wondering how to find the petrol to get home, any labouring craft that his hands had not done?

In the first Sweepstake he told me that he had painted the drum with fine gold leaf, some of which he still had in the attic. He produced it, letting my fingers feel the weight of each page of hammered gold. He had worked as a carpenter on the first estates built around Dublin, then left for England when work was scarce, and had come home to tour around Ireland erecting Esso advertising hoardings. All his life he had simply worked on, cursing politicians, believing only in the skill of his hands.

His two daughters lived in England and Boston now. They coaxed him to live with them but he would be like King Lear, he claimed. A man without his own home was not a man.

'If I want to get up in the night and shite in the corner of my own bedroom then I want to know that I can do it without asking permission off anyone. Now I hope to Christ that I'll never want to, but I always want to know that I can.'

And it was hard for me to imagine him being toured around to family parties in Britain or elsewhere. He fitted into that kitchen, those smoke-stained prints, that shed in the garden filled with every conceivable tool, including a device for – as he once explained to me in graphic detail – castrating horses.

But it wasn't just his loneliness that I was responding to, it was the fact that his life added up and made sense. It was an arc of years moving on to an inevitable conclusion. Once he gave me a leaflet for the Japanese Gardens which he had visited years before in Kildare. They were laid out like the path of a life, he said. When I read the journey through the stages of the garden described on the leaflet it was his life which I saw, from the Cave of Unknowing on through the Stepping Stones that joined in marriage and the Hill of Ambition, and the pause to gaze back over the quiet waters at middle age before the path wound steadily down to the

Tree of Mourning. Nick was eighty-seven and yet I envied him. His life added up, it made sense. Often I wanted to confide in him about Maggie, whom he still asked after, but I could not even be sure of my own feelings towards her. I was terrified of being summoned back to face her illness again and yet my life without her was barren.

On New Year's Eve I went out to join the crowds that were flocking up for the bells at Christchurch. Groups of excited friends, whole families together, solitary drunks lurching into people, young couples making vows for the year to come. At half-eleven I thought of Nick. I stopped at the top of Dame Street and couldn't go on. I had to run to get to Breffni Street before midnight. I bought a bottle of lemonade for him at the twenty-four-hour shop. Although he was pleased to see me he made no fuss. I had whiskey up in my room. I got it and at midnight we toasted each other in his kitchen. It felt good to stand there sharing that moment with him. It was so long since I had felt that good. I knew that he respected what I had done. Even though he would have loved to talk he made no effort to keep me there.

'Happy New Year,' he said one last time as I climbed over the fence.

'Happy New Year, Nick.'

The letter from Maggie came in early January, the letters big and awkward as though written by a child. She had been out briefly, been taken down the country by her mother, relapsed and then been moved to an asylum near where her mother's sister lived in Enniscorthy. The express bus to Wexford left me at the gates. The building stood

161

cresting the ridge of a river valley. The bus driver told me
the plans had been mixed up in London at the end of the
last century with those for an Indian palace. I remembered
the hospital where my mother had died, the same red brick,
the same Victorian flourishes. How many buildings did the
legend relate to? Maggie's hospital near Swords had been
an open and almost welcoming establishment but here, when
I climbed the long drive, there were bars and security gates
to pass through.

There was a small glass panel in the door of the ward. A
nurse was writing at a table inside. Maggie sat fully dressed
on her bed. Beside her another girl was turned to the wall
crying. The door was padded. The nurse called Maggie
sharply when she didn't respond at once. Now that I was
there she didn't seem to want to come out on to the corridor.
She stood in the doorway and then put her hand out for me
to support her.

'Mammy comes in with Aunt Kay every day,' she
mumbled. 'They say they can make out the light of my
ward across the valley. Do you know what? I've forgotten
how to walk. How can you forget something as simple as
that?'

'Of course you can walk. Come on, let's just take a few
steps.'

Maggie almost cried with pride when we made it the eleven
paces from the door of her ward to the locked window.

'I look awful. I know I do. You don't have to pretend
otherwise.'

I remembered Nick telling his old neighbour that he was
fucked, the honest humour between the two old men in the
face of death.

'You look fine,' I lied. 'Though it's the last time I'm going to bring you to the pictures.'

It was an old joke which she had always laughed at in the hospital but now she simply stared out at the country patients being led around the grass below.

'This place is terrible,' she said. 'Girls screaming, deranged at night. The constant bloody weeping is the worst. Day or night, there's always someone crying in that ward.'

The nurse was calling her. I hated the tone of her voice. Maggie looked towards her and began to obey meekly. I kept my arm around her as we counted the steps back.

By the third weekend I visited her we could manage the whole length of the corridor. There was a stench of disinfectant there that I could still smell even after I had showered in the evenings.

'Have you a girlfriend?' Maggie asked as she leaned against my arm.

'You.'

'No. A real girlfriend. You must be sleeping with someone.'

'No.'

'We never did get the sex right, did we? Maybe if we had had more time. You tried your best. Don't feel bad about it.'

'Maggie?'

'The nurses are watching. We should go back.'

This was the time to say something, either *I love you and accept you are the way you are*, or *Maggie, you know that it's over between us*. Was she waiting for me to speak and would she be able to cope with either statement? I couldn't

163

even decide which one I wanted to say. We had reached the door of her ward. Maggie tapped on the glass to be admitted back in. I watched her shuffle over to take her place on her bed.

When I came back the following Saturday I could see Maggie through the glass, sitting hunched in the same position like a wax doll dumped in a basement after a spring sale. She kept her back to the glass when I tapped. The nurse looked up, produced her bunch of keys and came out to me.

'Maggie thinks it might be better if you didn't come again.'

The nurse was younger than me. I looked down at the soft white leather of her shoes, then up at her face again.

'I'm sorry, Mr McMahon, but it would be better if you were to leave now.'

When I got off the bus in Dublin I stopped outside a new shoe shop which was having an opening sale and went in. I didn't care what anyone there thought. I was sick of caring and thinking. I picked cheap pair after cheap pair until all my wages were gone.

'I'll just wrap them for you, Sir,' the nervous young assistant said.

'It's okay. I'll eat them here.'

I couldn't stop laughing at the joke. She put the shoes into a bag and retreated beside the other girl behind the counter until I had left. The afternoon was freezing, weekend shoppers moving like ants around the shopping centre. I was at the top of the stairs when Nick knocked. I threw the shoes into my room and came down.

'I saw you come in,' he said. 'I've some homemade soup

inside. Sure a freezing afternoon like this you'd catch your death.'

I stopped and thought of the plastic bag in my room and then of the old soup spoons laid out in his kitchen. Nick was not a man to judge or be shocked by anyone. For one wild moment I felt that I could talk this out with him. I needed help and advice. Nick was grinning, anxious that I go in and share the meal with him.

'I've had it waiting on the stove for the past hour for you to come home. You look frozen, boy. Sure we'll be dead if we stay around too long in this weather.'

'I'll be dead if I don't go upstairs and lie down,' I said.

That's how I remember him, trying not to show his disappointment when the door slowly closed in his face.

My mother's favourite film was *The Lost Weekend*. I never forgot the title, nor her description of the alcoholic floundering about in his private hell. I had lost days before but that was my first lost weekend.

Lying there on Saturday night and hearing the couple downstairs come in, the country music, the grunts of their love-making. Half waking in the dark to the sound of the chain flushing in the toilet next to my room, feeling the shoes pinching my feet and putting my hand out to touch the other pairs scattered on the eiderdown. The sleepy panic I felt that Aunt Maire would come in and catch me. Then waking up fully to remember where I was and that Aunt Maire had been lying for three years in a grave which I had never visited. The chair leaning back against the handle of the door, even though it was locked. The stain above my head in the half-light which Maggie had once claimed was the devil's head. When I looked at it now it seemed more like a diagram of an empty womb.

I was sweating even though I was naked and the room was cold. I had to start my life again, to take that chair away from the door and to walk out into the grey light of Sunday morning. But it was safe there, sweating beneath the eiderdown, feeling the clasp of those shoes on my feet. Nothing could change in that room as long as I lay there. I could remain the age I always was, alone in Emily's house wearing nothing except Emily's shoes.

Before dawn there were movements downstairs, the noise of things being shifted and then the front door slamming. Later I heard footsteps on the stairs and later still a radio on somewhere. I stared at the rim of dust where the holy picture had once been. I would like to think that I remembered Nick going about his life next door. Sunday was his most hated day. I heard the strong wind outside. I should have known that he would be imprisoned in his kitchen. 'I can't beat that breeze any longer,' was his new phrase. But I only thought of myself, marooned inside my own problems. I still had the smell of disinfectant from that asylum on my flesh. 'You keep things bottled up,' Maggie had once told me. 'It would be better if you learnt how to cry and got the hurt out of you.' All I had learnt in my life was how to wear other people's shoes.

On the Monday I rose early and phoned in sick. I was over the worst, I told myself, I was going to claw my way back. On my way home from the phone box I called at Nick's door to see if he wanted messages. I had a joke ready to tell him. I knocked again, feeling guilty for having refused his soup. Although there was a radio on inside I got no reply. I remembered how he always joked that every time he went to the toilet the phone or the doorbell rang. I left him there, meaning to call again at lunch-time. I forgot.

In my room I tried to decide what to do with the shoes. The best thing was to make a clean start, to dump them all and remove the temptation. The only shoes I had ever kept were Emily's old red high heels in my father's wooden chest. I swear that I was packing them all into a bag. It was just that there was one pair which I realized I still hadn't worn. I would just try them on me for one minute, I decided. I had paid for them after all, I could control myself. I put them on, then found the strength to take them off. I put them with the others in the bag. I couldn't bring myself to throw them out.

It was only when I went downstairs that I noticed how the door to Joe's old flat was open. It was empty inside. The couple had done a runner on the landlord. I went in and lay on the old battered sofa listening to Nick's television blaring through the wall. I spent the whole afternoon lying there in limbo. At five o'clock I went out walking along the canal. I climbed out into the centre of the old lock gates and dropped the plastic bag over the side. I watched the shoes scatter out and bob in the water among the broken sticks and sacks of rubbish.

When I got back, Eamon, who had moved into the front room upstairs, was looking around Joe's old flat. The couple had left milk and tea behind. He offered to make me a cup and we sat, enjoying being in a different room, and joked about how much the landlord had been taken for. And like every time that anyone talked about the house, what we really talked about was old Nick next door. I told him how the girl used to ride her bike down the hall to avoid him, about the decoys we had used to escape out the back door. We swapped our favourite Nick stories, his tales about travelling in the west of Ireland during the war, the way he tackled the canvassers in the local elections and had them fleeing down the road. We evoked Nick so well it was as though he were in the room with us, grinning at his own stories, enjoying our good humour.

We were still there at half-seven when the builder called. I recognized him from seeing him going in and out of Nick's.

'Is the man about?' he said. 'I was due to call in to him this evening to arrange about a job on his roof. I can hear the television but I can get no reply.'

Why hadn't I noticed how long Nick's television was blaring at the one station? I knew how he switched it on and off, torn between the company it gave him and his disgust at the stupidity of the programmes. I banged on the wall, as I sometimes used to when visiting Joe there, to see if he would bang back. None of us wanted to express our fear.

'I'll check around the back,' I said. 'He might be out in the shed.'

There was a light on in his kitchen window. I knew he was there before I clambered over the broken wall. His hat was what I could see first, then his shoulders as he sat in the chair. He was staring at the back door. The key for it was lying on the ground. His body was slumped slightly with one hand stretching down to touch the wire surround of the two-bar electric fire. And spread out around him were a set of tools that he had been carefully cleaning in preparation for a job which he was obviously about to do.

I climbed on the sill and I tapped my fingers lightly on the glass. *Don't you dare die on me, Nick,* I wanted to say, *I want to talk to you. I want you to tell me about your life again. Turn your head towards the window and look at me. I want you to make soup for me and I want to take it. I want to bring you a sliced pan and carrots and parsnips mixed. You can't just leave me with that last memory of closing the door on your face.*

The builder had come out into the garden.

'Can you see anything? Is he in there?' he asked.

The small top window was locked this time. I didn't want to look back and say the words so I picked up the piece of lead piping from the sill and, breaking the glass with it, put my hand in. There was a faint scent of burning in the room. I climbed in and lifted Nick's hand up; his fingers were slightly singed. Nick's eyes were open, a look of amazement on his face. I picked the key up and opened the back door. There was a touch of frost in the air. The forecast on the news had said that the really cold spell was due to start later that week and would last well into February or early March. Apart from the brief snow in November it had been quite mild until now. Nick had died on the last good day of the year, he had cheated the winter. The builder came in and made the sign of the cross as he looked at him. I put my hand over Nick's eyes but I couldn't close them. There was a list of phone numbers in Nick's handwriting pasted up beside the receiver. His daughters' numbers were outlined in red. The builder and I looked at each other.

'You better phone them,' I said. 'They wouldn't know me. I'm nobody here.'

I had left Breffni Street in April when the letter came. It took two weeks before anyone thought of forwarding it to me. Maggie and her mother had returned to Canada by then. The house in Clonsilla was to be sold in their absence. The letter gave a flight time and a number. I thought of Maggie waiting at the sign which read *Passengers only after this point* while her mother fussed and checked the departure boards. There was no back field for me to get lost in this time, no pack of children for her mother to pass sweets out among, no neighbours to wave out of windows, no bright clean pages called tomorrow. Just Maggie's same search for a boy's face in the crowd, her same feeling of turning away, betrayed and disappointed.

PART THREE

The intercom on my desk is buzzing, the library outside crammed with Saturday afternoon borrowers. I lower my pen, set aside the monthly return statistic sheets and, flicking the switch, tell the staff I will be out shortly. Another complaint about the increased fines, I think, another special request to borrow a reference title until ten o'clock on Monday morning. This old Carnegie Library is my kingdom; the rare and most expensive titles safely filed behind me, the view from my private office of the ugly shopping centre with the mountains pressing up behind it, the Coola Press first editions behind glass in the reference section that overlooks the dilapidated Protestant graveyard where the Yeats sisters are buried.

I carefully brush the sleeves of my jacket before opening the door. The girls are working through the long queues at the check-in desk, the borrowers intimidated into having their books already open. The porter is collecting a handful of oversize titles from the returns trolley. As people glance towards me I smile in acknowledgement, thinking how the staff cannot handle even the smallest difficulty without my guidance. I look around to locate the problem.

A woman holding a young boy by the hand is staring at me from beside the counter. Her clothes are old-fashioned, grey and dull against the bright track suits and slacks of the women around her. I walk towards her, smiling in reassurance, wondering what sort of trouble her son has caused. The boy begins to smirk, then his eyes grow uncertain and fearful as she draws him towards her. Her own eyes are *making me uncomfortable, aware of how hushed the entire library has become. Then the light seems to change as though the sun has slipped through the clouds and the mousy green carpet tiles are suddenly lit up. And I know with a sudden instinctive fear why the borrowers have grown quiet and are now staring at me. I remember what I had been wearing, alone and thinking myself safe, in my office before the telephone had rung. I had forgotten to change them, but how could I have forgotten? After all the years that I have managed to hide them, how could I suddenly be exposed, trapped between the catalogue and the stairs on a busy afternoon? A girl at the desk sniggers as borrowers deliberately begin turning their backs. Only the woman and her son remain staring. I notice that he is wearing short heavy corduroy trousers. His mouth opens wider until it seems like an infinite black hole that will keep expanding forever. I know her face suddenly, I know the lines of hurt in it. And her son's voice seems to reach me across a vast distance and time.*

'Why is that man wearing ladies' shoes, Mammy?'

I hear the word spoken and I wake. That same sudden awful jerk as though my body was being pulled back to earth. The sensation of sweating between hot sheets, the anger at being caught out by the same dream again. Only the location changes; caught out in the library, found out on the bus, exposed in the busy supermarket. The same woman in the drab clothes holding the same boy close to her, and always the same anxiety for hours afterwards like a weight on my stomach.

I cross to the window and then out on to the balcony.

Part Three

Beyond the amber security lights a horizon of moon-grey trees and walls lurks where the leaves of sycamores sway like yellowed crinkled paper. In the compound below the roofs the cars glimmer like flattened, indecipherable grave slabs. And here on the balcony this figure I cut in the faded dressing-gown is barely discernible in the grainy light that filters against the dull concrete wall of the apartment block.

The cold night breeze against my face, the feel of rough concrete against my bare feet. I am thirty-eight years of age and naked beneath this dressing-gown. My stomach hurts. I grip the wrought-iron railing so tightly that my knuckles hurt. Soon this side of the apartment block will receive the first tints of light, but it is not the dawn that I seek, just this grey anonymity.

The apartments are quiet, as they almost always are. Fifteen minutes of car engines revving in the morning, the rusty creak of the security barrier being closed in the evening. A person could die here and it wouldn't be noticed. The intercom beside the telephone buzzing occasionally, the mail piling up in the wooden box in the hall. Residents pass like visitors in a hotel corridor, their eyes down, their vices hidden. Only when leaving the rubbish out in the wooden compound do you catch the clink of bottles that have held whiskey and valium. Set back from the public road like a tropical Governor General's compound, a quarter-mile from the seafront, this place is no place, sterilizing the acne behind the word *home*.

A cat stalks the wall of the old terrace of houses beyond the car park. It eyes me with mistrust and vanishes among the grey foliage. I take the plastic bag at my feet and hold it above my head. I want to fling it down at the expensive cars parked below, to hurl myself on to the concrete after it. But I know that I won't. Instead I will find a quiet lay-by on my route to work and dispose of the contents there. When I worked in that condemned library with the yellowing damp books off Thomas Street I remember the early morning drinkers that I had to pass, the dead look in their eyes as they shivered, waiting for the early houses to open. Sometimes I would pause to glance in the pub windows and see them struggle to get the coins out of their pockets, how they scattered them across the counter and the way the barman would turn his back when he had poured the measures of whiskey so they were left alone to cope with the slow calvary of trying to raise the glasses to their mouths.

Once I watched a well-dressed man who could only manage the task by leaning his head against the wall and pushing the glass with both hands up along the cracked paintwork until he could just get his lips around the rim. As he tilted the glass his hands twitched apart and he fell backwards and lay among the overturned stools, his tongue frantically trying to lick the splattered whiskey off his chin. He looked up and saw me at the window as the barman came around to evict him. How pathetic he looked, unable to hide the shame and self-disgust in his eyes, but at least he would know the brief respite of a cure, a moment of release when the trembling temporarily stopped.

My hands now are steady, my knuckles white as they grip the iron railing. Nobody watching in the filtered light could ever guess at the shame and self-contempt that is hidden within this solitary and motionless figure reliving the events of yesterday.

Part Three

Yesterday had been like all the other days, yesterday was the day when I swore that I had stopped. Driving home from the library the idea lodged like the faintest buzzing in the back of my skull. I shook my head and half smiled. I had thought it all out and my will-power was stronger than that. I would not surrender to any of my mind's tricks. But already I was searching among the heavy traffic for a parking space.

I parked the car along the Southern Quays. A Guinness boat was tied up, the pumps at work unloading the empty tanker drawn up beside it. The cobbles were wet and there were just a few bollards between my wheels and oblivion. I lied to myself, or I thought I did, my finger brushing the car keys as though they were chimes. A woman passed with a pram, two boys with bent heads lost in anoraks. I was in control, I told myself as I locked the car. I would just take a look in the shop windows to prove to myself that I could do it, just take a stroll for ten minutes and then resume my life. But already I knew by the awful purpose in my step that my words were hollow. Now I was living again, now I could feel excitement. I forgot about the car, the stack of defaulters' tickets that I had promised myself to sort at home that evening, the Ad Hoc Residents' Committee Meeting in the apartment block in two hours' time.

I slowed my step only when I reached the shop. I looked behind, wanting the street to be clear. Nothing should have been easier than simply stepping through those glass doors, but this is always the hardest part, when I am balanced between shame and an unleashed insatiable yearning. Most days I lose the courage and walk on past the shop window, fists clenching and unclenching inside my jacket pockets. I

177

throw my head back as if it were stiff with grief and yet when I reach the car I always sigh with relief like a dried-out alcoholic who has managed to make it past his favourite public house.

Yesterday I lunged forward towards the shop doorway filled with just enough false bravado to get me inside. I no longer cared who might be watching as I gripped the handle and entered. There was nothing conspicuous about me, I told myself, no reason for them to stare. But they knew that I knew they were not deceived, those young assistants with their amused smirks of recognition from the time before. I closed the door behind me, stepped forward and stopped. New leather has its own unique smell. My hesitation was gone. I knew what I wanted and for now nothing else mattered.

'Are you sure that you know her size?' the assistant asked. 'Sizes vary you know, they might not fit.'

I pointed again authoritatively.

'I know what I'm doing, I always buy them for her.'

She was still explaining how I could change them as I snatched the receipt and left the shop. Outside I began to walk, varying my route back through different streets. I knew that nobody could be bothered following me, but still I took no chances in my terror that I might be recognized.

Often I think that it is those moments walking back to the car, when everything seems possible, which are the greatest bliss. Everything is heightened in the way that they say the final moments are before death. I had overcome my inhibitions and escaped discovery. I touched the bag and felt the outline of their shape. I longed to take them out and run my hands across the smooth leather. And all the grey tedious evenings in the apartment block were gone, the red line that I drew across the attendance book in the library each morning at half-nine like a vein sliced open. I might have been twenty-six years younger, rushing home exhilarated to Emily's bedroom with that red candle next to my shirt. I was almost running when I saw the river, my car parked at an angle, the tanker pulling away from the Guinness boat.

I cursed the evening rush-hour traffic, staring at those blank faces behind their windscreens. Off home to wives and children. Good Jesus, how part of me wished that I was doing the same. I stopped at the lights near the small park by the bridge in Drumcondra. A small cluster of people were gathered by the statue of Our Lady of the Tolka, earnestly praying, staring at the grey stone eyes, beseeching them to come to life. A row of poplars leaned in the wind by the bank of the river. As I watched them pray in public with a vague disgust I could feel the tension that was building inside me, the knot in my stomach, the indescribable ache. I was no longer the person who left the apartment that morning, the Grade A librarian who had sat at his desk with his neat row of pens.

And yet in the midst of that animation I knew the despair that would follow, the sense of dislocation that the night would always bring. Caught between two worlds like a fallen spirit, I would stalk this apartment with the lights out, thinking of all the things that I have never been. Where had I tilted away? I could have been the most ordinary of men with a dog on a lead in the park at evening-time. I could have known what it was to be woken at half-three in the morning by the tiniest of cries from a cot in the corner.

Instead I knew that I would sit hunched by the window while individual lives withered in the neat packages of rooms above and below me. All single professional people like myself, their footsteps overheard in the corridor followed like an echo by the plop of an automatic light-switch going out.

The cluster at the statue began another decade of the rosary. I thought of the girls in work who passed in and out of my life, a succession of moccasins, sandals, suede boots and clogs. One slice of corned beef at lunch-time from the supermarket, one white roll, a cigarette burning itself out in an ashtray when some boy they met at the weekend rings them. They cycle off after work or run for buses, leaving me suspended at my desk. A figure of authority in a dark blue suit to be distrusted, an unsmiling face with a reputation for being kind. They reach their plywood flats and sneak out the stolen toilet rolls that I pretend not to miss, the books stolen for their friends. Once I overheard them discussing how many thousand they thought that I earned. Who do they see as they knock respectfully with requests for holidays or for special leave? Phoning in sick on the weekends of open-air rock concerts, a boyfriend's sweat drying into their flesh as they sleep together in small canvas tents.

Two of the girls at the statue might have been them. The same age, the same hopes. One girl with black hair was gazing at the crude stone face with such intensity it disturbed me. Lately this has been the cause of most requests for leave. Crammed up in private buses trundling down pot-holed lanes to where crowds await the Blessed Virgin's next appearance in some ugly grotto. Ballinspittle, Asdee, Carns in Castleconnor. Each lunch-time I hear them chart the latest apparition, the obscure place-names like a gig guide for a third-rate showband. I want to tell them the stories half-remembered from Maggie's mother about the crowds in Kerrystown in Annagary when she was a girl, about the time that a whole family were reported to have seen the outline of Mary cradling the Infant Jesus in her arms on the face of a rock after a late night game of cards.

People are the same, I imagine myself telling them, generation folding into generation, the same desperate hopes, the same need for signs and visitations. I know that they would just smile and nod in embarrassment, their talk drying up as they wait for me to leave the canteen. Could they imagine me walking home with Maggie to her tiny bedsit on those nights when we had decided to drink the bus fare? Or coming in once at Christmas, after a night's drinking with Joe, to fall asleep wrapped around the heater in that very library? Often I want to take one of their hands and say, *Listen to me, I have lived too. I also sat in my flat broke till pay-day, I too once rushed out to parties in the rain.*

Where did it happen, where did I become separated from the rest of them? Was it Maggie's illness or Nick's death or was I always set apart from the afternoon I first tried on Emily's shoes, or even before then? Why could I not have settled for the same compromises, have been content to grow older, cursing the mortgage? A wife broadening out now with flattening breasts, a youngest child, like an afterthought, running in with a bruised knee to be cured with a kiss from us both.

But part of me has always been alone in Emily's house and has dreamt of nothing except her shoes. For how many years have I tried to block that image out, how many dances and tacky night-clubs, the brief succession of girls after Maggie, the feel of their flesh through blouses, their nervous laughter?

'You're so shy,' they would say, noticing how my gaze was always drawn back down to their shoes. And I would look up and smile at them before my gaze shifted down again to the high heels trapped in slow motion by a strobe light, my mind struggling to shake off their mesmeric attraction. But always it was like a bubble which I have never been able to break from. I would imagine myself free before it closed on me again until I was only putting off the moment when I shattered the brief intimacy between us.

'Leave them on, please.'

They'd stop, half-undressed, and look quizzically at me. The bright posters on the wall, the scattered clothes on the armchair of the flatmate whose turn it was to stay out until midnight.

'Don't you want . . .?' The smile already leaving their faces, to be replaced by unease and confusion.

'Just your shoes I mean, just leave them on for me . . . please.'

They would walk towards the bed, unsteady now and awkward in their shoes as if suddenly unused to the shape of them, feeling vaguely threatened and exposed. But without shoes they were just a blur of white flesh, shapeless contours somehow without sexuality. Afterwards we'd lie on in the cheap single bed, so far apart now in that cramped space.

'My flatmate, she'll be in soon . . .'

'I know.'

Part Three

How many hours would they have spent clearing the flat or sitting at the mirror by the window fixing their hair back?

'I'll phone,' I'd say and receive their stiff nod. They would pull the bedclothes further up to their neck and as I rose I would notice the shoes that had fallen to the floor when they had managed to slip them off.

The girl with black hair lowered her gaze from the statue. A small child was running among the flower-beds, his knees covered in muck. The lights had turned green. The car behind me was beeping. I felt cold and rational. All I had to do was wind down the car window and toss the bag out over the parapet of the bridge as I drove past. But yesterday, like all the other times, my foot moved like an uncoiled spring. I left the crowd at the statue behind. I swerved into the outer lane that led out towards the airport, in the flow of that torrent of glinting chrome, with no need to think as the car powered its way there.

I parked in a lay-by behind the airport with spent condoms scattered around the trampled weeds. Beyond the wire fence the landing-lights shone dimly in long rows snaking through the grass. A sign warned cars against halting for the next three hundred yards, a plane with dipped wheels descended along the flight path. It was too early for lovers' cars to inch into line in the lay-by, too late for van drivers to sit smoking, dodging their bosses in the depot. I got out and crossed the flattened grass. The place disgusted me with its beer cans and litter, but it was safely deserted. I removed my shoes and socks and bathed my feet in a tiny dark stream obscured by brambles. The freezing water hit my flesh like a numbing slap. When it felt as if all circulation had stopped I lifted my feet out, avoiding the broken shards of glass as I limped back. I took the plastic bag from the back seat of the car and squeezed the beautiful shoes on, wincing as they cut into my flesh. For days afterwards my skin would be sore with scraped flesh and blisters but at that moment I no longer cared.

Because I was alone in the car and I was wearing her shoes. I could feel the pain of them like it was the pain of something new. I closed my eyes and for a moment Emily walked before me, taller than me then, up the stairs of my mother's house. And I was breathless and confused, balanced on an edge of grief that I could not comprehend. I wanted comfort, wanted life to remain warm and tight and familiar. The shoes pinched into me as I let myself remember. The past became a sepia tone filled with strangers' handshakes and pats on my forehead; the cloying smell of incense and the shuffle of feet, and when I looked up Emily was kneeling among the women on the female side of the altar rails. And I knelt with my uncle on the male side, unable to prevent my eyes from staring at the vibrant sheen of her shoes. My uncle prodded me and I lifted my head as the priest's massive hand brought the white host down. But as it touched my lips all the weight seemed to drain from it so that I was left barren, consumed by an emptiness like a phantom pain.

All my life it has never left me, that hunger, that ache which can never be filled. And I have seen it in other people's faces without them ever realizing. My library girls praying that years of freedom will give way to a mortgaged house and a husband who will love them, their mothers praying for a peaceful death and a God who will remember.

I have seen it in the faces of public men, peering into their eyes at night with the sound turned off on the television. Yesterday I could see it, too, behind the prayers of those gathered around the statue in Drumcondra, in the crowds that have been gathering again for these last few months in desolate grottoes and boggy lowlands desperate for a sign that their lives mean more than they can comprehend. And when, crippled with loneliness, I have stalked the weekend streets when the pubs are closing, I have heard it behind the raucous laughter of crowds tumbling out; the cars speeding off, the bodies twisting on sweaty leather car seats in that same lay-by while the airport lights sparkle like glow-worms.

A plane was beginning its take-off down the long runway as I sat in the car. I watched it speed towards me until the nose lifted off. I pictured all the passengers inside staring out while the stewardess demonstrated the safety procedures, trying not to think of mechanical failure as they leaned their heads back. And I thought of how alone and powerless they must suddenly feel, and how if they looked down they would see below them a car parked on the grass, the middle-aged man inside rapidly becoming a speck. I watched them vanish into the sky. I had felt that mesmeric moment so often before, those last few seconds before I came. And I raised my feet up on to the dashboard so that the red leather shimmered at dusk in the runway lights. And how I would gladly have died in such a moment as that, when I was alone in her house and I wore nothing except her shoes, when I could feel nothing except her shoes, with that ache within me suspended, that hunger trapped at bay, and just me at the window on an English street, standing behind the white lace curtain with my body tingling, my nerve ends shredded. And no more fears of death to face now, no more changes and world endings, just eternity stretching outwards to fill that single, infinite afternoon.

There is one door which I have never opened in this apartment that I have rented. The landlady, who is practising as a lawyer in America, has left most of her belongings in the spare bedroom still uncollected. Only twice in the seven years that I have lived here has she returned, ringing the silver buzzer on the front door which still bears her name that I have never bothered to change, smiling apologetically as she vanishes to rummage through the boxes in that room. Both times I left her alone in what I think of as her home and what she probably now considers as mine. When I returned, the only sign of her presence were the coins left by the telephone for the call for the taxi to take her to the airport. She is an account number which turns up monthly on my bank statements, a telephone voice which calls every eighteen months when the service charges for the apartment block are increased. She talks of selling the apartment but cannot seem to break the connection with her native place. I offer no encouragement, still frightened of the commitment in buying a home. I agree to pay the charges and she hangs up quickly before I can question her about anything else.

Old Nick would have called them luxury apartments but he would have spat on his fist and banged it against the hollow wall. *What class of building work is that?* I can almost hear him say. *Sure you could hear somebody having a shite two floors up.* The grounds are manicured, floodlit at night. Mrs Brennan, the cleaner, hoovers and dusts the outer corridors for an hour each afternoon. Sometimes I

still remember the bedsit in Breffni Street with the noise of
card-players wafting up past the cobwebbed altar on the
dark landing and the damp outline of rafters emerging like
an apparition on the ceiling in winter. I recall the coldness
of that room with its single-bar heater, the window perpetually occluded from the sun by the stone bulk of the flour
mills that are now themselves converted into apartments.
Even the burial chamber at Newgrange received more
sunlight than that window. Nick would grin and say that I
have risen in the world, but it hasn't been the opulence of
these apartments that has kept me here, but their crisp
impersonal sterility.

I remember locking the door on the night I moved in,
lifting the phone off the hook and turning to survey the
empty white walls. Here was a world where lives had not
been piled upon lives, where the ghosts of children in black
boots with stout laces could not run. Here the past had no
rights. In Breffni Street, alone there in the evenings, I had
often felt an atmosphere which I couldn't define, had
hesitated before turning off the landing light, had lingered
with my back against the bedsit door, listening as if other
footsteps had followed mine up the stairs. And yet even in
these apartments there was no escape. A month after I
moved in I met the builder who was trying to trace down a
water leak. He was taking me into his confidence, he said,
as he described how when his men were digging the foun-
dations for the apartments they came across what must have
once been the dried-up bed of a stream in which a neat
procession of eight adult skeletons were laid in a row.

'Of course, we had to keep it quiet,' he said, surveying
the neat paving of the car park from my balcony. 'Property

prices, you know. People feel funny about where they live. They don't want to know there have been skeletons gazing up at their living-rooms for the past thousand years.'

Yet over the years it hasn't been those hunters with their wooden sticks and myriad gods that have disturbed my sleep, but that locked door of the spare bedroom. I know that it's why I've been able to rent this flat so cheaply, but even now I still glance instinctively towards it when I go into the dark hallway to use the bathroom at night, as though somehow I expect it to be open and some figure to be watching me from the shadow of the curtained room.

Some evenings I have taken a chair out into the narrow hallway and climbed up to peer through the glass pane above the door. Little light filters through the curtains. The landlady's past is neatly parcelled on the floor there. Her clothes and books seem to be waiting for her to return through that locked door and resume her life. I can barely discern the shapes of two suitcases, of cardboard boxes crammed with clothes and plastic sacks filled with old books. Yet I always feel uneasy, convinced that my memory is playing tricks on me and that a particular box had lain on the other side of the suitcase before or some plastic sack was tilted at a different angle.

There are no windows in that hallway or in the bathroom at the end of it. Heavy fire doors block out any light at either end of the long communal corridor outside. Often when I stand up on that chair in the silence of the apartment block and peer through the glass pane I feel that, if I could only make out the shapes clearly in the room, I would see that it is my own life which I am watching in miniature. All the bric-à-brac which doesn't add up, the memories and emotions talcum-powdered with dust. And I am stranded, a ludicrous figure in that unlit hallway, waiting for something or someone to return who will make sense of it all.

How does it happen that a man slips suddenly into middle-age? There was no single moment when it occurred and yet it seems that I went to sleep one night still young and woke up the next morning in an older and greyer world. Was it after Maggie left, after Nick died? Was it during the moves between a dozen flats before I found this apartment block? How did I suddenly feel comfortable being called Mister, suddenly become aware of the distance in people's eyes in work when I entered a room and began to fall into their image of myself? Why did dark blue suits suddenly appeal to me? How did my life one morning feel like a drink which has been left out all night on a bar counter? How can I have never taken one decision in my job and yet find myself over the years being propelled up a ladder? Senior Assistant, Grade B, Senior Librarian – titles that grew to fit me like suits of clothes. How did a day come when the phone line in my office was broken and before I used the public call-box across the road to request relief staff I found myself soaking a handkerchief in disinfectant and holding it over the receiver that I had to speak into? How did I wake up one morning to discover that I was renewing the lease on an apartment for the seventh year without knowing the name of the person on the floor above me? Why do I still listen to make sure that the communal corridor is empty before ópening my door to collect the post in the box in the hall?

One morning two years ago I went out to purchase a newspaper and met a woman who lived on the top floor. I held the door open for her as she came in. She smiled in acknowledgement and I smiled back, the same tight smile with our eyes avoiding contact. Then she stopped.

'This is ridiculous,' she said. 'I've been passing you for years and we have never introduced ourselves. I mean to say, we *are* neighbours.'

She looked weary, I thought, as we exchanged names. I gazed at her face fully for the first time. It was impossible to discern her age. I said goodbye and the door swung shut behind me. When I returned ten minutes later she was sprawled unconscious on the carpet. I tried to call her name and discovered that I had already forgotten it. What I found most shocking was that I felt more pity for myself than for her, that what I really wished was for me not to have opened the door, that I had gone for a walk instead and somebody else had found her body. I glanced behind me, wondering whether I could step back outside. Then I remembered her voice, how musical it had been. One of her shoes had fallen off. It was scratched and shabby and had obviously been heeled a dozen times over the years. Yet it gave her an identity beyond the bag of scattered groceries strewn about the hall: a small tin of beans, a cling-wrapped portion of steak in a carton, the five new potatoes in a plastic bag, all the ingredients for a solitary dinner. Her shoe said *I have suffered hard times, I have had to skimp and fight hard to own this flat, I do not deserve to die here like this.*

I knelt down quickly beside her. She was breathing faintly as though in the most serene of deep sleeps. Instinctively I heard myself from somewhere trying to summon up the words of an act of contrition. The few phrases that I could remember sounded hollow in the spartan lobby. I rose and knocked on the door of my nearest neighbour. She was a tiny, anxious old woman who never changed out of her dressing-gown. All I could see of her was one eye with a drooping lid as she peered at me through the narrow slit of light at the chained door.

'There is a woman out here dying in the lobby. Will you phone an ambulance or a doctor? She's from upstairs on the top floor. Do you know her name?'

She undid the chain and blinked in the harsh light of the corridor.

'Dying?' she said. 'In the middle of the night?'

'It's morning,' I told her. 'Half-past ten in the morning.'

Through the doorway I could see that the heavy drapes which reached to the ground were still pulled, the small red reading-lamp casting a dim light through the room. The television was on with the sound off and just the test card with the picture of a little girl and a blackboard on the screen. There was a half-empty whiskey bottle on the table and through the open kitchen door I could see a carton of cigarettes and a row of tins of different baby dinners and desserts. Her apartment smelt of smoke and musty talc. She looked back behind her, holding on to the frame of the door.

'The dizzy spells,' she said. 'I get these dizzy spells.'

She repeated the phrase again as though it answered every question that could be put to her now about life. I had only ever really spoken to her once before on the night of a violent thunderstorm when I had heard a scraping noise out in the corridor. I had opened my door and found her trying to drag a hard chair out from her apartment in her night clothes. She had obviously been crying. The lightning frightened her, she said. She always sat up in her own hallway when there was lightning, but now even though the drapes were pulled she still thought that she could see the flashes underneath her living-room door.

I remember asking if she wished to come into my apartment but she said that she was happier out there in the dark corridor away from all windows. There were stories about lightning which she had heard as a little girl that still frightened her. When her husband was alive he had laughed at her but she would still get up from their bed during thunderstorms and hide under the stairs. I had brought her out some whiskey and sat up talking with her. After her husband died, she told me, she was frightened of being robbed in her old home. The neighbours had told her about these lovely new apartments, they had said they would come to visit her but they were all as old as herself and it was a long bus journey. She felt secure here and she loved the television, *Live at Three* in the afternoon and especially the Christmas toy fair on the *Late, Late Show*. The gardens were kept beautiful and she could see them from her window and she had never imagined that she would wind up living in such luxury as this. I refilled her glass and stuck a match in the timer switch to jam it. 'Such lovely apartments,' she said half-heartedly, 'such luxury.'

Her hand shook as she raised the whiskey to her lips and I remembered a night in Breffni Street during one of the worst thunderstorms I have ever known. I had gazed out of my small bedsit window to see Nick silhouetted in his garden, one hand resting on the faded bird-table as he gazed skyward from beneath his old cap. For one moment I had thought that he was a ghost as his features were lit by a sheet of lightning beyond the flour mills. I had dressed quickly and gone down to check that he was okay.

'Okay? Why in the name of God wouldn't I be? Isn't it grand, boy, eh, just grand? Nature's grand opera. Sure you can see nothing of it stuck there inside the house.'

And then he had leaned back against the bird-table and told me stories about being out in thunder and lightning during the war in the Local Defence Force or earlier up on Bray Head as a boy, while the garages and bushes around us were being illuminated with flashes of silvery light. I remembered how good it had felt to be standing on the far side of the tumbledown wall from him, with the old rose bushes grown wild between us.

There had been another distant muffle of thunder and my neighbour shivered in her chair on the corridor. I went to take her hand but found that I couldn't bring myself to. Here in these sanitized apartments loneliness and fear were not words that one could feel comfortable with. I had remained with her in the corridor until the storm ended, both of us feeling vaguely exposed and embarrassed.

We hadn't spoken again until I had knocked on her door that morning. As I used her phone to call an ambulance she hobbled down into the lobby. When I returned she was kneeling beside the woman's body.

'The lady with the blue car,' she said. 'She's new here, like yourself. Bought the apartment upstairs around five years back. She never used to say much at the committee meetings.'

That is how they would think of me, I thought, if I were to be found dead here. The man with the brown Volvo.

And how would they think of my neighbour when she was found dead? The lady who kept the drapes pulled. She began to cry suddenly and I thought that she was praying for the woman, but instead it was more like a whispered curse repeated over and over.

'Jesus, Mary and Joseph, what's to become of me in this place?'

The woman on the ground gasped with a rattle-like moan. Then her breathing went quiet again and stopped as we heard the noise of the ambulance arriving.

'Don't worry, she'll be all right. The ambulance men are here now. They'll take care of her.' I tried to sound reassuring. The old woman rose carefully, holding on to the steel banisters. Her eyes were clearer than they had been when I knocked on her door. She let go of the banister and stood steady for a moment.

'I worked forty years in an undertakers in Aungier Street, Mister. The lady's a stiff and that's all there is to it.'

She limped her way back down the corridor and chained her door again. All that day I remember thinking that I should put something down in the lobby, a few flesh flowers on the spot where her body had lain. I even stopped outside a florists on my way home from work. But somehow it felt indecent to do such an act in that apartment block. The only other corpse that I had found had been old Nick's. Breffni Street came back to me, with the tumbling lines and crooked angles of those crumbling back walls, its irregular extensions and battered corrugated iron sheds. And the way the neighbours there had kept calling all that evening after his body was found until it was almost like a street party, with everybody talking at once, each trying to tell their favourite story about Nick. It was twelve years and two miles away, but not only might it have occurred in another city in a different era, but, more frighteningly, it felt like it might have happened to another person.

I remained on the balcony in my dressing-gown a long time the morning after I had visited the lay-by at the airport. It was dawn when I dressed myself and silently left the apartment block. In the grey first light seagulls were wheeling above the waste ground near the apartment, marauding scavengers shrieking as they tore at the plastic refuse sacks among the weeds and brambles that were forcing their way through the cracks in the old house there. Half a storey remained with windows merging into the skyline a few feet above the stone sills. Old tyres and broken wing mirrors were all that was left from the trailers of the three tinker families whom the developer brought in to live there before the residents dropped their objections to his proposals. Now the *For Sale* sign emphasized that outline planning permission was available for another apartment block.

I gazed back at the deserted junction before stepping through the gap in the wire. That same old man stood like a ghost near the traffic lights with one foot balanced on the pedal of his ancient black bicycle. In every weather I had seen him standing in the early morning, as though dropped from the sky, either there or in other parts of the city, always with the tightly buttoned ancient black coat, a felt cap and the unlit cigarette held in his right fist. I had never seen him actually cycle the machine. He just stood waiting with one foot poised on a pedal as if part of a long, invisible queue.

He never looked towards me as I slipped through the

wire. A rat scurried through the wet grass as I approached the split refuse sacks. How many pairs of shoes had I deposited in that or similar places, dropped from bridges at midnight into rivers, flung out into hedgerows from a speeding car, left in bins at bus-stops that I would return to nights later, hoping they would still be there? This was the final worrying part of the whole ritual, trying to camouflage the shape of them beneath my overcoat as I left the apartment determined to be rid of them before a new day began. Pledging to make a fresh start, dressed impeccably as though somehow cleansing myself, resolving never again to put myself through such humiliation. And always, when I climbed back out on to the street and walked purposefully away, I would remember Alice.

Alice. It was four years since the evening that I had met Alice, four years since I had run like a criminal along the roads. Four years since those nights when I used to walk through the nearby streets at half-eleven when lights were being switched on in bedrooms along the terraces of flats throughout that part of the city. How long was it since the last affair with some girl in work had petered out, how much more careful had I become since my promotion in work, more frightened of ridicule? How many weddings had I attended over that last decade, lads who had once cursed around Joe's poker table in Breffni Street looking vaguely embarrassed as they posed in tails with their in-laws? And how many flats had vanished where I might once have knocked, as hesitantly as at Liam's house twenty years before, and pretended to be part of that world of tea in cracked cups, five-skin joints, digestive biscuits and a place in front of some second-hand television set?

In those years silence and reserve had formed like a glacier around me and I was preserved within it, each day a replica of the one before, thawed only by my brief and solitary encounters with shoes. Yet somehow within that isolation I had begun to find solace in those walks through the late-night streets. Often I would be halted for a moment, stunned by the glimpse of a bare arm drawing a curtain shut or of a girl's back as she cooked a late meal in her makeshift kitchen. Watching, I tried to visualize their struggles to hold on to the rent money until Friday evening, their exhilaration at an unexpected tax rebate, the ebb and flow of their wages, pounds saved each week for holidays and Christmas, prices checked carefully in their baskets in the supermarket. Without a wife or a child, with a dozen increments on my salary and even the money from my mother's house still untouched in the bank, I had stepped so far from the ordinary worries of life that I found it hard still to conceive of life in these plywood rooms. All I knew was that their lives contained a spark which had flickered out in the stale web of days I was caught in. And yet those half glimpses of lives at night seemed to grant me some kind of fulfilment, as though I were now merely an observer, no longer a participant, in life.

I do not know how many months I had been walking those streets before one night, down a small terrace backed on to by the gable-ends of two other small redbricked streets, I came across a lit curtained window through which I could see the outline of a girl removing her clothes. She could never have known from inside the way in which the bare light bulb projected her shadow on to the curtain so that she existed as a silhouetted strip-tease for some thirty seconds. I might have just paused a moment and then passed on had it not been for the manner in which, after she had removed her blouse and skirt, she had put each foot in turn up on a hard chair to slowly unlace her shoes, seeming to derive great pleasure from the act as though they had been hurting her feet. I could only guess at the near naked figure with the slim bust, but I could see clearly in my mind the high shoes which she removed. As soon as her shoes were prised off, the light went out and I was left in the shadow of the lane-way to imagine her crossing to a single cheap bed, her bare feet gradually being eased down between the cold sheets. That first night as I lingered there I looked up and thought for a moment that I saw the corner of the curtain being flapped back into place.

I had christened her Alice before I even left the corner. The name seemed to fit her, it sounded right in my mind. In work I was even more withdrawn than usual. I relived her silhouetted movements. There had been something curious in them, something that I knew intuitively to be different, something which was important to me that I solved. It became obsessive with me, like a name that you wake up in the night trying to remember. I began to build my nightly walk around trying to reach her corner about a quarter past twelve which was when she normally retired. I knew how dangerous it was to linger there but each night I was back, halting my walk when a door opened along the street or a car pulled up, often missing those few magical seconds if people were passing home along the street from the pub; then I would have to walk back to my apartment nursing a sudden aching loneliness. But most nights, almost as though she had been waiting for me, the light came on soon after I turned the corner. I would lean against the dark gable-end and manage to watch her unlace her shoes not with any real feelings of lust but with both a strange tenderness towards her and also a sense of bafflement, as though I were missing something.

Each morning and evening on route to and from work I drove down that street, hoping for some glimpse of her among the people I occasionally saw leaving the house. What if she's an old woman, I asked myself one night, shrunk back with age into a schoolgirl's frame? What if she is too feeble ever to go out, if her movements have been rendered slow and awkward by arthritis? Yet still I haunted that corner every night.

As a small child I once felt that if I covered my head so that I couldn't see other people, then they in turn wouldn't be able to see me. I began to take risks to ensure that I would witness her undressing, stupidly imagining like a child again that if I avoided looking at passers-by, then they too would avoid glancing at me. And yet I could never approach her corner without a tremor of deep unease. Often during those weeks paranoia took hold of me. I became convinced that I was being followed by a small man in his forties built like a flyweight. I glimpsed him behind me on the street and once or twice in the supermarket or sitting a few benches down from me in the park. Always I felt convinced that he had been staring at me just before I turned my head to look back at him.

One night as I lingered near the back lane across from Alice's house a squad car suddenly turned the corner, cruising slowly along with the guard in the passenger seat shining a flashlight out through the open window, scanning over the back walls and gardens. I stepped right into the lane-way of back entrances and threw myself down among the filthy puddles on the broken concrete, watching the torch beam pass a few feet from my head, with my heart pounding and my whole body shaking.

After the squad car had gone I was still afraid to come out. My cheek bone hurt where it had struck the ground. I knew it would be bruised. This is what I have been reduced to, I thought, a peeping Tom hunted by the police. Liam's voice came back to me across more than half a lifetime, on the night the pair of us had lain in his father's trailer to stalk out the underwear thief. *The sick bastard isn't going to come tonight.* I could see the newspapers suddenly, the small paragraph on the court case photo-copied and sent around as a joke to all the libraries. And me sitting at my desk waiting for a phone call, an object of pity and ridicule like those sad little widows up in court for shoplifting.

When I finally left the lane-way I ran all the way to my apartment, glancing over my shoulder, convinced I was being followed. I cried that night for the first time in years. There were two pairs of shoes hidden in the apartment. I took them out to wear for comfort, then suddenly flung them against the wall. I smashed them against the cooker and the kitchen table. If it were not for them I might have had a normal life, I might have been happy. I felt the heel give way and began to stab at the soles with a bread knife, ripping the leather into shreds, cursing at it until I heard footsteps in the apartment overhead.

The next day I phoned in sick to work, my first day absent in three years. I hadn't slept, my nerves were still unsteady. I desperately wanted help, I knew I needed to talk to somebody. If I had committed a murder then I might have known where to go, if I had pulled off a serious robbery I might even be able to brag about it to the police with a certain bravado, but who could I turn to with a shoe fetish?

All that morning I was afraid to go out, embarrassed to meet the neighbours after the noise I had made. In the afternoon I was frightened every time a squad car passed me on the street. Towards teatime I found myself outside Berkeley Street Church. There was stained light coming through the porch, the rhythmic muffle of voices. Even when I walked as far as the porch I still didn't think that I would go in. How many years had it been? The scent of floor-wax as I pushed the door open was an echo from my childhood. Thirty or so people were kneeling in the semi-darkness, young office-workers among the old women, incongruous in their bright clothes. I sat stiffly in the last pew, unable to kneel. I couldn't decide if I wanted the words of the mass to mean anything or not, phrases which I remembered from my childhood that now seemed so utterly bizarre. Body and blood and death on a cross. I watched the priest move through the ritual with a curious fascination, a sense both of something lost and something rejected, recalling an innocence which repulsed me now.

And yet I had never felt more alone and I knew that I needed help. I wanted a sign, a clue to my predicament. I sat there long after the mass was over, having nowhere else to go. Then I noticed the queue forming outside one of the confessionals. I watched them go in and come out every few minutes, the way they knelt to say their penance then slipped out through the gloom of the side aisle. The last penitent had gone and the priest's door had clicked open as he prepared to leave his box, when I surprised myself by suddenly lurching across the row of pews and stepped through the door of the confessional. I slammed it behind me. The darkness made the enclosed wooden space seem like an upturned coffin. After a moment the little slot opened and a mesh of light poured through. I was still standing up, as though confused by how I'd got there.

'You are supposed to kneel,' the priest said gruffly. Then after a moment when there was no reply he spoke in a softer voice.

'Do you not remember the words, my son? *Bless me Father for I have sinned. . .*'

'Don't call me son,' I said.

'What will I call you then? How do you want me to help?'

I didn't reply. I heard him sigh. Just when he thought he was finished for the night, I imagined him thinking, he gets landed with one of the silent types. I wanted to say that I was sorry for bothering him, that it had been a mistake, and to back out of the box. And yet I wanted to speak to him, to convince myself that he would do as well as any other stranger, to lift this unbearable loneliness from myself, to bring my secret out, if even just for that one moment, into the world.

'Is it something that you've done? Something in the past that you have a problem talking about?'

My mother's voice, it's funny how the sound of it came back to me at that moment. I could hear her teasing me when I asked her how she knew something and she had smiled and replied, *A little bird on a branch told me. A little bird on a branch.* I leaned my head against the wall of the confession box. I felt the sweat on my forehead turn cold against the wood. That same dream that I had killed someone came back to me, the image of limbs inside the fertilizer sacks buried in the garden. I knew that I had dreamt it recently without even remembering after I'd woken.

'Fuck,' I said softly.

'What's that, my son?' the priest asked.

'Don't call me son. Fuck. Fuck, fuck, fuck, fuck!'

I repeated the word louder and louder as I banged my head in time on the wood. I expected that the priest would come out to pull me from the box or phone the police. Instead he remained silent until I finally stopped. Then he whispered.

'God bless you in your trouble, my son.'

The slot of light closed over. I left the box. The church was empty. His door never opened until my footsteps were gone. I walked back out on to Berkeley Street. Curiously, I found that I was feeling better. I needed a drink though. I chose a pub on the corner at Phibsborough where I'd never been before, and sat alone at the mock Victorian counter, feeling the brandy sooth my nerves. I had escaped discovery but it had been a warning. I resolved for the hundredth time to make a fresh start with my life. I would go out more into places like this, I would look up people that I had once known. I ordered several more brandies, savouring the brash anonymity of the pub, the office-workers gossiping in clusters at the tables, the prison officers discussing Gaelic football down at the far end of the counter.

I am not sure how long I had been drinking before I glanced up and saw the man sitting two stools away from me. I looked down at my drink, gripped with terror. It was him, the same man that I'd seen in the park and the supermarket, and this time he had definitely been staring at me. I was frightened to stay at the counter in case he approached me, yet frightened to leave in case he followed me back to my apartment. I ordered another drink, realizing that I hadn't eaten anything all day, and asked the barman for the newspaper from behind the till.

I could hear him move up a stool as I tried to read the shaking newspaper. Now he was only a few feet from me. He seemed relaxed, self-assured, waiting for me to raise my head. Eventually I did and looked at him.

'You're getting careless, pal. You almost spent last night in a police cell, eh.'

Even until he spoke I'd been convincing myself that his presence was just coincidental. Now I felt a cold dread pass through my body. All those years I'd kept myself hidden only to be exposed like this. Money, I thought, I don't care how much it costs, I will buy him off. Then the dream came back. Had it been a premonition, over all those years, that I would one day kill this man? He smiled as if to reassure me and discreetly patted my hand.

'Listen, pal, I know you're scared but that's normal. Everybody is scared the first time. It is your first time, isn't it?'

The voices in the pub seemed to have all gone quiet. I felt as though my own voice was amplified and filling up the entire place.

'I don't know what you mean.'

'Listen, pal, it's okay, honest. I didn't phone the police on you. That was some old biddy across the road. I mean I still didn't even know if she was phoning them because of me or you.'

'So what are you to Ali – to that girl?'

'What did you call her?' He smiled.

'Alice,' I muttered, embarrassed.

'Nice name. I'm her twin. So tell me, what do you like about her most?'

He had been a boxer, I decided, possibly when he was in the army by the stance of his shoulders. He had that hard-edged scutty look. Yet although his voice was thick it was also somehow soft. His question wasn't phrased in a dirty or aggressive manner. Rather there was a frankness in his tone, a genuine curiosity. I decided that he probably didn't even know my name. After the drinks I found it suddenly easy to talk to him.

'Her shoes,' I said. 'The way she seems to get so much pleasure from simply taking off her shoes.'

He smiled and nodded companionably as he took a sip of his pint of lager.

'I used to wonder a lot about that. I hadn't put you down as a shoe person though. You like doing things with shoes?'

The question sobered me suddenly. I put my glass down on the counter and went to rise. He put his hand on my shoulder, calming me, glancing round to make sure that nobody was watching.

'Jesus, you're like a scared fifteen-year-old. Listen, don't get so embarrassed. I didn't have to follow you in here, you know. It's not me that's been plaguing you. It's been easy for you, turning up for five minutes and going home again. Did you ever think of the risk you're putting me to? Now I'm only trying to help you.'

I understood everything suddenly as my mind finally made the connection. Those limbs in silhouette, the way they moved, unable, despite the feminine clothes, to disguise their masculinity. It was so simple and I felt so stupid that I started to laugh. He looked offended.

'Oh, Jesus Christ,' I said. 'Oh Jesus. No offence, I'm sorry. The joke is on me.'

'Here, wait a minute,' he hissed. 'You mean you thought it was a girl and you're just a fucking peeping Tom? You fucking . . .'

He stopped. We both looked at each other. One or two drinkers had glanced round at the raised voices. I knew that he had been about to use the word pervert. I felt I had to justify myself some way.

'I wear women's shoes,' I said.

He sat back, slightly appeased, as though waiting for more information.

'That's it,' I said.

'Where? Where do you wear them?'

'At home. Not with other people.'

He shook his head and looked at me closely.

'You need help, pal. You need to talk to somebody. I mean you're nowhere, pal. What are you? You're not one thing or the other. I always presumed you'd followed me home from the club that night. I can't tell you the fright I got when I looked out and saw you there. I mean I always thought you knew. Night after night watching out for you to come. I figured you were lonely and kept trying to give you chances to make some approach. I mean listen to me, pal, the hardest thing is just coming out. Then you find there's thousands like you. Do you want to come back home with me now? Try on some of my shoes? I've all sorts and I've got dresses, lovely silk slips, leather skirts. You've only tried shoes, but there's a whole world of clothes just waiting for you to try, pal.'

I looked around the bar and then back at him. His eyes were genuinely concerned. I knew he really did want to help. But my flesh was crawling. I knew that clothes were not what I needed or wanted. Looking at him, I knew that it wasn't even shoes. It was something else, something that had been torn from me years before, an empty ache inside me that I could never fill.

'No,' I said. 'Thanks but . . . well, no thanks.'

He looked offended.

'Why, do you think I'm trying to seduce you? Don't flatter yourself, pal, you're not even my sort. Maybe I've been a bit pushy but I'm just trying to help. Listen, there are clubs you can go to, there are help lines you can phone, people you can meet. You don't have to be alone in this.'

'No,' I said, 'it's just that it's different with me than for you. I can't explain it and I know you're trying to help but for me it's more than just the shoes, it's . . .'

'You're stuck up, eh, is that it? Or are you just too chicken? Dressing up when little wifey is away, shitting yourself every time she opens the front door. Listen, there's nothing different about you, pal, except that you're a snob. Roaming the streets looking for your bit of rough trade and then frightened when you meet it, eh? If I had an upper-class accent now you'd be all over me, eh? Right? Am I right or what?'

Although his voice was still low, the agitation and hurt in it made the prison officers stop talking and look towards us. I got up quickly. My legs were shaking so much I wasn't sure if they would hold me. I began to walk towards the door aware now that suddenly everybody was watching. The man was hurt. He seemed near to tears. Yet when he turned on his stool to face the prison officers I knew that he had snapped back into the safety of the scutty little boxer.

'Fucking queens, eh,' he said, 'you get them trying it on everywhere. In the army we'd have given his sort a good bayonet up the arse.'

I heard him laughing with them as I reached the door. I ran home, staggering from side to side, no longer even caring that people on the street could see how I was crying.

That morning, after dumping the shoes in the derelict site, I washed myself carefully in cold water, closing my eyes as I felt the electric shaver on my check, returning to the bathroom twice to rinse my hands after finishing shaving. It was the morning that Mrs Brennan, who cleaned the outer corridors, came in to do an hour's hoovering and dusting in the apartment. I never liked to be there when she was working. I let her in at nine-thirty, half listening to her babbling as I slipped out. Her presence reinforced the feeling I had of having lived for years in a hotel. Neither the furniture nor the prints on the walls were mine. Everything there was white or grey, colours without colour.

I spent the hour in the local coffee shop on the seafront, glancing through the paper. Scandals in the semi-state bodies; monster expansion plans for St Patrick's Athletic; crowds still gathering for prayer vigils at the site of the apparitions in Kerry, West Cork, Mayo and now, after two children were visited there by the Blessed Virgin, in a field in North Dublin; the GAA official found naked and in a state of sexual arousal by police in a massage parlour in Harold's Cross, who claimed he was receiving treatment for a sports injury.

The owner of the shop came in and nodded. Soon the shop would be flooded with girls from the convent next door. I knew she took a quiet pleasure in seeing me there, clean-shaven in a neat suit reading the *Irish Times*, as though my presence were somehow a reflection on her trade. How far away the previous evening seemed, how bizarre and grotesque the figure with his feet encased in red shoes on the dashboard, out by the airport. I smiled on the way out and she smiled back, lifting her eyes from the display of cheap cakes she was arranging.

I was a few minutes early so I waited outside the apartment to avoid having to listen to Mrs Brennan's gossip about the other residents in the block. At half-past ten exactly I opened the door and saw her standing in the narrow hallway of the apartment, still with a duster in one hand as she stared at the door of the locked bedroom. She looked startled when I came in and, without taking her eyes from it, asked me about the door again.

'It's kept locked, as I explained to you,' I said. 'You can just ignore it. Nothing in that room is mine.'

'Have you been tampering with it, Mr McMahon?'

I remained out in the corridor looking in at her. As always when asked anything unexpected, I felt guilty and vaguely threatened. Where has she found the shoes? I asked myself quickly.

'I haven't touched that door since I came here. It's in no better or worse condition than any of the other ones.'

'No. Look.'

She pointed to a knot of wood near the brass handle. It was clearly discernible in the varnished door with rings flowing downwards from it.

'It's a very nice finish all right, Mrs Brennan. Now can I pay you, please?'

'No, Mr McMahon. Surely you're having me on? Can you not see it with your own eyes? Last week I wasn't certain, I thought maybe it was just my imagination. But this week sure it's as plain as your nose. Now don't tell me you haven't been touching up that face in the wood with a paintbrush every week for the past month.'

I wanted the old woman to take the money and leave. I had never really liked having her nosing around the flat. I always worried that there was some incriminating evidence, like a bag from a shoe shop, which I had forgotten to hide.

'Mrs Brennan, I'm afraid I will be late for work.'

'Do you mean to tell me that it's been happening in your home and you haven't even noticed the face of Our Lady?'

She sank down on to her knees so suddenly that I thought she was going to faint. She made the sign of the cross and began to pray. I felt both relief that she knew nothing, and embarrassment. Thankfully the other doors along the corridor were shut. I stepped inside and picked up her brush and the open tin of polish. I put them in the cardboard box with her other cleaning materials, and then placed it out in the corridor with the Hoover. I remembered the cluster around the statue in Drumcondra, the fresh reports in the paper. The whole country seemed to be going hysterical. Soon you would be scared to take the plug out of the sink in case the Blessed Virgin's head popped up. I was finding it increasingly hard to control my agitation. The woman's mumbled prayers were unsettling my nerves. I hated to be in the presence of anyone who was praying. It always made me feel slightly nauseated. I kept my back turned to her.

'Mrs Brennan, I'm afraid that I'm going to have to ask you to leave now please and not to return. I will pay you for the next six weeks as your notice.'

'. . . *full of grace, the Lord is with Thee, Blessed art thou amongst women and blessed is the fruit . . .*'

'Mrs Brennan!'

I screamed her name to drown out the prayer. Churches and stained glass, nurses kneeling at a bedside around a corpse, promises unkept, souls clambering their way out of purgatory like teams climbing up a table in the football league. Mrs Brennan's face looked terrified as she turned towards me. I grabbed her shoulders and half helped her, half shoved her out into the corridor. She looked back towards the locked door and then up at me again. Her eyes were suddenly reverent as though about to ask for my blessing. I threw whatever money was in my wallet down on the carpet beside her and slammed the door. My hand was shaking so much that I could barely get the chain on.

When I got my breath back I approached the locked bedroom door. The knot of wood was slightly larger than the size of a fist, a fairly standard small kink in the natural pattern of the timber. When I stared at it for long enough I could almost see how she might have imagined that it represented the outline of a face, in the same way as you could distinguish figures in ink blots if you really tried. I felt that I needed a brandy, though it was only a quarter to eleven.

I hated any argument or fuss in my life. In work I was about to tell the girls about it at lunch-time and then I stopped. I felt embarrassed by it, as though the ludicrous affair had been my fault. I recovered myself in the routine of work and felt calm again when I turned into the driveway of the apartments that evening and discovered Mrs Brennan across the street with another woman. I could have sworn I saw her bless herself in the rear-view mirror after I had passed. Inside the flat I poured myself a drink. This time I really did need one. My own imagination was starting to play tricks. Now I seemed able to make the face out more clearly in the knot of wood.

I had had several more brandies by eleven o'clock when the buzzer on the intercom went. I knew who it was.

'Go away, Mrs Brennan,' I said down the receiver before she had time to speak.

'Mr McMahon, I have a priest here who wants a word with you.'

I put the cupped glass to my lips again and realized that I was slightly drunk. I knew that later on I would have a desperate craving for shoes. The voices were babbling away in my ear. I lowered the glass.

'I am a private citizen,' I said. 'I have the right to be left in peace.'

'Mr McMahon, we will just take up a few moments of your time.'

The man's voice was brisk, trying to sound friendly but firm. I knew that he must have a beard even before I saw him, I could envisage the earnest eyes, his smile which made old women swoon. I hated beards. I heard a young voice as well, that of a girl whispering, and then Mrs Brennan saying that she would ring the bell of another woman she cleaned for upstairs who would let them into the front hall. The last thing I wanted to do was to get neighbours involved.

'Stay there,' I said angrily. 'I'm coming down.'

The priest was how I imagined him, only tackier, as though down on his luck. The girl seemed by her clothes to be in her late twenties. Her face was even more youthful, yet there was something about her eyes which seemed older. She had dark hair and a vaguely familiar look.

'What the hell do you want at this time of night?' I demanded. Mrs Brennan stepped back awkwardly while the priest practised his smile.

'Just a moment of your time,' the priest replied, 'just one glance at your door.'

I could see him noting that I had been drinking.

'No doubt the whole thing is probably an optical illusion, but I can see the worry which it has been causing you. These last months Our Lady has been trying to tell us something very serious about the state of the world. It is not for us to question how or through whom she sends her messages. Mr McMahon, I'm sure that I can help to put your mind at ease.'

The girl's eyes unnerved me slightly. I stopped looking at her face. Instead my eyes made that old slow progression downwards. She wore a blue jacket and white jeans which tapered out just before her ankles. Her flesh was bare down to her red shoes. The priest coughed. I had to look back up at him before my mind registered what he had said. I knew that at any moment he was about to call me 'son'.

'Go and fuck yourself the hell away from my door,' I said.

His smile quivered but remained fixed. I could see his mind working again, slotting me into the applicable category, dredging up the appropriate set of responses. He glanced briefly towards Mrs Brennan as though reproaching her. His voice took on an ingratiatingly reasoned tone.

'Mr McMahon . . . there are ladies present.'

'What church are you attached too?'

Mrs Brennan touched my sleeve, and blurted:

'They put him out, Mr McMahon, would you believe that? For saying the mass in Latin like Our Lord told us too. It's why the Blessed Virgin is appearing all over the place, to warn us about the vipers who are dragging the church down into hell.'

'I am having some theological disputes with my bishop at the moment,' the priest injected. 'We are living in a difficult time for the church with Our Lady having to come back because they won't release the Third Secret she gave the world at Fatima.'

I was about to close the door when the girl suddenly spoke.

'Please, Sir, I beg you. Just for one moment let me see the face of Our Lady.'

Were it not for her red shoes I would never have let them in and led them down the corridor. I stood, blocking the door of my apartment, and pointed.

'The girl can go inside. You two wait here.'

The girl looked hesitantly at the priest who considered for a moment and then nodded. The brandies and the late hour added to the surreal atmosphere. They made me bold and almost giddy.

'Your shoes,' I said to her. 'Those heels will mark my carpet. Give them to me here, I'll hold them for you.'

She leaned against the doorway to take them off and hand them to me. The leather was cool but inside I could sense the warmth of her skin. The figure 7 was barely distinguishable in gold ink. The priest tried to lean forward, peering towards the knot of wood as the girl approached. She gave a sharp intake of breath and knelt down, leaning forward on her knees so I could see the outline of her panties through the white cloth. Her bare feet were twisted sensually and almost painfully by the way in which she knelt. I held her shoes tight against my chest, suddenly feeling almost as faint and breathless as herself. She stared at the wood for a few moments and then cried out.

'Oh Mary, Mother of God.'

In the doorway Mrs Brennan knelt. I remembered where I had seen the girl now, in the cluster of people around the statue of Our Lady of the Tolka, lowering her gaze to look at the small boy running through the flower-beds. The priest flexed his shoulders, confident now in himself. He stepped forward as though about to brush me physically aside. I stood my ground and he stopped, unable to disguise his irritation now.

'You don't fool me, Mr McMahon. I deal with your sort every day. The lapsed Catholic, the black sheep. Who are you fooling? Do you think I couldn't see the look on your face as the girl was praying? You're just too scared to admit to yourself how overcome you are.'

His voice was slightly raised now. I knew that people would be listening along the corridor but I couldn't help snapping back.

'Keep the fuck out of my flat. I say who comes in here and nobody else.'

'Really, Mr McMahon . . .'

'I'll take an axe to that blasted door if you don't step back.'

The girl turned towards us, her face enraptured.

'Would she be saying something, Father? I think her lips are moving but I cannot hear the words. Please, can I stay here a little longer, Sir?'

The priest looked threateningly at me.

'The girl will be safe if she wants to remain for a while,' I said, 'but you are not welcome here.'

'Please,' the girl pleaded with him. 'I think it's what Mother Mary would want.'

'I can't just leave you alone with this man.'

'How can you say we'll be alone?' I said, pointing towards the knot of varnished wood. 'Unless you really don't believe in any of this stuff.'

The priest might have been just a joke, but the girl's almost desperate sincerity made it seem improper for me to remain in the hallway watching her kneeling in prayer. I went into the kitchen and put on the kettle to make tea for her, then poured myself another brandy. How long was it since I last had a girl in my flat? I thought of the priest outside, scowling in his car, and wondered how long it would take for his patience to evaporate.

The girl appeared behind me at the kitchen door and tapped.

'Did you really see something there?' I asked.

She looked offended but also a little unsure of herself without the priest.

'Why wouldn't I? Didn't Mrs Brennan and others?'

'What others?'

'She said there were others. That's why the priest came down.'

'What did she look like?'

'She looked incredibly . . .' The girl stopped and held her head sideways to observe me. 'Can I have my shoes back now?'

'No,' I said, 'I'm still minding them for you. My carpets. Would you like tea or coffee?'

I knew how ludicrous I looked with her shoes in one hand and a fresh brandy in the other. She shook her head and laughed.

'I think I could use a gin if you have one.'

I found some vodka which she settled for and sat drinking cross-legged on the sofa. I know that it was mainly the drink which was making me so relaxed with her, but it was also something else. A sort of recognition. She reminded me of somebody else. I had been expecting a gushing diatribe on religion, instead she seemed anxious to avoid any reference to the door.

'Are you planning to keep me here as your bare-foot prisoner?' she asked.

'Mrs Brennan is harmless, but that priest, Bluebeard or whatever his name is, is a headcase. Do you know that?'

'He claims I have a vocation. *Me?*' She laughed incredulously.

'A vocation for what?'

'He says God will let me know. He's even had some nun phone me up, but nuns are not that keen on recruits with three-year-old sons.'

217

She laughed again. I liked her laugh. It was unselfconscious.

'He's a very powerful man to hear him talk to you. The people around him, well a lot of them are dry old sticks, but he is . . . I don't know . . . he makes you feel like you'll never need to make a decision again. He's talking of recruiting me and some other girls to go to Iceland with him.'

'To do what?'

'Convert the natives.'

I saw her trying to suppress a laugh again at the absurdity of it.

'You're having me on.'

'That's what I thought, but he's deadly serious. It has the highest level of atheism in Europe with all the problems it leads to, alcoholism, drug abuse. He says the main street of Reykjavik is just one line of sex shops full of little Eskimo women buying magazines of blonde Swedish girls for their husbands.'

This time she couldn't suppress her laughter. Reykjavik. I thought of the stick of rock which my father had brought home for his new-born son with that name curved down the side of it. It was a quarter of a century since I had dumped it, along with everything else relating to him. How much I would have given to have back those tattered telegrams and newspaper cuttings.

'And will you go with him?'

The intercom buzzer in the hallway began to go in long bursts. She glanced back at it and then at me.

'I don't know yet. I was never much good at decisions.'

'I saw you yesterday,' I said. 'At that statue in

Drumcondra. I was passing in a car. You stood out. You were younger, different from the rest of them.'

'They're good people,' she said defensively, jumping as the buzzer went again.

'I never said they're not. I just said you stood out.'

'So I suppose you know it all, eh?'

The priest had his finger on the bell now. I knew I had insulted the girl without meaning to. With anyone else I would have slipped into my professional librarian mode, but with her I felt a compulsion to be open.

'I don't know the first thing anymore about anything. I barely know how to breathe.'

It was impossible to ignore the buzzer any longer. I went out to answer it, shocked by the nakedness of my own words to a complete stranger. I snapped down the receiver at him to take his finger off the bell.

'Send the girl out or I'm coming in. Do you hear, man?'

'She'll come out when she's ready, Bluebeard. Now put your shagging cutlass away. We're just after finding out about the Blessed Virgin.'

'What, man? What?'

'She was made in a joinery in Taiwan.'

'Clare, what is he doing to you? Just scream out and I'll break this door down.'

'I'm okay, Father. Honest. I'll be out soon.'

She took the receiver from my hand and put it down.

'You're funny,' she said. 'Mocking everything like you had enough anger inside you to burst. You're still carrying my shoes around. I think I'd like them back now.'

We both looked back towards the locked door.

'It's just a kink,' I said. 'A kink.'

219

I repeated the word again before I released her shoes.

'Maybe you're just too scared to look into it.'

Her eyes were so serious as she took the shoes back that for a moment I thought she understood what I was talking of. I wanted to tell her, even though I didn't know her. Perhaps it was the fact that she was nobody, that I would probably never see her again. She was waiting, expectantly, then the buzzer went again.

'He's getting impatient,' she said. 'We'll be late on the canal.'

'Where?' I asked, suddenly incredulous in turn.

'The canal. He brings myself and some other girls there at night.'

I leaned back against the door, trying to control my laughter. I realized how drunk I was.

'Bluebeard is a pimp and he wants to bring you to Iceland?'

'It's part of the group he's formed. We work along the canal in shifts. We're there to help the call-girls. To give them coffee from flasks if they want it or just let them talk to us.'

'And do they?'

'Well, curse at us might be a better description. We keep driving their customers off. When a man pulls up in his car we try and talk to him but they just get embarrassed and drive off again. Last week I put my head into one car and offered the man a miraculous medal. He said he'd give me fifty pounds for it if I threw myself in as well.'

She laughed and then stopped, with a sudden glance at the locked bedroom door.

'It's just a kink,' I said. 'A kink.'

Part Three

She put her hands down the neck of her blouse suddenly and produced the miraculous medal which she had been wearing around her neck. I stood there, helpless, as she reached up to place the thin ribbon of blue wool around my own neck. She smiled, as though embarrassed by her own actions, genuflected towards the bedroom door, then opened the hall door and ran, still barefoot and clutching her shoes in one hand, down the long corridor towards the front lobby while the intercom buzzed angrily beside me.

I lay awake half that night, feeling the shallow little medal like a lead bullet weighing down on my naked chest. All my life I had hated religious ikons, I had never imagined that I could bear to wear such a thing. Yet when I put my fingers up to remove it I would remember the feel of her shoes in my hands, the shocking whiteness of her bare soles vanishing down the carpeted hall into the night.

The giddy sensation of drink had worn off. Instead I was left with the same sickening feeling in my stomach that a drunk knows when he wakes up aware that he has disgraced himself in public again. Apart from two occasions, I had passed twenty-five years without seeing the inside of a church, without being swamped by ugly plaster-cast statues and badly sung hymns. Twenty-five years of finding something slightly sordid about seeing people at prayer. Of Sunday mornings, if I was too long shaving in the bathroom, I would come in to find mass being broadcast on the radio and shudder as I reached for the plug in the same way that I had shuddered as a child at the sight of worms. I had been born and I would die. I would be cremated and forgotten. That was my right, to be left alone in oblivion. What frightened me most about death was that perhaps at the end I would give in to that final mirage of familiar, long dead faces beckoning down a burrow of pure white light. The last terrible trick of the brain, the cortex dissolving into whiteness as its oxygen supply was shut off. Life's final chemical hallucination. And the terror that my mind might go and they would rush in priests with their anointings and muttered prayers as I lay there, too weak to refute them, with my last shred of dignity stripped away.

I'm not sure what was unnerving me most, that knot of wood in the doorway or the memory of holding Clare's shoes. I got out of bed at three in the morning. I knew that if I didn't do something I wouldn't sleep. I thought that I was going to take out the battered and padlocked wooden box which I had kept with me all those years, the one which my father had carried home from his ship, the box where those very first shoes were still hidden away. But I found there was a greater compulsion driving me. I felt a stab of irrational fear before I opened the door into the hallway as though I expected papier mâché figures of martyred saints to populate that windowless narrow space. I switched on the light and stepped back. I seemed to be able to see the face in the door quite clearly. I shuddered, sinking my teeth into the knuckles of my right hand. Two eyes which might have been carefully carved into the wood, a secretive smile and flowing shoulders which now almost reached down to taper away at the elbows. The wood was glistening as though a bright light was shining off it. It looked sticky like fresh sap was oozing from it. I felt sick and gripped with fear. I remembered Maggie, that night when she was left alone in Breffni Street and claimed the devil's head was in a stain on the ceiling. I felt cheated. This was a new place, a clean sterile structure. There should be no room here for ghosts or spirits. I wanted to throw up, to run out screaming down the long communal corridor to the floodlit gardens.

I lowered my eyes and when I looked again it seemed to be no more than a kink in the wood after all, a silly optical illusion. I glanced away and then back again. This time I saw a face shining there as though a slide was being projected on to the door. *Pray*, a voice in my head was whispering, *fall down on your knees and pray*. I found myself sinking down until my bare knees touched the carpet. I leaned my head forward and suddenly slammed it against the door.

'Get the hell away out of my life,' I cried. 'This is my home, mine! Do you hear? Do you? Do you? I don't believe in any of you. Are you listening to me? Not now, not ever!'

I began to scream obscenities at the shimmering wood. I remembered Mrs Brennan once cornering me to describe a charismatic revival meeting. I was speaking in tongues now too, summoning up curses I had never even heard, slamming my palms against the wood which seemed to be warm and damp, feeling the saliva frothing in my mouth as I screamed. Above me I could hear footsteps and realized that I could be overheard throughout the entire block. Regulation 13b of the Ad Hoc Residents' Committee was being broken, lunacy was rampant on the lower floor. When I tasted tears trickling into my mouth I realized that I was crying. I knew that I had gone into a state of shock, knew that I couldn't prevent my legs from trembling, that I was probably unable to stand up. It was a joke among the lower library staff;

since I had started that job eleven librarians had been signed into John of Gods after nervous breakdowns. I knew that at a big table in headquarters there was a lottery going about which of us would crack up next, that some young library assistant had a ticket with my name on it. I felt so small, kneeling there naked on the carpet, so utterly insignificant. The eyes in the wood were watching me, the smile troubled and disappointed. With an absurd stab of fear I checked my palms for signs of stigmata. I wiped my mouth and leaned my head forward in despair until it was lightly touching the wood.

'Whoever the hell you are,' I whispered, 'please just go away from me. Can't you see that you're not wanted in this place? You're only causing trouble here. I'll smash this door down if you don't disappear from it. I have the right to be left in peace. Holy Mary, Mother of God, don't let me go insane like this.'

Next morning I left the apartment block early before the other residents were up. When I checked the locked door before leaving all I could make out was a dull and unfocused knot of varnished wood. I went over litanies of half-understood diseases in my mind as I drove to work, Parkinson's, Huntington's, Alzheimer's, Legionnaires'. I checked my face in the mirror at each red traffic light, searching for some hint of premature senility.

I spent the whole day in my office, sending one of the girls out to get me a sandwich at lunch. She brought it in with coffee, looking at me with genuine concern. I smiled to reassure her, flattered that she should have any interest in my welfare.

Part Three

All day I had been dreading having to return to the apartments and when I got there my worst fears were realized. Mrs Brennan and six other women were kneeling on the steps with a child in a wheelchair in their midst. They had vases of flowers on the top step and candles stuck in little glass bowls. The other residents awkwardly passed them on their way in from work as the women recited the rosary. I resisted the awful temptation to plough into them with my car. I parked the car a small way off and kept my head down as I approached the door. I could hear Mrs Brennan calling as I walked past them up the steps and already had my key in the lock before the woman tugged at the sleeve of my coat. I turned, ready to lash out, and found myself staring at the eyes of the young boy in the wheelchair. His limbs were twisted and wasted. Although his head was shaking from side to side his eyes seemed totally still as he looked at me with desperate hope.

'Please, Sir,' his mother said, 'can my son not see the face of the Blessed Virgin? I beg you, Sir, the child is dying, we've been all over the country with him. To every grotto where she's appeared. Let him in, Sir, it's his only hope.'

I turned to lean over the railings that looked down over the side passage to the car park and vomited up everything in my stomach. Then I turned the key in the lock, slammed the front door and ran the length of the corridor.

All that evening I lay on the bed like a haunted man, the repetitive hum of the rosary just reaching me from outside. I heard footsteps along the corridor that paused outside my door and could guess at the contents of the note from the

Residents' Committee. My coat was hung on the door handle to obscure most of the knot of wood which had been waiting like a conscience for me when I came in, although I had refused to look down at it. I covered my head with a pillow, feeling that same sense of shame and exposure in my mind that I associated with my dreams of being discovered wearing a pair of ladies' shoes. The murmuring stopped after a long time, the intercom stopped buzzing, but just when I'd begun to savour the silence, the phone rang. It startled me, jangling at my nerves. I walked out on to the balcony and saw Clare standing among the parked cars staring up at me. The amber security lights had come on and she looked like a prisoner standing near the barbed wire at the edge of a camp.

'It's okay,' she called up softly, 'the posse has been called off. Is the face still there, what can you see of her now?'

I lowered my head. The phone behind me stopped, then after a moment started ringing again.

'I don't know,' I said. 'Fuck it, I don't want to know.'

We were both still for a moment, each watching the other.

'Do you mind that I came?' she asked. 'I can go if you want.'

'No,' I said, 'don't go. Don't . . .'

The phone had stopped. I could suddenly hear that faint electronic buzz which came from the large bulbs overhead. She smiled at me and looked down. I knew that she was feeling foolish.

'Do you want to come up?' I asked.

'No. But I want you to come down.'

'Why?'

Part Three

'Bring your car keys. I want to show you something.'

I saw the curtains twitch in my neighbour's window as I got into my car with Clare. Firstly there's queues of people praying on the front step because of him, I could imagine the old woman thinking, and now he's sneaking off with some young girl. What did she make of it all? I wondered. I pointed out her window to Clare.

'Maybe she'll appear in the midst of it all tomorrow in her dressing-gown like the mother in *The Life of Brian*,' Clare said, 'and harangue them all for following her son home.'

It was the first time I had been able to laugh at the whole business.

'I don't think Bluebeard would approve of your choice of films.'

She said nothing and I noticed that without the priest she seemed less sure of herself and yet more natural.

'Twice a week the grocer brings over the messages that she has telephoned him for,' I said. 'The only sound I hear from her is the hiss of a tap through the wall when she fills her kettle. On Christmas morning she frets out in the lobby, waiting to be taken out by some relation. From half-nine till midday you can see her face peering out through the glass beside the door.'

'Why do you live here?' Clare asked.

'It fits me,' I said, realizing just how much it did. Clinical and impersonal like a cast-iron structure in an art exhibition. Clare had changed her shoes, now they were shapeless, bulky sneakers. She put her hand out for a moment to cover mine on the gear stick. I could only dimly see her features in the half-light of the car.

227

'It doesn't really,' she said, 'so why are you fooling yourself?'

How long was it since anybody had touched my hand, had stroked any part of my flesh, had shown me the least sign of affection? She took her hand away, suddenly embarrassed.

'I don't know why I did that. I'm sorry,' she said. 'I don't know why I came. You probably think I'm half crazy. It's just . . . I dreamt of you last night.'

'What sort of dream?'

'Nothing really. Nothing that makes much sense. It was some place that was overgrown, like a big garden or an allotment or something. And you were going around, almost out of your head, trying to find something that you'd buried, and I was trying to help you. But you wouldn't tell me what it was. You kept pushing me away and I knew you were scared too. What's wrong? Are you all right?'

It took me a long time to open my eyes and lift my head from the steering-wheel.

'Who are you?' I asked and she looked frightened.

'What do you mean? I'm nobody. Did I say something to upset you? I didn't mean to, it was just a dream.'

I started the car and put it into reverse. I opened the security gates and drove up past the side of the apartment block, slamming on the brake and jerking Clare in her seat. I got out to close the security gate and slammed the car door when I got back in.

'Where are you bringing me?' I asked.

'You don't have to go . . . it was just an idea . . . maybe it's better . . .'

'Where?'

228

I startled myself as much as her with the violence in my voice. I could see her trying to undo her seat belt.

'I'm sorry,' I said. 'I really am. I would like you to take me wherever you were going.'

She was silent for a moment, then said, 'It's a fair way. A small turn-off out in the fields between Ballyboughal and The Naul.'

She was sharing a house on the road parallel to Breffni Street with three other girls. The layout of the house inside was identical, the same air of gloom. Religious pictures like the ones Joe and I had taken down over a decade and a half before watched over the hallway, their cross-eyed Saviours following Clare as she climbed the stairs. I felt that if I followed her there would be an altar beyond the bend of the stairs, Lourdes bottles and religious ikons cobwebbed by decades of dust. The door from the kitchen opened and the small boy whom I had seen two days before running among the flower-beds came out. He had a Transformer truck in his hand. He came up the two steps into the hall and leaned against the banisters to eye me up.

'You came in with my mother.'

I nodded. He ran the wheels of the truck along the banister, then flicked a switch to show how it transformed into a rocket launcher. He held it out warily for me to hold. I knew that he was trying to decide if I was his friend or his rival.

'She's my mother,' he said.

'I know.'

'I don't have a father. We don't need one of those. Have you a mother?'

229

Clare called his name from the top of the stairs and we both looked up.

'Susan is going to put you to bed. Will you come up and find your pyjamas for her?'

The boy took the Transformer from my hands and went up to her. I walked out into the front garden. It was almost ten o'clock. Two girls in their late twenties came out behind me, dressed as though on their way to a night-club.

'Are you another one of those off-duty priests?' one of them asked as they eyed me coldly.

'Do I look like one?'

'You should see those bastards sniffing around her like she was a bitch in heat. Always the same Clare, never knowing what she wants. When we all came to Dublin together first we had to rescue her from the Hare Krishnas. Up eating with them in a tent she was, with all that chanting and some weird video playing. I mean a free meal is a free meal, and Jesus we were hungry often enough, but we had to reef her out. You know, one moment she's up here at a party in the house miming to *Patricia the Stripper* and the next she's out seeing visions of Our Lady.'

'She sees what she sees. You can't take it away from her,' her friend butted in.

The other girl took a small bottle of nail varnish from her shoulder-bag and brushed up one of her nails as she shrugged her shoulders.

'Listen, I see Our Lady smiling too and I sleep around. So what does that prove? That Our Lady is saying *Girls Just Want to Have Fun?*'

We heard the clatter of Clare's heels running down the stairs and the girls shut up. She had changed into black, flat-soled shoes. She came out and all three girls followed me to the car. Her friends seemed to presume that I knew where we were heading and so I just drove, following whispered instructions from Clare in the seat beside me. Along the desolate road which I turned down beyond Bal-lyboughal there were two mobile chippers with a fluorescent sign for *Larry's Chuck Wagon* on the roof of one of them. I could see tail-lights of cars beyond them and began to make out the arrows beside the hand-painted signs on the Tarmacadam which read *The Visions Field this way*.

I had to park the car at the end of a mile-long row of vehicles with their left wheels down in the shallow ditch. We got out. I saw the nail varnish still lying in the back seat as I locked the car and put it in my pocket to give back to her friend when I caught up with them. There were people coming on bicycle and foot beside us, families crossing the fields and helping each other over gates on to the narrow road. Two old men with strips from a torn red shirt tied around the sleeves of their overcoats were trying to steward the crowd into lines and to make room for the John of God ambulance men who were struggling to bring a stretcher down against the tide of people. Somebody whispered that the man they were carrying had fallen backwards after seeing Padre Pio in the sky. In the distance I could hear an amplified intonation of the rosary. Clare's two friends had wandered on ahead. I stopped, causing confusion among the crowd behind who had to fan out on both sides of us. I felt flushed and sick in the midst of the throng.

'Listen, Clare,' I said. 'I don't know why you thought I should come here, but I can't take this place. I don't believe people see things up there, and even if they do see things I don't want to know about it. Now I'll wait in the car and I'll drive you back when you're ready.'

'Please, Michael,' she urged. 'Don't chicken out on me now.'

She took my hand and I snatched it back. The decade of the rosary had stopped and a male voice could be heard over the loudspeakers.

'*Our Lady, Queen of the Heavens and Star of the Sea,*
I beg you on my knees to appear before me.'

The crowd in the distance took up the chant and I could hear it spreading among the people walking past me. Many were looking up towards the dark night clouds as though expecting a revelation to appear above their heads. One of the elderly stewards tried to nudge me into moving on and I shoved him away from me with what was either fury or terror. I turned back into the surge of expectant faces and tried to fight my way out. Clare had wrapped both hands around my elbow and I could see how near she was to tears as I struggled to shake her off.

'For the love of Christ, Michael, will you just stop,' she said. 'Can you not see that I'm not some stupid little girl trying to convert you? I'm more terrified of this place than you are. I brought you here for my sake, not for yours, for my own. Now don't just fuck off and abandon me.'

I stopped and she relaxed the pressure on my arm. An old woman in front of me smiled as she pushed her way past. I turned back reluctantly.

'Listen, your friends will find their own way home,' I said. 'Just turn your back if you're scared. Walk away with me from here.'

'No,' she said. 'I've got to make some sense of this. Come with me. Please, please.'

'What do you want me to do?' I asked.

'Stay beside me. See if you see what I see.'

I found that I could not refuse. She let go my hand as I began to walk beside her. Some of the crowd were singing hymns now, others staring around them in curiosity. Two farmers behind me were arguing about the merits of the fields which we were passing through, a woman nearby describing the sheer bliss of black tea against her throat after ending the fast on Lough Derg. Memories were coming back to me, unwelcomed and unannounced. Lying in bed in the boxroom waiting for my mother to come home from the women's mission in the church. The joy on her face as she described the visiting priest's sermon, the catch-phrase he had made them repeat over and over with their hands raised, *The family that prays together stays together.* The feel of lino burning into my knees every evening after the Angelus as she listed her special intentions, my father lost at sea, her sister in the soil of Glasnevin, her parents, and then the prayers for the souls in purgatory with nobody left to pray for them. And from nowhere another memory came back, suddenly important. The wet November morning when she had told me how she had dreamt that the world was about to end and the local priest was going around to break the news at each house.

It was less than two months after the dream that her world really did end. My boasts came back to me about all the prayers I had told her I would say if she ever came to harm. The last time I had bothered visiting her grave had been at old Nick's funeral and I remembered the strange chill I had felt reading the inscription on the single plastic wreath that was left: *From all of Michael's fellow pupils in fifth class.* It was so long since I had even thought of her and now she could have been any of these women striding through the dark, their clothes and views transformed by three decades of Gay Byrne and piped television but still walking with that same secure belief. Some people had young children trotting beside them, excited by the crowds and the darkness and by the freedom of that late hour. I took Clare's hand and squeezed it for a moment, not certain if I was trying to reassure her or myself.

The crowd fanned out as we came through a gap in the bushes into the main field. There was an overgrown mound in the centre of the large field, a pagan tomb made by men before the time of Christ. On the crest of it two thorn bushes swayed in the light breeze with branches that were sparkling in the spotlight shone from the roof of the parked car on which the loudspeakers were mounted. It took me a moment to realize that the shimmering was caused by hundreds of religious medals which had been tied on to the bushes. A young girl and boy knelt between the two bushes with their hands raised and joined in prayer. They were so still that I thought they were statues until I saw the wind flicking away at the girl's hair. Their faces were transfixed as they gazed upwards towards the sky.

The huge crowd was being arranged into rows of eight who were allowed to come forward and kneel for ten seconds at the foot of the mound like a queue going forward for communion. Some people just blessed themselves as they stood up, others cried out or had to be helped to their feet. Often they were led away, oblivious to the crowd around them as they stared towards the heavens. A woman screamed that she had seen Saint Bernadette. The man beside her held her hand as the next row of people moved eagerly forward.

I thought of Jim Jones and his cult of followers out in the jungle, how they had come forward eagerly to receive the poison from his hand. It is said that they were smiling as they shot their children and calmly waited arm-in-arm for their turn. And yet there was nothing sinister or deranged about the crowd around me. They waited patiently for their turn, making room for elderly people to get in front of them, kneeling when their turn came, rising again at the signal from the stewards and vanishing into the dark mass on the far side of the hill. Although the prayers never stopped there was little sign of hysteria. They clustered around in the dark corners of the field, discussing what they had or had not seen.

As the row we had been shepherded into got closer I could see a small chipped statue of the Madonna and Child standing between the thorn bushes, like dozens that I had seen as a child in bedroom windows. There was an antiquated bath-tub behind the mound which had served as a drinking-trough for cattle. I couldn't help staring at the kneeling boy and the girl in her communion dress whose white skin glistened in the strong spotlight. I have always found something vaguely obscene about first communion dresses, the girls like miniature brides or children in the windows of a Bangkok bordello. I remembered suddenly Graham Greene's review of Shirley Temple's sexual innuendoes in *Wee Willie Winkie* and the venom with which Twentieth Century-Fox had sued him. I tried to read what was written on the label of the boy's jacket. It was only when the wind died slightly that I made out the words *New York Mets – Baseball.*

We were being ushered forward now. I caught sight of Clare's face. There seemed to be both anticipation there and sheer terror. I wasn't sure what I was supposed to look towards. Some people had gazed at the sky, others at the kneeling children, more at the chipped statue or the shimmering branches. I felt the damp of the trampled grass seeping through the knees of my trousers and kept my hands in my pockets, refusing to join them in any pretence of prayer. A woman beside me let out a long slow gasp. Her face had gone into genuine rapture. I followed her eyes to beyond the tinkling thorn bushes. There were only the distant lights of an isolated bungalow glowing through the hedgerow.

Our time was up. I could hear the next row approaching, the stewards gently urging us to make room for them. The woman whose face was still in rapture had risen. She genuflected and then looked towards me, searching for reassurance. I found myself nodding as though I had witnessed something too and she smiled and touched my arm before walking off. When I looked back Clare was still kneeling, her eyes fixed on the boy and girl, her face showing only terror now. A small knot of people was forming as the queue began to clog up behind us.

I touched her shoulder and she rose. She pressed against me and I put my arm around her. She was crying as we made our way out in the darkness behind the mound. Many of those who had knelt were standing there, saying another rosary together. She lifted her head slightly and I could feel her tears on my chin.

236

'What did you see, Clare? Was it something that frightened you?'

Her head was lowered again and I could barely distinguish her whisper.

'Nothing. I saw nothing. I never see anything. I'm not worth shit. I wasn't worth her appearing to.'

'Don't be silly, Clare, don't . . .'

'Those two children, they see her all the time. She speaks to them and gives them messages. Why are they singled out and I'm left in the cold? Why?'

I found myself comforting her, unnoticed among that vast crowd. Stroking her hair, running my fingers down her cheeks, cupping her chin to try and make her smile and then kissing the dampness away from her eyes. A woman screamed something in the distance. The voices nearby at their rosary did not even turn. The crowd felt like a cloak covering us, made me feel that there was nothing I couldn't do among them, no depth of pain which I couldn't express. The field had taken on the unreality and freedom of a dream.

'Good God Almighty,' an old man nearby, who had been staring intensely at the sky, said. 'The moon is dancing. Dancing up there in the clouds.'

Clare twisted her head, either to lift her face away from my hands or to follow his gaze.

'Nothing there,' she said after a moment. 'Nothing.'

'He's been gaping up at the moon since we've arrived. Sure the man is half blinded. The eye can't cope with light like that.'

'Nothing,' she repeated bitterly. 'Nothing now, nothing on any of the nights that I've knelt in fields like this. Do you know how many grottoes I've travelled to, how many people I've seen fall backwards, paralysed with joy? What's wrong with me? I keep asking. What have I done to make me different from everyone else who can see her face?'

'But you said you saw her image on the bedroom door in my apartment?'

'Nothing,' she said again. 'Nothing but the grains in the wood. Oh, I wanted to see so badly that I half fooled myself into thinking I did. I had begged Father O'Rourke to take me along. You were all watching me so I lied to him, I was ashamed of letting him down. He'll think there's something wrong with me if I can't see it too, I thought, but I knew it was just the shape that the wood had been wrapped into.'

I thought of myself kneeling in the hallway that night after Clare had gone. Even when cursing at the wood I, too, had been trying to fool myself into believing.

'I'm frightened,' Clare said suddenly. 'Frightened of growing old. Maybe it's different for a man. A girl comes to a time in life when . . .'

She laughed suddenly, that same self-deprecating laugh which I had loved in my apartment the previous night. I knew that she was thinking of her son being minded by the fourth girl sharing the house. And I remembered from nowhere that conversation on the stairs a quarter of a century before with Emily on the night of her birthday.

'I know. I already have a family in my child and I don't want any other. It's not that I'm looking for a man either, though not that I'm not, it's just . . . and it probably makes no sense to you . . . but you could feel your life going stale. You get too old to still be open to things. You see your future, that house or some other, the other girls getting married, starting homes of their own, and watching your son grow until one day you find you are just his mother. And the frightening thing is that you don't mind, the frightening thing is that you'll settle for it.'

'Clare, why are you out here in this God-forsaken place?'

'I don't know. Because I want more than that. Maybe it's to ask her what to do with my life. Maybe . . .'

The noise of music started suddenly from across the fields, a Country and Western band in some back lounge, even though it was past closing time. I caught sight of Clare's flatmates among the crowd chatting to two young men who were pointing towards the music and playfully trying to put their arms around them.

'Every morning I promise myself that I'm going to sort out where my life is going. But it doesn't matter what I resolve to do, by nightfall I'm back to square one again. Maybe that's why I need a sign from somewhere, Michael, because basically I don't know my arse from my elbow.'

'I know,' I said suddenly, 'Good Christ, you don't know how I know. It's not enough just to rise up every day and pass through the motions of living. There has to be more, or else we would all just lie down in that ditch there and never bother getting up.'

She turned her head back to look up at me. A girl had come over to lead the old man away. He held one hand over his eyes as she helped him through the crowd. Clare's voice was startled.

'But you have everything. That lovely apartment, whatever job you're in, it must be good. I heard you stand up to O'Rourke. You seem so strong, like you've no room for doubt or faith inside you, no need for anybody or

239

anything. And yet you're not happy, are you? There's something wrong . . .'

'God, you're Emily, do you know that? You really are Emily.'

It was more a sigh than a sentence. I hadn't meant to speak out loud. Clare was looking at me, confused.

'Emily?' she repeated.

'Who christened you Clare?' I asked her.

'My mother.' She was perturbed by the question.

'You're an Emily like myself,' I said. 'Stomping around in this mucky field in Emily's shoes.'

We both turned as the heavy voice called her, stepping apart as if caught doing something wrong. O'Rourke strode towards us, his smile souring as he recognized me before it turned into a leer.

'"*And those who came to mock remained to pray,*"' he quoted.

'I suppose you're going to offer me your blessing?'

'Not until you modify your tone of voice. You remember where you are.'

'I'm in a field in the arse of the bog, so stuff your blessing.'

He grabbed Clare's arm, pushing her away from me and turning her face around until she was staring at him.

'Did you see her?'

His voice was accusing. Clare glanced back with what I thought was fear. His eyes were pressed close to her. She swallowed and then nodded. He glared at me in triumph and began to stride away, gripping her arm so tight that she almost had to run behind him to keep up. Yet he gave no sign of even being aware that she was there. She had gone a few steps before she halted, causing him to stop. One of her shoes came off in the muck. She was looking back at me. I couldn't be sure if she was trying to say something. He tugged at her arm impatiently.

'Come on out of that,' he muttered. 'Do you want us to be late, girl?'

She staggered as he pulled her arm again and she only just managed to snatch up her shoe. He never looked around as he strode through the crowd. When she was almost out of sight she glanced back towards me and opened her mouth. I could not be sure if what she said was 'Emily?' or 'Help me'.

I can't explain what I mean, but I didn't leave that field alone. I'm not sure when I first noticed it, maybe after a mile of lonely country roads, but at some stage I knew that there was a presence in the car. The convoy of tail-lights began to break up, turning right off side-roads leading away to Drogheda and Balbriggan or left towards Ashbourne and out into the fields of Meath. I drove on in what I hoped was the direction of the city, dogs coming out from farmyards to bark when I passed. And all the time the feeling persisted that if I turned my head I would see someone in the back seat, somebody who had always been there watching over me, somebody whose presence I had never noticed before. From decades back I remembered the nights alone in Emily's house when I had lain with my face to the wall, convinced that the shirts in the open wardrobe were swaying souls.

And yet now I didn't feel scared. There was an atmosphere in the car as I drove which gradually overwhelmed me, a glowing sense of compassion and concern. I no longer felt that I was just myself, but in some way I was also outside myself, as though part of me was hovering overhead watching as I drove. And it felt that I wasn't just driving back to the city, but right back through my life. Things which I had forgotten were suddenly startlingly vivid. Three faces, feminine, familiar, leaning over a cot; the feel of clothes-pegs being pushed along the concrete as wet sheets dripped overhead. There appeared to be almost nothing that I could not remember, though even as I went back my mind always halted at the same hospital corridor, the sight of my uncle's face, the neighbours hurrying me along. And it is hard to say if I was even driving the car as my arms seemed to move automatically.

It was like those evenings when I kept telling myself that I was going home even as my arms were steering the car to a parking space near the shoe shop. This time I watched with the same bemused fascination as I drove down all the old streets where I had lived. My mother's house first, that once perched on the edge of the city and was now encircled by new estates. There were ugly aluminium frames on the windows, the front garden concreted over to accommodate a motor car. I sat outside with the lights off in the car and gazed up at the window of the box-bedroom where I had lain awake, frightened that ghosts would fly through the hole above the door. Maggie's house next door had a name-plate now and a new porch. The garden path had a mock cobble finish. I remembered a little girl, her legs balanced on a mound of bricks and the feel of a limp penis spurting in my hand. Where was she now, Maggie of the red hair? A hundred nursing jobs in Canada, a hundred flats where tenants passed on the stairs, a hundred returns to her mother? All the nights that I had decided to fly there on a holiday and try to find her, all the mornings that I had woken up scared of the responsibility it might bring. Ever decreasing circles, the doctor had said. The words were like a warrant, *ever decreasing circles*.

Aunt Maire's bungalow was knocked down, a small road driven through it to provide access to the tiny estate of twelve town houses in the small space behind where the glasshouses used to be. I stared at the unbroken white line running down the blue Tarmacadam. I had never even bothered to come back and check what had happened after the bungalow was sold. It felt like reality was playing a trick on me.

I drove on in circles until I reached Breffni Street. I stopped on the corner, then drove up slowly past old Nick's house. I half expected his ghost to be standing on the doorstep, a hand raised in greeting, cupping an untipped cigarette. There was a row of teddy bears in the window of the front room where he had slept. The engine hummed in neutral as I tried to decide what to do next. I wanted to turn my head but I couldn't. Would there be just an empty space behind me or would there be a shape whose eyes I might recognize, and could I be sure if I wanted to see something there or not?

I couldn't think of anywhere else to go, so I drove back to the apartment block. Only when I reached there did the atmosphere inside the car change, as though the air had turned cold. I stopped beside the metal barrier to the car park and undid my seat belt. I tried to pull myself together and longed for a cigarette. *Look behind you*, I told myself, *look behind*. I turned my head quickly. All I could see was the few scattered flowers left on the steps of the apartment through the back window.

The apartment block was as quiet as death. Inside my own hallway I examined the kink in the knot of wood on the door. Looked at from certain angles it did almost look like the shape of a woman, except that the rings tapered out before they could form her feet. Inside my pocket I felt the small bottle of nail varnish. I carefully drew in two red high heel shoes underneath and then like a halo over her head I scrawled the letters EMILY. It was the first time that I had changed or defaced anything in the apartment. I held the brush against the white wall so that it left a long red stain all the way from the hall into the bedroom. It was a good feeling.

I'm sure that I must have woken up from my sleep – surely no dream could be as vivid or last as long. I stirred in the bed, aware of the yearning emptiness of the apartment block, the muffled security light edging through the gap in the curtain. I was leaving the bed then and yet my feet didn't feel the carpet. I knew instinctively that the other bedroom door was unlocked, I was walking towards it, both frightened and prepared. The windowless bathroom looked like a torture chamber which had been washed down, the front door was locked with its mock brass chain. Slowly I turned around to face the small unlovely hallway leading down to the plywood door.

The figure had retreated back into the knot of wood, so that only the red streaks of nail varnish stood out on the door. I knew that if I pushed my hand forward the door would open. Before I could touch it, it began to swing inwards. I could see a strip of carpet widening as it opened, then boxes and plastic bags filled with the landlady's clothes. But then the carpet wasn't there anymore, there were rafters instead, an attic-scape of copper piping and wooden beams. Dust lay everywhere, mixed with tiny shreds of fluff from the worn insulation. A pram with three wheels lay upside-down where the roof slanted down in one corner. There were toys scattered beside it that I should have recognized – toys that I don't want to remember – Christmas annuals and smudged copybooks where my hand had struggled with the awkward nib in primary school. When I looked behind me the white hallway of the apartment had vanished and there seemed just a solid wall of emptiness. Only the bedroom door remained, with its knots of varnished wood.

Then I stepped forward and found that I was falling back, down a blurred succession of days traversed in reverse. I felt weightless as the first cosmonaut, I was pitched about like a plane in turbulence. *Oh Jesus, help me*, I cried, *Jesus if you exist, Jesus of all the nights that I have avoided trying to solve the puzzle of you. Jesus of every pair of women's shoes.* Yet I wasn't alone; something which I could not fathom or comprehend was consuming me, like the presence in the car only magnified a hundred times. The warmest love, as though it were a physical force field. And I was radiating it, it was glowing inside so warm that I was no longer afraid. There was a name I was calling, a name which I know, which I hadn't pronounced for decades, a name which I was still calling when I hit the wooden floor.

I knew where I was. That attic in my mother's house which I had always been too scared to enter. My mother had to bring a table out from the bedroom and balance a chair up on top of it. Once or twice I had stood on the chair, terrified to look down at the huge fall beyond the banisters, frightened to lift myself forward to where her arms were reaching down to help me up when she was storing away old bags of clothes. Now, without ever having been inside it, I recognized everything. An electric cable ran along the raised board close to my nostril. When I put my hand out I could feel the cold brass of a water pipe.

I knew that I was looking for somebody whom I had abandoned. I turned my head to where the coffin rested above the ballcock, balanced on the edge of the water tank. How long did I lie there frightened to get up? I know that the lid was off, the body inside staring up, incorrupt. And I remembered that on both occasions when I was brought to see that body, how I leaned forward but at the last moment was afraid to kiss those unfamiliar painted lips. How I had sat at home on the crook of the stairs after the first occasion in the hospital and promised myself that I would find the courage to kiss goodbye the next day. And yet among the crowd jostling in the funeral parlour at the final minute I had once again been too scared. I had carried away only the icy parchment of her forehead on my lips and the feeling that I had failed her even in that last act.

This is just a dream, I told myself, *I am lying in bed, I will rise with the alarm clock and remember nothing of this.* Yet how distant everything in my life seemed. I rose up from the boards. The dead did not frighten me any longer. All my life running from them but now I was ready for anything that I might see in that coffin. I crossed the beams carefully. All the knick-knacks of a life were scattered about, the Cub Scout cap which I could never find, the first pair of long black trousers purchased in Clery's. My mother had cried suddenly that day, telling me about how her own mother had cried the time that workmen came to the parish to lay a new road and the baby of the family had to be fitted out in long trousers so he could be taken away from school to earn his first week's wages working with them. *The first long trousers are the end of childhood.* I could hear the very tone of her voice which I had blotted out.

I reached the coffin and as I bent to look down into it I could sense the eyes watching me from the corner of the attic. Now I knew the meaning of true terror. My hands were sweating, my teeth grated with a chattering sound. I knew he had been waiting here for me to find him through all the years since he had been abandoned. If he spoke I knew that I would know his voice and every word of the childish prayers which he would lisp. I looked down. The coffin was empty, what had been there had long passed on. It was the boy in the rain who was trapped here as my prisoner, the brave little soldier whom everyone had praised. I raised my head and returned his gaze. His eyes were glazed, both vulnerable and guilty, like in a photograph I had seen of a concentration camp guard kneeling in a concrete chamber, gazing into the camera before being casually shot.

He stood to attention like a sentry in his Cub Scout uniform, bareheaded with the blue neckscarf, the navy jumper and corduroy shorts, the long grey socks and Emily's red shoes. He stared ahead, convinced that soon she would return to him. All the years that I had left him there, walking away from his pain, refusing to let him mourn, freezing him in time. And all the longings which I had invented to fill the ache left by that pain: the shoes of a thousand strangers; the coldness of hard leather which was impervious to grief. He was staring at me now as though beseeching me to speak. I could not bear his gaze. I closed my eyes but now I could feel him inside myself, like something that had been frozen there, an embryo that another skin had slowly formed over. I knew suddenly that all the time he had been there like a hole inside me, like an ache without a name. His was the body that I had always dreamt about, buried beneath the long grass in fertilizer sacks, the child I had spent a lifetime fleeing from. I opened my eyes and knew by his eyes that I was crying, wordlessly and hopelessly, as if the tears could wash away my skin. And as I cried I watched him cry with me.

It's okay kid, I wanted to tell him, *we're going to make it through okay. Just you and me together now that mammy is gone. We'll grow up now and we'll be able to remember her and then to pass on. We'll become a father and we'll watch over our children at evening-time. I'll let myself be you until you become me and then we'll be one together. No more nights for you in this attic in your uniform, no more walking from shop to shop for me with shoes under my coat.*

He opened his mouth to speak. I leaned forward, straining to hear. That single word spoken across the rafters, her name which sounded golden and warm as it echoed through my brain.

Sometimes, when the loneliness seemed too much to bear, I had thought of going down there at night but I had never gone. Something always held me back. I would like to think

248

it was self-respect, but I suspect it was simple fear. I had dreamt about it at those times, the girl paid to wear the shoes in the back of the car, my hands running over them, touching her ankles as she looked out through the window, bored.

I had sat in the car park for a quarter of an hour after I woke, my palms thumping against the steering-wheel until they were bruised. Before leaving I had checked that the bedroom door was still locked, the plastic bags and boxes in their rightful place. The painted name and red shoes were all that remained of the figure in the wood. I knew why her features had disturbed me, I had carried them inside me all these years. The first memory, the first face, feminine, familiar, bending forward into my line of vision. The same features as the woman whose shoes I had just taken out from that old wooden box.

When I had started the engine I picked them up in the headlights, lying there on the concrete after I had thrown them from the balcony. How scratched and battered they looked, lugged around with me for quarter of a century. Would the residents comment on them as they got into their cars in a few hours' time, or would they just drive past, preoccupied in their own worlds? I put the car into gear and drove away from eight years in that apartment block.

The office buildings along the canal were empty, pyramids of glass and electric light. The night-clubs in the basements beneath the insurance brokers and shipping agents were still finishing up, a bouncer on the corner of the street speaking into a walkie-talkie with a torch like a baton in his hand.

I saw the first three girls in the shadows under the bridge

at Baggot Street. They were small and plumpish, trying to hold back forty. They looked frozen and bored in their short skirts. They came out into the lights of the tow-path as I slowed down. I looked around nervously, there was nobody else about. One was tapping on the passenger window as she walked along beside the car. There was no longer any sense of a presence in the car, I just felt alone and foolish and scared. The women shouted mockingly as I drove off. I circled the area, not certain what I was looking for. There was a shadow in the car park under an office block. I slowed and wound the window down. It was a girl in a leather jacket who moved her head into the half-light to glance around at me. I could see the bottom half of the man whom she was giving the hand job to. Her other hand held a cigarette which she took a pull from and then blew the smoke towards me with a defiant smile as she worked away leisurely.

A police car cruised past and I ducked down in the driver's seat, acting more guilty than any of the girls who lounged against the park railings further down the street. The car stopped a few yards behind mine and I watched in the rear-view mirror, convinced that they were taking my registration number. When they moved off I began to drive out of the area. I felt sick now and dirty. I had reached the corner and was turning down Lad Lane when I stopped. There was an argument taking place across the street. I recognized the figure of O'Rourke keeping well back in the shadows as three prostitutes cursed the group of girls who were watching the car with the prospective punter drive off.

Before I had time to lose courage I did a U-turn in the

middle of the road and drove towards them. The prostitutes broke free and crowded around my window.

'Come on love, any of us here will give you a good time. Just pick one of us quick before these gobshites close in.'

I heard the passenger door open and turned to see Clare leaning in. There was a miraculous medal in her hand which she closed her fingers over in surprise. Her mouth was open.

'Fifty,' I said to her.

'What?'

'You said the man offered you fifty pounds if you'd get into the car as well.'

She looked at me and then laughed.

'What are you doing here, Michael?'

The prostitutes were beating their hands against the glass.

'Jaysus, it's bad enough driving our punters away without the feckers stealing them from us as well.'

'What the hell are *you* doing here, Clare? Just get into the car and let the pair of us get away.'

Clare had climbed into the passenger seat and closed the door when the prostitutes were pushed back from the window. O'Rourke stared in at us, his eyes wild with rage.

'Clare, get the hell away from that car! What the hell are you playing at, man? Step out here now and I'll take off this collar and floor you with one hand.'

'This is not happening,' I heard Clare say as she gazed out at the other girls and tried to stop laughing. I grabbed the medal from her hand and wound my window down. I pressed it into O'Rourke's fist as I hit the accelerator. He

ran alongside us for a few moments, trying to pull at my
face through the window, then, as the car picked up speed,
he stumbled and drew his hand back, staring down at the
silver medal.

'Keep the change,' I said and rolled the window shut.

We drove in silence through the night-time streets. Forty-
eight hours before I had lain awake, hating myself, with
two high heel shoes in a plastic bag beside the bed. More
seemed to have happened since then than in the previous
five years.

'Do you always kidnap women like this or am I special?'

I looked at her. Her face was serious but her eyes were
amused.

'Jesus, Clare, you didn't need too much persuading.'

'Fifty quid could be useful. Shoes for the child, a whole
new outfit. Are you going to give it to me for just getting in
or do I have to do anything more to earn it?'

I turned on the radio. There was classical music on one
of the stations.

'I haven't thought that far ahead,' I said. 'I've never done
this type of thing before.'

'You don't look the type.'

'Neither do you. I'd be too scared.'

'No, it's more than that.'

We stopped at the traffic-lights at the end of Tara Street.
I didn't know where to go. Even when the lights went green
the car remained there motionless.

'You're not exactly the masterful type, are you?'

'Stop making fun of me, Clare, please. I'm a middle-aged
man stuck here without a shred of dignity left. I have to

know. When that O'Rourke fellow pulled you away in the field what did you call out after me?'

Her smile was gone. She looked uncertain and almost scared for the first time since getting into the car. The lights had gone red again. A taxi pulled up behind me.

'If it was *help me*,' I continued, 'then it was what I was calling out in my mind to you. Now these lights are going to go green any minute now and I've never been more lost. So get out if you want to, but don't mock me.'

The lights turned green. Clare ran her teeth over her lower lip.

'Have you a cigarette?' she said and I gave her one. The taxi beeped twice, then swerved past before the lights changed. Clare inhaled and let the smoke out with a slow sigh.

'Do you know the way to Howth?' she said.

I nodded.

'Deirdre's on a late tomorrow, she'll get the child up. I'm not due home for a few hours yet. Take us out there. Somewhere near the Bailey lighthouse.'

We crossed the North Strand, Fairview, Clontarf. The tide had gone out and an expanse of dark muck lay between us and Bull Island. Her face was pensive, alternating between shadow and light as we passed under the neon lamps. The classical symphony on the radio seemed as if it would never stop and I wanted that journey to Howth to last for eternity. Just the pair of us trapped in that bubble of chrome, the world outside the car suspended as we journeyed through the dark with no decision ever to make at the end of it.

'How old?' I asked.

'Thirty-two.'

She didn't ask the question in return and I had to ask her to guess.

'I don't know,' she said. 'Forty-three, forty-four I would have said in that apartment, but I can't tell anymore.'

'I can't even tell myself anymore,' I said. 'I mean, I know the year I was born, but ... you have to live your life to grow old, don't you? Long ago I stopped living, I woke up one day and I was just existing. Now I'm two people and I'm not sure which I am. One of them is a hundred years old and the other hasn't even begun to grow. A kink in the wood, eh, a kink in the shagging wood.'

We had reached Sutton Cross and I swung right, taking the road up through the start of light fog towards the summit. My hands had started to shake so much I found it difficult to steer the car.

'Thirty-eight,' I said with difficulty. 'I'm only six years older than you.'

She was silent as we passed the graveyard beside the school on our right and the entrance to an estate of houses. And then the engine revved, facing up to the steep climb through the dark.

'You're like a coiled spring,' she said. 'You're going to burst apart on me at any moment. Who was Emily? You said I was walking around in Emily's shoes.'

'She was the aunt I went to live with when I was a boy. She didn't know her arse from her elbow either and I loved her for it. I used to go through her things and wear her shoes. I never felt scared in them, never felt alone.'

We had turned right and then right again when I made out the red sign in the stone wall for a private road. *Visitors*

254

are not admitted to the lighthouse premises without a permit from the Commissioners of Irish Lights. I struggled to read the lettering in the wisps of light fog.

'Go down it,' Clare said.

'But the notice . . .'

'Jesus, Michael, we've gone this far. Just drive down the road.'

The road plummeted down in a long curve with much of the surface of the Tarmac gone. There was a small valley where the sea could be guessed at along either side of the cliffs. The music station had gone off the air and the car was filled with the hiss of static. Neither of us reached out to turn it off.

'I'm the one who's lost,' she said after a moment. 'Not you. Bluebeard, you call him. Jesus, how low can I fall when I'm reduced to tagging along behind Bluebeard. It's just power to him, everything is power. Phoning me if I haven't showed up for a day or two, turning up at the house, saying that he needs me, me telling myself that he does when nobody else could give a curse if I vanished from the face of the earth. But I know anyone else will do as well as me for him. We're all just pawns in his private war. The scrap-book he keeps of his own photographs. Only reason we're on that stupid canal is so he can get his mug in the press and embarrass the bishop in whatever stupid bloody quarrel they're playing at. I hate him and he frightens the wits out of me and I don't know how to get away from him.'

'Iceland's off?' I asked, and for a moment her face lost that anxiety and she smiled.

'Iceland. Maybe he really means to go. He'll find people

255

if he does. He can smell us out. Any fear, weakness, vulner-ability. The rat-catcher, Bluebeard. Never saw anyone stand up to him like you did in your apartment. You made me laugh and it seemed like nothing could bother you. I don't know what I thought you could do for me.'

'Sometimes when I'm on my way to work,' I said, 'when I get out into the fast lane and there's nobody looking, I turn up the radio full blast and I scream. I'm not even sure why. I just scream with all the windows closed and the car speeding away.'

'I'm so tired,' she said. 'If you had told me that six hours ago I wouldn't have believed you.'

Looking back I could barely believe myself. Those mo-ments screaming in the car or rocking myself to sleep at night curled up in a ball around the pillow, they were times when I had ceased to be myself. I had never spoken of them to anyone, they sounded unreal as we sat gazing at the city lights beyond the cliff.

'I'm carrying around this pain,' I said, 'that I just can't shake off. A hole in my heart that I don't know how to fill. You think there would be something, some drug, some sensation . . .'

'Michael,' she said, 'it frightens me, how I came to be here with you.'

I leaned my head back against the seat. I closed my eyes and put my hand out on to the dashboard and when she touched it I screamed so loud and for so long that the voice seemed to be coming not from my throat but from somewhere deep within my skull, from some memory, some person imprisoned there. The boy in the dream came back to me, I could see his mouth opening. The scream I heard didn't seem human. I wanted it to stop and yet was terrified because I didn't know what I would do when it ended.

The scream died away with a choking noise. I opened my eyes. I was afraid to look towards her but I could glimpse the side of her face, the frightened eyes, the open mouth. She was going to get out of the car and run, I thought, but her hand squeezed mine tighter.

'Don't feel sorry for me,' I whispered. 'Good Jesus, I could stand anything but that.'

'I'm not frightened of you,' she said, 'I'm frightened for you. What do you want me to do, how can I help?'

I leaned my forehead against the steering-wheel until it hurt. I felt so foolish and yet I felt good.

'I don't know,' I said. 'I don't know anything about ordinary life. All my life I've lived just for images, for illusions, moments when time stood still. I could never trust what was real, what was flesh. People always went away on me, died or went insane. Images don't do that, neither do shoes.'

I found I still couldn't look at her. Clare drew my hand up until I could feel the warm outline of her breast.

'That's real,' she said. 'Feel it. It's alive. It has known pain and suffering and joy and hurt.'

'I'm frightened. Frightened that it'll be snatched away from me again.'

'I'm not talking about again, I'm talking about now. I'm a mother staring at middle-age. I don't know if I'll ever see you again or want to, I just know that nobody can bear that much pain alone. I want you to touch me now, Michael, I just want to be needed for now. Come on, Michael, only children think that things must be forever.'

I could feel the outline of her nipple through the cloth, its warmth pressing against my palm.

'I want . . .' I said, but I could get no further, just kept repeating the words like a prayer. 'I want, I want.'

I opened the car door suddenly and ran out into the darkness, up through the gorse and the rocks, almost stumbling on the edge of the cliff and falling down into the white foam below. As I crested the hill I was caught suddenly in the sweep of the Bailey light as it swung its way round the tower. The beam swept out to sea and a moment later was answered by the winking of the Kisk light out on a sandbank in the depths of the bay. I heard her behind calling. How long was it since I had last touched a woman? I wasn't afraid of her but of the hurt that would follow, the brief joy that would fade into the greyness of those mornings when I would wake alone and remember her. And yet I desperately wanted her, I longed to feel alive again, even if it were just for that moment. I stumbled down the slope towards the sea. There was a small outcrop of rock jutting out into the waves, just about still bridged by a ribbon of grass to the cliffs. I ran down towards it, then stopped, scared by the steepness of the bank. The light came round again and caught me. I shivered suddenly. Clare had stopped running. She approached now, awkward over the rough ground in her shoes. She stopped a few feet above me.

'You bastard,' she hissed. 'Don't just run away on me, you bastard. I'm not one of your pairs of shoes or whatever it is that you just throw away. You came for me down the canal like some God-forsaken knight in your car. maybe I don't want a knight, but I don't want a coward either. If you want to mess around like this there are enough girls down there who will let you babble away all night if you put the money up front. Fifty pounds, you said. That's above the going rate, but if you're going to just ditch me here then I'll take it. Now I'm not your judge and jury, Mister, so you do whatever it is you do, but just do something.'

She shivered; I wasn't sure if she was going to strike me or break into tears. I reached into my pocket and took my wallet out. I laid fifty pounds down on the grass between us. She never moved to pick it up. After a few moments the wind swept it away out over the cliffs.

'At least Bluebeard never made me feel dirty. Now you've paid your money, Mister, what is it you're going to do?'

She looked eerie and silver in that light. She could have been any age and from any age. The beam of the lighthouse caught her and she seemed like a grey statue come suddenly to life.

'Unbutton your blouse,' I said, 'and your bra. Some way that I can see your breasts.'

Her breasts were smaller than I thought they would be, more pointed. One had a few specks of hair growing near the nipple. Her anger was gone. She looked more vulnerable again now and uncertain. I opened my shirt and ripped the vest underneath. Then I knelt forward, reaching out to touch her foot. I drew it towards me until the hard sole of her shoe was resting on my naked chest. I closed my eyes, feeling the weight pressing against my heart, the heel cutting into the flesh. I opened them again and looked up. She was watching me, expressionless.

'All my life this is what I've yearned for,' I said. 'I can't explain that to you, can't explain it to myself. The smell of

259

shoe leather and foot sweat. The feel of it, hard and secure. All my life dreaming of a moment like this, carrying this fantasy around inside me.'

'What happens next?' she whispered.

I closed my eyes and tried to remember. A hundred different rooms came back, a thousand pairs of shoes, a thousand sobering mornings when I woke up with a stale taste in my mouth.

'That's the joke,' I said. 'I've never been able to figure that out.'

I knelt back and as I did I felt something being squashed beneath my sole. My whole body shuddered. I knew it was a slug or a worm, something slithering and wet which I had made contact with. The dreams of worms which I had known as a child came back, the terror which still turned my stomach. Clare's hand reached out to touch my forehead. She was trying to soothe me, not even sure what was wrong. *The worms crawl in, the worms crawl out.* Oh Sweet Christ, death inside a coffin, dissolving from within. The feel of wriggling flesh and all which it had reminded me of.

Clare's hand felt cool against my sweating forehead. It gave me courage, I didn't lift my shoe away, even when it felt as if the wetness of the slug was penetrating up into flesh.

'What happens next?' Clare whispered again. I looked up at her grey breasts through her blouse, her anxious face. I fondled the cool, hard leather of her shoe. It had no room for thoughts or fears.

'I don't know. I'm scared that you'll vanish, I'm scared of dying, scared of being just an ordinary man. How the hell did we come to be here, Clare, scrambling around looking for gods on the mountainside?'

'Take off my shoe for me.'

I looked at her, her face was grave. I prised her shoe off, smelling the warm sweat from her released flesh. I turned and flung the shoe down the slope. It clattered far down among the cliffside rocks, disturbing seabirds into flight. When I turned back she brought her other shoe up to press against my flesh. I eased it off and flung it behind me also. She put her foot down on the dew-drenched grass.

'Now yours,' she said, 'you do the same.'

I felt foolish as I unlaced my shoes, put the socks inside them and handed them to her. She flung them out with a shriek into the mist. The noise of the waves was so strong that I didn't hear them splash into the sea below.

'So are you going to kneel there forever or what?'

I got stiffly up and took her hand. Small pebbles and tufts of rough heather scratched against my soles as we walked. Although the mist was lifting we still could hear the low moan of the fog-horn at the Bailey, filling the air with its warning to craft every ninety seconds. We could no longer see the sweep of the city, just the lights of a few isolated houses along the rim of the hill behind us. We were walking towards a stone wall with a sign that read *Danger-ous Cliffs. Keep Off.* Beyond it there was a helicopter pad beside two old stone houses. The beam of the light picked them out and then blinded us as it swept past. I waited for the Kisk to answer it with two short flashes.

'That was my home once,' she said, 'that second cottage. My father worked here for four years when I was growing up. So many homes I had, the Bailey, Rockabill, the Fastnet, Tory Island. It's a little private world, lighthouses. The same families, the same names, generation after generation. If I'd been a boy I would be in there now, alone in that big control room like the deck of a ship. Always thought I'd marry a keeper when I was a little girl. I'd look at the boys in other families in the houses and see them looking at me.'

'And you didn't?'

'Automation. This is the last manned light left. What's the point in marrying a keeper's son who is going to be a civil servant or a mechanic? No, it was having to face out into the big wide world for me.'

We stood together to watch the stained face of the rock being illuminated as the beam moved along it like a magic lantern, then swept out to sea.

'Every ninety seconds it lit up the wall of my bedroom,' she said. 'Every night the same. I could get up and look out at it, like a vision moving across the water. Made me feel so secure here in its magic little universe. *The Star of the Sea. Pray for the wanderer, pray for me.*'

I remembered my mother down in the kitchen still listening to the long-range shipping forecast, thought of the father that I never knew, smoking at the rail of a ship, watching the last glimpses of Ireland, a beacon flashing in the dark every ninety seconds. And Clare's father climbing down the ladder from the tower where the huge lamp swung, watching the ship until it was lost beyond the horizon. Two men face to face across the dark water, unable to see one another, not aware of each other's names. The lights of a passing ship, the flash of a revolving beacon. And here their offspring were, decades later, lost on the edge of the world.

'My father died at sea,' I said. 'A man I never knew to mourn. My own father.'

'Come on,' she said, 'let's go down.'

'But what if we're caught? It's against the law.'

'Maybe it's time we started breaking a few.'

There was a road in the sharpest of Vs leading down the cliff and then an old outhouse where a car was parked. Steps led down to a concrete yard where a light was on in the house where the off-duty keepers slept. The fog-horn was housed in two huge metal drums. It hummed like an animal straining in the intervals before going off. Beyond it there were steps leading down to a flattened expanse of rock where somebody had been burning rubbish in an old metal bin. Small flames still guttered about in the wind.

Our bare feet made no noise on the second set of steps. The door of the lighthouse opened inward to a hallway of empty chairs. From somewhere we heard the swish of a washing-machine. We climbed two flights of steps and came to a landing. To the left was the tower where curving steps led up to the light. We could hear the crackle of a radio and the noise of the keeper moving about. To the right a small corridor led down to a set of cell-like rooms, each with a single bed without covering, a built-in wardrobe and a mirror with a light.

'This was a training school for keepers once,' Clare said, 'built before they decided to make all the lights automatic. Soon even this one will be just a machine turning by itself in the night.'

There was no curtain on the window of the last room on the corridor. As we both sat on the narrow bed I stared out at the dark sea through the dirty pane of glass. How much the room looked like a ship's cabin, I suddenly thought, a space where a man might take four steps, might drink unbonded whiskey or read the long night away, dreaming of home where a wife and a newborn child waited. This was the space where my father had lived out his life. A cabin like a prison cell, lurching at the mercy of the sea. A photograph of me in his wallet beside the crumpled telegram telling him that I was born. Weighing anchor and docking in a dozen ports, sending money orders by registered mail so that I might have a home to grow up in. And what had I done with the life he had given me? This spartan cell felt more like a home than my rented apartment with its drapes and manicured lawns. If I had ever thought of him it was to imagine how pleased he would have been at my rising up in the world. Now in that bare room I knew what his ghost would plead for: *Give me a grandson, let my name live on. I lived in the world until the sea claimed me. What are you doing, son, rotting away your life in that tomb?* I discovered that I was crying. Clare put her arm around me. She wet her finger on my cheek and then put it to her lips.

'Can you mourn someone you never even knew?' I asked.

'Do you need me?' she said.

'I need you so much I'm frightened my need will scare you away.'

'Somebody else needs me even more,' she whispered.

'I know. All my childhood I pretended I didn't need one.'

'You get in his way and I'll ditch you faster than you've ever known.'

'I may have run away scared long before then.'

'But I can't be just his mother for ever. I want to be needed by somebody else too.'

'I'll be an Icelander for you,' I said, 'if you'll convert me.'

'And we'll live in an igloo somewhere out in the frozen wastes.'

'And teach your little boy to acquire a sweet tooth for fish eyes.'

There were footsteps along the corridor. We huddled back against the dark wall. Outside the sea turned bright for an instant as the beam swung round. The fog-horn moaned and we heard a toilet flush. The footsteps retreated again.

'Shoes are all right,' she said, 'but feet are nicer when you learn to play with them.'

'Do you think you'll ever teach me?'

Clare smiled, sitting up on the bed so that I could rub her bare sole with my palm.

'The world always seems a little crazy this time before dawn,' she said. 'People imagining that they see or feel all sorts of things. It will be a big cold morning outside soon when you might just head back to your flash car outside and your spick-and-span apartment.'

'Or you might run back to your priest.'

'I might too. At least Bluebeard is a bit more dependable than you. There's no fear of him breaking his neck climbing down the cliffs to steal one of my shoes.'

I hadn't heard a splash when I threw them. They would be still there like two black pearls perched half-way down the grassy cliff. The instincts of a lifetime made me calculate if I could recover them. I took the miraculous medal from around my neck and hung it on the door handle.

'No more shoes,' I promised for the thousandth time in my life, 'no medals, no miracles.'

'If shoes are all we have to worry us,' Clare said, 'then we'll be doing all right.'

The fog-horn suddenly stopped outside. We could hear gulls clamouring as they hovered beyond the window. The wind at Howth Head. Howth, *Binn Eadair*, where the Fianna warriors had run. My Cub Scout uniform with the wolf's head. If a Fianna warrior returned now he would kneel on the wet grass before this beam, he would worship the light swerving around to catch him on the cliff-edge. And here I was hidden inside its stone belly with a girl of flesh and blood. It was half-six, time for the radio stations to come back on the air. I thought of the car parked up on the cliff with the driver's door still open, the low hiss of the stereo suddenly exploding with music.

'I know I'm not very good at this, but would you like to stay the night?'

'That depends, Michael. Are you asking me?'